I0561915

Big
White

Big White

Keith Weaver

IGUANA

Publisher: Cheryl Hawley
Editor: Amanda Feeney
Front cover design: Jonathan Relph

ISBN 978-1-77180-669-5 (paperback)
ISBN 978-1-77180-668-8 (epub)

This is an original print edition of *Big White*.

Other Works by Keith Weaver

An Uncompromising Place

Un endroit sans compromis (Traduit de l'anglais par Jean Forest)

The Recipe Cops

Balsam Sirens

Mr. Drumlin's Orchard (Novella)

Sicilian Refuge

Rolls

Walking with Albert and Other Stories (Short Stories)

Fool's Cap and Other Stories (Short Stories)

And Then There Was Maggie: A Memoir

Flight

For Maggie.

Again.

And always.

1

Windstorm

I went partly because there were no downed trees blocking the railway line and partly because the doghouse had been crushed.

"No. The dog's all right", John told me over the phone. "He was inside with me eating when it happened."

We talked a little longer, then I ended the call and made my travel booking. My train would leave that afternoon at four thirty, which was four hours away. It would be a short fifteen-minute walk to the station.

The rain had stopped, the terrible wind had blown itself out, the sun was shining, and I felt that I could smell the forest already. For the next little while, until it was time to set out for the station, I busied myself with work I had brought home from the office, although I did stop regularly to look around and think. It seemed that I'd been doing quite a bit of that lately.

Rather than a home away from home, John's place is really a second home for me. I've been going back to visit John now for more than twenty years.

It's likely that I sound a bit flat, and I can tell you exactly why. Joyce died just eight months ago. Still seems like it was yesterday. The doctors had done a full hysterectomy and removed both ovaries, but it was just that bit too late. The cancer raged like a wildfire, and that was probably the least horrible aspect of a supremely vile thing. She died, my beloved Joyce died, just four weeks after the operation. Four weeks of complete hell. But at least not four months or four years.

Three colleagues from work proved themselves true human beings by keeping me company before and after Joyce's funeral, despite my claims that I was fine. I wasn't, of course. And it took very little time for me to admit to myself that having them around was a lot better than being alone.

I take time off work whenever there's a chance to do something different that might interest me, otherwise I work steadily. And here I am now, taking some time off, ready once more to make that familiar trip to see John, and I find that I'm looking forward to it.

I got to know John at another funeral, that of my father, who died when I was ten. Cancer was involved in that one as well, or maybe I should say it might have been involved. My father, Damion Boscombe, died in a single car accident on his way home from the marina in Cobourg, where he worked. They looked for a cause. He hadn't been drinking. From what they could tell, he hadn't been speeding. He wasn't forced off the road. His car had just gone straight into a huge oak tree.

What they found was an inoperable brain tumour, but there was no sign that he knew anything about it. There had been no visits to doctors or hospitals, no records of any tests, and from what my mother said later, there had been no evident change in his mood or behaviour. The mortician probably suspected that my father did know that something was wrong and that he'd driven deliberately into the tree. But it could also have been a blackout, not common for that sort of tumour but not impossible either. Or he could have swerved to miss an animal. But it was the lack of any tire marks on the tarmac that caused possibilities to be raised and discussed. In the end, my father's death was ruled accidental.

My sister, Sylvia, is six years older than me. We exchange polite notes at Christmas now, but aside from that we have no contact. I wanted to stay in touch with her. Back then, when she was sixteen, I thought she was gorgeous, and, judging by her popularity, many others thought so too. But she and our mother, Carol, fought from morning to night. My father was my mother's second husband, and Sylvia came from her first, short-lived union. Strangely enough, Sylvia liked her stepfather but couldn't abide her mother. Sylvia left home a few months after my father's funeral and never came back.

Ruminating on this brought back snapshot recollections of my father's funeral. It had been a sunny day. There wasn't a large crowd, but death seemed to have cast the same feeling over everyone — we were in the right place but, at the same time, somehow also in the wrong place. The brief service had ended, and we were outside, standing around. I had no idea what to do next, or what should happen next, how things would move forward. All the people around me smiled wanly, but somehow they seemed to be familiar strangers. The wind ruffled my hair. Suddenly the light seemed brassy, and I wanted to be somewhere else.

"Steven, your tie is crooked", my mother said and fussed around in the way that irritated me no end. But I said nothing and did nothing. I just let her straighten a tie that was already perfectly straight.

Having worried my tie, my mother went off to speak to some other ladies who were chatting nearby. She smiled faintly on one occasion, but mostly her expressions and hand motions looked utilitarian, as though she were borrowing a cup of sugar. My sister was dabbing at her eyes, standing on her own, so I went over to her.

"Okay, sis?" I said, putting an arm around her shoulders, since I was tall for my age. She nodded and mopped up some more tears. I think we both knew, and she certainly knew, that even though we cared for each other, we would go our own ways and our paths would diverge for good. She was right.

Because of the violence of the car crash, the casket was closed. My sister and I approached it, bowed our heads, and said our silent goodbyes to the man who had always been there for us, even though he hardly ever knew what to say. At that moment, I felt sorriest for him. He and my mother had been moving apart for a few years, and now the future was hers, not his.

"Steven?"

I turned at the sound of my name. The man before me was tall and lean and had brown eyes, a dimple in his chin, skin bronzed by the sun, and slightly wavy blond hair streaked in white just above the ears.

"I'm John Stanley. Your father and I worked in the forest together for a few years. We kept in touch after that. I'm sorry. He was a good man."

I think I mumbled "thank you".

Conversations were concluding, small clutches of ladies were dissolving, the last people had left the small church, and the pastor was closing the doors. The hearse had pulled up to one side of the church and the attendants were standing around, probably waiting for everyone to leave.

"Can I drive you both home?" John said as he looked across the nicely mown grass in front of the church to where our mother was getting into a large car. It occurred to me that either she had asked him to make sure we got home all right or, being the man I eventually came to know well, he just offered. There was hardly any need, since we lived less than two hundred metres away. But I guess it doesn't look right for the newly bereaved to have to go home on foot.

We accepted.

As we were climbing into John's car, Sylvia stopped.

"Could we go somewhere first please? I'd like a glass of coke or something."

"Certainly", John said, and he drove us three kilometres to The Forest Inn, a restaurant and B & B.

That's how I first came to know John Stanley, more than thirty years ago. And I smiled now as I looked at my watch and came back to the present with a thud, reminding myself that my train would leave in an hour. I grabbed the bag I had packed, locked up our condo (I wasn't yet entirely comfortable at calling it "my condo"), and began a leisurely walk to the station.

It was a brilliant day, and although I wasn't really cheerful, my mood was more upbeat than usual. I felt that it was okay to have expectations for this trip. The walk to the train did me good. I mooched around the old station a bit, sat for a while on an isolated bench, and read my book. Eventually I made my way to the platform, climbed into my assigned carriage, located my seat, and got ready for the trip that would take an hour and a bit. Going to see John was always a bright spot, always something to look forward to. This time, judging from what John had said as he offered the invitation, it sounded like there was work to be done, and maybe a puzzle to solve.

I enjoyed the train ride. I always do. But this time I had the impression that we arrived sooner than expected, and for some reason, sooner than I had hoped. A forewarning, perhaps, that the time with John would pass too quickly?

John met me as I emerged from the station in Cobourg. Despite having just turned seventy, he was still straight, lean, and tanned. His hair retained quite a bit of sandy blond, and he moved without any of the halts or hindrances usually conferred on us by age; he might have passed easily for someone in his mid-fifties. His firm handshake and his smile, restrained but at the same time most welcoming, were typical of John. One arm was flung unselfconsciously over my shoulders, and we headed for his car. We chatted about all and sundry as John drove at his stately pace from Cobourg along Highway 45, heading for his cabin. Although I call it a cabin, and have always done so, John's cabin is larger than many houses in the area, and he has equipped it with everything modern while keeping evidence of those changes subdued or even hidden completely. The place thus retains the feel and spirit of a cabin. Even though the basic structure is more than 160 years old, and at one time probably was primitive, the cabin that was passed down to John has moved forward with the times. Inside and out, it drips TLC.

We passed by the turn to Ranleigh, the village where I was raised until shortly after my father's death. Each time I see the signs to it and its access road, I have that odd feeling of combined relief at having left it behind and nostalgia at no longer being there. John says it's part of that sorting mechanism that's become a hallmark of modern life, the rarely defied urge for people of a certain outlook to move to a city and for people of a different outlook to remain country bound. I know what he means, even though it's hard to put the idea into words without appearing to condescend or to give offence. It has always been a useful idea for me simply because John is himself a glaring and extraordinary exception to it, appearing to be a natural city dweller who has chosen to live in the country. In a way, I think of myself as something like a contact print, a sort of complement to John, the country boy who somehow has lapsed and lives in the city. Maybe we're each a bit of both.

And John lives deep in the country, about five kilometres from Ranleigh, in a large clearing near the edge of what is now the Northumberland County Forest. As we turned into his well-kept lane, the cabin sat before us, greeting us with a beatific smile, or as close as it is possible for a dwelling actually to do that. John's spaniel, Dougie, stood by the front door, tail wagging. Normally John would have driven past the cabin to the garage that sits to one side of it, part of a large lean-to structure that combines garage in front, well-equipped woodworking shop in the middle, and woodshed in the rear, all of them accessible from the house. But pulling into the garage wasn't an option today. A large but not exceptionally old white pine lay across the way leading to the garage, and beneath this fallen tree, about two-thirds the way along from the large uptorn root, lay the shattered remains of Dougie's dormitory.

John spoke about cutting up this fallen tree in a voice that revealed regret, even pain, but he said that it would yield a good deal of firewood in addition to a good deal of raw material for woodworking.

"This has also uncovered a mystery", John said as we got out of his car. I lifted out my case and set it down, fussed Dougie, and then turned toward John.

We walked up to the bole of the tree, and I could share John's sadness at such a great living thing having been brought down and, at the same time, also his understanding of the benign but directed and purposeful violence of nature.

"What's the mystery?" I asked.

John motioned me to come with him, and we walked to the huge root system now reaching up irrationally nine feet into the air. We walked around the upturned root.

"I found this just before I set out to collect you", John said and pointed into the hole left by the root. At one side of this hole was a scattered collection of bones.

"I called the police as soon as I saw them."

And when I looked further past the root into the hole, I understood why. Partially covered in soil, what looked back at me was the obscenely grinning lower half of a human skull.

2

Police

I moved away from the upturned root, and it was like stumbling into a different time and place. Although it was a warm late afternoon in the second half of May, it no longer felt like that. The sun had bathed my bare arms in what felt almost like a caress, but now a chill had descended on everything. Instead of being inviting, the bright sky suddenly was sharp and piercing. Everything now had a gritty ominous feel. All at once, I felt as though I didn't belong here, didn't belong anywhere. The visceral icy grip that I had come to know well over the past eight months, since Joyce was taken from me, returned now with a vengeance. I stumbled toward the picnic table and sat down heavily. Without warning, I began to weep silently.

John was beside me instantly. He said nothing at first, just put an arm over my shoulders and waited silently until I regained control.

"I'm sorry, Steven. I'll be right back", John said in a soft and sympathetic voice. I sat there in my unhappy alien world, looking without seeing. A glass appeared on the table before me, and John sat again next to me, holding another glass. "Drink", he ordered. I could see John from the corner of my eye. I had the impression that he was kicking himself silently.

Picking up the glass like an automaton, I put it to my lips, tasted cognac, and suddenly took a large mouthful and swallowed. A surge of warmth flowed through my chest and abdomen. Without saying a word, John encouraged me to take another mouthful, and another, and over the space of five minutes we both emptied our glasses. I looked around at the table, at John's cabin, at the grass, at the pine forest, at the long trunk of the white pine to my left lying there helplessly, doomed, moribund.

"Come on", John said. "Let's go for a short walk."

With John at my side and guiding me along a path that led among the trees at the edge of the cleared area around the cabin, it took only about ten minutes. The long cold fingers that had slithered out of the hole left by the fallen white pine and taken a grip on my intestines slowly released their grasp and slunk back to the hole. The image of the skull was still there before me, seeming to hang threateningly in the air, but it was now fading. The shock that had flooded through my nervous system was being overpowered, and my rational mind was reasserting itself.

Ending our short walk, we moved away from the trees back onto the grass surrounding the cabin and headed toward the picnic table.

"Let's sit", he said.

John had prepared a welcome, of sorts, and it was resting on the picnic table. It was clear that he hadn't anticipated the impact the skeleton would have on me, but he was evidently determined to try to move quickly away from it and get back on script. I looked at John as we took our places at the picnic table once more, and his expression was almost inscrutable. Almost. There was a hardness in his face that might have been a sign of self-recrimination at failing to tread gently around any reminder of death, something that had been such an unwelcome companion for me so recently. John's welcome, sitting on its tray before us on the table, was something that normally would have raised smiles, laughter, and relaxation: a bottle of wine, two glasses, and a bowl of nuts.

John hesitated, seeming not sure of what to do next. Without saying anything, I reached out, opened the bottle, and poured two glasses. John accepted his glass and reclaimed the initiative.

"Let's start again", he said. "Here's to you, Steven, my great and wonderful friend."

I felt as though I might begin to weep again, but a smile slowly crept across my face instead.

"Thanks, John. What would I do without you?"

The question was hypothetical. We sipped at first, then drank more deeply. We both smiled hesitantly, then with faint enthusiasm, and then we laughed softly when John picked up the bottle to pour and muttered "Good God!" on realizing that it was already half empty.

***

It took more than an hour before we were close to being back on track. I spent most of that time nodding at John's quiet background conversation as he got the barbecue going. But I wasn't really focussed on things. I gazed around at the stand of pines that enclosed John's cabin. I had known these pines for decades and now it was easy to see them as friends. In fact, I was forest bathing. The scent from these hundreds of trees was soothing my rough edges.

For our evening meal John had prepared his trademark hamburger patties, incorporating generous splashes of red wine and a dash or two, or five, of balsamic vinegar. Eventually we both stood together and cooked these patties on John's barbecue, a stone construction of his own design. It was definitely an old-school appliance, since it took the best part of an hour to produce a bed of coals just the way John wanted.

As we watched the charcoal transform, I put a great deal of effort into living in the moment, recalling what John and his cabin and his pine forest meant to me. And some of the familiar comfortable feeling began to reassert itself. I recognized how good it felt to be out of the city, to know once again the sense of slowing down, something that was a consequence of that escape from noise and concrete and hustle. The breeze, the pine-scented air, the chorus of birds, the absence of background urban growl, the whole package that came with a visit to John's place, collectively, was a balm that was now seeping back into my being.

We had sat at the table and then stood by the barbecue for a longish time without saying anything. I turned and looked at him.

"It's good to be back, John", I said. "I love this place."

John smiled. "That makes three of us", he said and reached down to rub Dougie's head.

And it was true. It was relaxing to be in the country, even though during each visit I still felt residual guilt at no longer being able to share it with Joyce. But Joyce had shared my love of John's place, and, after not very long, she and John had hit it off. She always looked forward to "John visits" and she encouraged me to see John on my own as well, knowing our background and close bond. Joyce knew that John and his cabin was truly happyland for me. And her statement, made to me quite a few times once the final verdict had been given on her condition, was both a wish and an order, and it came back to me now: "Be happy, Steven. Be as happy as I've been with you."

"Wine or beer?" John asked.

I looked up suddenly, still not fully in the moment, still aware of making considerable psychic effort to move out of my familiar reverie, to ignore the fallen tree, the hole it had produced, and what was in the hole.

"Why 'or'?" I said, trying for some levity.

"That's the stuff!" John said with a smile. "Could you go inside and get it? Pick whatever you'd like."

Coming back from the cabin, I deposited another bottle of decent red wine and four bottles of Pub House Ale on the picnic table that shared space with two large and comfortable garden chairs on John's deck.

"Is that going to be enough?" John asked, an eyebrow raised in surprise.

"Probably. But that problem can be solved if it arises."

"I'm relieved to hear it."

The bed of coals passed a final test, and the burgers went on the grill, hissing and sizzling. Just nicely pink inside and large enough to protrude everywhere from the homemade kaiser rolls that John had pulled from his oven that morning, the burgers were items of perfection, straight from Plato's world of forms. The first bite was ambrosial. That intensely sensual first moment of taste and aroma, both anticipated and recognized, filled my awareness. It was almost as though my mind was looking for a diversion back to the reality it wanted and grabbed it with both hands at just that moment. The rich blend of juice and condiments ran over my fingers and down my chin, and I just allowed it to happen. John had often said that there was no way to eat a decent hamburger politely and no reason to bother trying, and this was especially true of John's creations, loaded in Dagwood fashion by all the extras he considered essential.

We munched and nodded at intervals.

***

My hard-won partial grip on equilibrium was shaken somewhat at about eight o'clock when the police cruiser turned up. The involvement of officialdom meant that the thing in the hole could not be excluded entirely from consciousness and had not gone away. A face unfamiliar to me emerged from the police cruiser. The face and John greeted each other, and I was introduced to Constable Cecil Olsen. Then John and the constable went to gaze into the hole left by the fallen tree. I sat sipping my wine. John cast me a reassuring look. I was within earshot but decided to do nothing about that.

"It's been a few hours since you reported this", the constable said to John. "I hope you don't mind the delay."

"No. Not at all. Why would I mind?"

"Well, some people would want the thing carted away immediately and the whole area sprayed with Windex. But it's hardly an emergency, and it's been a busy day. A lot of things more pressing than an old skeleton."

"How old do you think it is?" John asked.

"Oh! I've no idea. But there seems to be no flesh left. So, probably months. Years."

"What happens next?"

"The coroner will visit, and he'll decide whether an anthropologist should take a look."

"Anthropologist?" John raised an eyebrow.

"Yes. Could be Indigenous remains. We need to be quite careful about that."

"Of course."

"But the coroner will also want to see whether there's any evidence of foul play."

John just nodded.

"And on that front, I need to ask whether you know of any burial that took place here. You've lived here quite a while, haven't you?"

"Yes. All but a few of my seventy years."

Olsen stood looking at John, his pen poised expectantly over his notebook.

"No. I'm not aware of any burial here. But there's probably something here that can put a lower limit on the amount of time that body has been in the ground."

Olsen looked up sharply.

"Yes", John nodded and inclined his head to his right. "That tree."

"What about the tree?"

"Well, it looks as though the body was under the main part of the root system. It's ludicrous to imagine that anybody would tunnel under a root system as large as this and then stuff in a body."

"Couldn't someone just have cut through the roots and dug a grave?"

"I guess you've never tried digging up a live, mature tree, have you, Cecil."

A shake of the head.

"A tunnel might be easier. My guess is that this tree is at least eighty years old. Could be as much as a hundred and thirty. It's certainly been here during all my time." He cast a glance at the fallen giant that easily could have been a lament for a lost friend. "But it's possible to make a quite accurate age estimate. I presume it will be up to you or the coroner to order that. If someone buried a body here, it would have been before this tree began growing, or up until it was not more than five years old. After that, digging somewhere else would have been the only practical option."

Olsen had been writing continuously while John spoke, perhaps hoping to be seen as a Sherlock back at the station house. He looked up.

"Anything else?" Olsen asked.

"Not without payment of a fee", John said, winking.

They both smiled. Olsen took some more pictures, then tucked away his notebook, pen, and small camera. Olsen and John shook hands, then walked together back to the cruiser. Olsen climbed in and drove off.

Back at the picnic table, John cast me a "where were we" look and, in reply, I raised my glass and invited another shared mouthful of wine. We clinked and sipped.

"So, tomorrow we begin cutting up that pine?" I asked, wanting to move to a neutral topic.

"Yes. But we do it deliberately. I want to get a reasonable amount of wood out of it for my shop. It will need quite a bit of time to season, but there's a lot of value to be had out of a tree like that."

We both looked over at the fallen tree again.

"And I want to have a new house built for Dougie by this time tomorrow. You should have seen him when we came outside yesterday after the storm had passed. He was almost as devastated as his doghouse."

All this recalled for me John's great skill and productivity as a woodworker. He had been fashioning high-quality items from wood for decades: furniture, bowls, bread boards, various kitchen utensils, beautiful boxes involving exquisite inlay patterns, carvings and various ornamental items, in fact, just about anything. My guess was that he still worked at least three days a week doing commissions.

And he did all that in his shop, a surprisingly extensive work area. It was not visible at all as one approached the cabin from the front but was attached to the cabin and accessible from the pantry through double doors into the garage and then through another door into the workshop. This workshop, an enclosed and heated space measuring about thirty by twenty feet, stretched back along the side of the cabin. Inside his workshop, John had a radio, a fridge, a lovely old potbelly stove, all his woodworking machines and hand tools, what he insisted on calling a "draughting" table, and floor-to-ceiling racks where various woods lay neatly ordered, waiting to be used.

"Are you going to build the same sort of doghouse?" I asked, pouring the last of the wine into our glasses.

"No", John said. "I think Dougie would like a change."

"You mean with a TV room and flush toilet?"

John chuckled.

"How long would you like to stay?" he asked. "We didn't talk about that on the phone, but I invite you to stay as long as you want."

"Four days, if you don't mind, not counting today."

"With pleasure", John said, beaming.

I looked hesitantly toward the tree then quickly back at the table. "Do you think someone will come tomorrow?" I asked.

"I would bet on it", John said. "Everything is exposed now to the elements and I think they'll want to get to work immediately. They'll want some basic information and to know…" and here John hesitated, "er, how he, or she, died."

I just nodded, not wanting to think about it.

"What I mean is, they'll want to know whether it was a violent death."

At that I looked up sharply. And I recognized that the shock of seeing what had been brought to light had got my logical mind working. I became aware of thinking in terms of investigation, forensics, and hypotheses. I was beginning to see the situation at arm's length as a problem not linked to me at all. I could tell from John's expression that his mind was moving along the same lines. His connection was different, since this was something found on his land, and something that had been there for a considerable time. But it was clear to me, and probably clear to John as well, that the possibility of something nefarious being behind that skeleton was near and real.

John shook his head, as though to change reels in his mental cinema, rose from his chair, went over to the serving area next to the barbecue, and returned to the table carrying a pie, two plates, and some cutlery.

"You like rhubarb and strawberry pie, I hope", he said, knowing full well that it was my long-time favourite, never to be dethroned.

"How much would you like?" John asked, stringing me along as he glanced my way inquiringly and prepared to cut a generous fifth of the total pie. I looked at him, nodded in agreement, then waited for him to navigate around the many unasked questions we were both aware of. He fixed me with an assessing look, then evidently reached some conclusion as he set down the pie cutting implements.

"I've lived here for almost seventy years", John began. "For part of that time, and going back further, my father and mother and siblings lived here as well. Prior to that, my grandparents lived here. None of them was buried here. In fact, I would bet my boots that during all that time nobody was buried here. Certainly nobody has been buried here with any of my family's knowledge and permission, as far as I'm aware. I fully expect that whoever that skeleton belonged to, he or she was killed and then put in the ground here surreptitiously."

I had regained control, since the situation now posed just a problem to be understood and solved, and its role as a trigger to reignite my own personal pain was already fading. "Why do you say that?" I asked.

"I'm assuming you mean 'why here'. That's what we'll find out, I expect. You like puzzles, don't you?"

"Well, yes. But this…" I wasn't ready yet to begin trying to solve this problem.

"Back to the immediate task", John said briskly. "Anything with your pie? Whipped cream?"

"No, thanks. But John, aren't you—"

"No. I'm not", he said, through a mouthful of pie and a huge grin. He was toying with me again in a way that I had always found entertaining and never challenging.

"Our guest over there, having been disturbed from his long slumber, also probably wants things sorted out as quickly as possible. But another day won't make any difference. We have this pie to eat, and I must say I'm finding it good, we have a lot more to discuss, and there's another bottle of wine that might need company."

I smiled and shook my head at this, indicating that I didn't need more wine. But I rose from the table and went to retrieve another bottle in case John wanted more.

As I entered the cabin, a voice sounded in my head, a very familiar voice offering another variation on the words of encouragement that I had heard many times over the past months.

Stay calm, Steven. You're okay.

It was Joyce, and I could hear the familiar reassuring smile in her words.

3

John

Bats had been swooping through the air for half an hour when we finally gathered plates, glasses, and empty bottles and headed inside. At the edge of the deck, I stopped and looked around. The sky offered faint backlighting to the conifer sentinels that surrounded us, now silhouettes, well-defined shadows. But more than just sentinels, they were also guardians, companions, and witnesses from past ages. Many of them were pines. Some jack pines, some red pines, but the proudest of all were the great eastern white pines. There were more than a hundred of them reaching into the zodiacal sky, and there wasn't a larger stand of old-growth white pines within hundreds of kilometres.

"Good to be back?" John asked.

"Much more than good. This place is gorgeous, inspiring." I looked around again, my warm feeling of homecoming dulled once more by the frequently recurring stab of Joyce's absence. It will take time, my friends had all said, maybe quite some time.

John's cabin sits in a largish clearing on land that slopes gently toward the south. Behind the cabin, the land rises to high ground about sixty metres above where we were standing. From the front of the cabin, one looks out over a gentle grade down to a small stream about a hundred and fifty metres distant. From there the land rises steeply again to a crest that runs east and west. The entire area is covered in pine forest.

To the right of John's cabin, about fifteen hectares of land had been cleared long ago and converted to a cultivated field, but most of it had been reclaimed now by the pine forest. This cleared area had once been the land that John's ancestors, going back a century and a half and more, had hoped would feed the homestead. It had done that, just, but only for a time, and at the cost of back-breaking work. John had told me the story several times, but I never tired of hearing it again.

Back inside the cabin, we washed up our dishes and John offered me a seat on the sofa that stretched in front of his fieldstone fireplace. The sofa, large but elegant, was made from an old elm that had to come down years ago; it was a solid piece of furniture that John had fashioned himself. Its thick cushions converted what would have been a beautiful but hard puritanical bench to a sinfully comfortable lounging spot, and on more than a few occasions I had drifted off to sleep here in front of a fire.

"Digestif?" John asked.

It was probably the case that here, in what could reasonably be called "deep country", one wouldn't hear the word *digestif* this side of Gores Landing. I smiled and nodded, and John went off to get what I thought would probably be one of his favourites, sambuca. It turned out to be another of his favourites, Poire Williams. He poured, he sat, we sipped.

"Anything you'd like to do in particular tomorrow?" John asked.

For some reason, this conversational initiative caught me off guard. Something was being avoided. Just what, I wasn't sure. But I followed John's lead.

"Well, we should at least trim the branches off the fallen pine, cut it into whatever lengths you'd like, stack them, and in general clean up the area. The branches will give a lot of kindling and firewood.

That task alone will probably take four hours. Then we need to build a new house for Dougie. If there's any time left after that, I wouldn't mind making a short visit to Gores Landing."

John was nodding.

"We should be able to do all that. I've made a sketch for a new house for Dougie. I have all the wood we need. You don't mind an early start, do you?"

I shook my head. "Not at all."

John stopped here for a moment, held up his glass of Poire Williams, and peered through it.

"It wouldn't surprise me if the coroner comes by tomorrow", he said, "but in the morning I'll call Olsen and ask him what we should expect. I doubt that we need to be here. But … I want to know what the coroner comes up with. I'm afraid this is going to be a major event, locally."

The mention of "coroner" caused a dark rumble to pass through me fretfully. I did my best to brush it aside.

"So", I began. "We start on Dougie's house first?"

John nodded. "Yes. We shouldn't be doing anything that could disturb those bones before the coroner has had a chance to look at them."

John had regarded me several times during the evening, probably wondering how I was holding up, how I was coping without Joyce. But I wasn't going to start down that road.

"How is the forest doing?" I asked, diving off in a new conversational direction.

"The County Forest? Oh. Okay."

"Still not impressed at how they're managing it?"

Without answering right away, John rose, refilled his glass, the offer to top up mine having been declined, then retook his seat and held up his glass, turning it before his eyes, examining the contents in the light.

"They're not doing a bad job on the forest. It's just the old story. It's all too … disconnected." John stopped here and looked at me.

"As you know, Steven, the forest began as a rescue operation, to stabilize the soil after so much uncontrolled clear-cutting. It was necessarily a monoculture forest, all the same species of conifer. But as the decades went by, it was obvious that the forest would slowly convert to multiple species. But there was never any strategy to help the forest make that change. I guess I'm just old school. It was people who created the desertification problem by clear-cutting, so we should have done and should still be doing much more to help it grow back as a mature mixed forest. But I've already said all this. I don't want to bore you with it again."

"We both love forests, John. You could never bore me. And I've said before that you should write it up. You're in the best position to do that. And it's something that needs to be done."

John sat up suddenly and placed his glass on the table, then his face creased in a slow smile.

"You're right. And that's just what I'm doing."

"What? Documenting the forest? That's great! Long past time. Can I take a look at what you've done?"

John shook his head decisively.

"Not yet. Still too rough. And only about two-thirds finished."

"What approach are you taking?"

"I had started off, somewhat naively I soon realized, hoping to make it a story of a 'Once and Future Forest'. Now, instead, I'm just trying to write it up as the forest that was and the forest that it's become."

"So, pretty much a straight history?"

"Yes, but as well as just presenting a point-by-point history, I'd also like to correct the disconnected aspect of the whole business. It would be nice if people could see a forest as more than just some vague thing hiding behind the word."

"Lots of the people side of things then?" I asked. "Give credit to the people who raised the alarm about desertification, fought to have a systematic approach to deal with the damage, and spent so much time and effort getting a large replanting operation underway?"

"Yes. I worry though that I'll be seen to have an axe to grind."

I took another sip of my Poire Williams, wanting to get my reply right.

"People who don't have skin in a game don't play the game very well. They can't even describe the game very well. I think we've become much too accustomed to trying to stand outside things, so discussions can tend to take on that weird mock-disengaged drone of the passive voice. It's not convincing, but it suits people who want to stay uninvolved. To invoke a technical term, it's bullshit. So, tell it the way you see it, John. Straight from the shoulder as first draft. The massaging and finessing, if any is needed, can come later."

John just looked at me, practically open-mouthed.

"Well!" he said. "Something gave you a good bite on the ass!"

"I make no apologies", I replied. "You have this fantastic story to tell. Your family were players. Nobody could talk about this the way you can."

And I knew the outlines of the story well.

John's great-great-great-grandfather, Clifford Stanley, had been born in 1813 and had come to Upper Canada at the age of three when his family migrated here. The family struggled to make a go of it, but they did become established, and as soon as Clifford was old enough, he acquired a hundred acres of land in what eventually became Northumberland County. He cleared land to accommodate a house, a small barn, and a field to plant a first crop. The remainder of the hundred acres was left as virgin forest. That house and the cleared land is where John's cabin sits today.

Clifford and his wife, Abigail, survived the first few years and welcomed three sons, and Clifford cleared more land for larger crops. By the fourth year Clifford recognized that the soil wouldn't support the kind of agriculture everyone seemed to have in mind. A near neighbour of Clifford's, where "near" meant that he was six miles away, had been badly disabled in a tree-felling accident. Clifford had gone to help him whenever he could, and eventually they reached an agreement under which Clifford would work his neighbour's land and share the resulting harvest — grains, milk, and beef. His neighbour's land was flat and rich, not the sandy fragile soil of Clifford's holding, soil that needed much work to produce even modest yields.

Abigail was a tireless homemaker, and whenever Clifford returned home from working the neighbour's land, every four or five days, it was to a warm and inviting abode. The work was hard and it showed on both of them, but he and Abigail had come to cherish their home. Although abandoning it and moving elsewhere would have made their lives easier, they rejected that option. In due course, Clifford's eldest son, Cyrus, became strong enough to help, and that marked a turning point. They had named their homestead Bush Green after an area in Norfolk near Harlesden, the town they had left.

Cyrus took on more and more of the work as Clifford aged, and Cyrus's two younger brothers, Andrew and Richard, took over the neighbour's farm completely when the neighbour died and his wife was forced to give up their land and move to town. But the original farmstead that had been carved out by Clifford, hidden away in its protective pine forest, remained a spiritual home for all the Stanleys. They assembled there often, and when Clifford died, Cyrus took over the place, looking after his mother until she too died some years later. By this time Cyrus was married, had begun raising his own family, and had acquired several hundred more acres, about half of it pine forest and the rest good, arable land. He worked just as hard as his father had done, and he was soon aided by his own son, Donald, and later by a strapping grandson, William.

By this time, logging had become big business, and Cyrus was increasingly alarmed at the level of logging taking place all around them, and at the consequences that were already beginning to appear. It was a brutal business, a large-scale stripping of a natural resource that left the landscape devastated, an operation that Cyrus considered to be driven merely by greed for short-term gain. Cyrus refused to allow any logging to take place on his land. There had been several attempts by logging crews to fell the huge white pines on the Stanley lands, but these attempts had been thwarted, in one case by the Stanleys threatening to use their firearms. Their determination to prevent their land being logged was so evident, and their stances so fierce, that the logging crews took the safe and easy course and just gave them a wide berth. But in the process, the Stanleys had made permanent enemies of the Ballantyres, the family of timber barons active in the area at the time. The Ballantyres were a short-fused, argumentative bunch, and there was a serious crossing of metaphorical swords between Lorne Ballantyre, the ruling head of the family dynasty, and three generations of Stanleys, an aged Clifford, his sons Cyrus, Andrew, and Richard, and his grandson Donald. From an early date, Lorne Ballantyre had made it a personal objective to log the white pine on Stanley's land and this family imperative was passed down to other Ballantyres.

The story had more ins and outs, but eventually the area was essentially logged out, apart from the Stanley land, and the threat waned on its own. The Stanley family's skill at farming, their eagerness to acquire more land and to work land well removed from Bush Green, the place they all were determined to retain, meant that they were able to weather the problems in those early pioneer years.

Clifford, Cyrus, Donald, and William all were farmers, all raised families, and all shared the same fierce possessiveness for Bush Green. William's eldest son, Arthur, was born in 1921 and was the first of the Stanleys not to be a full-time farmer. By then, much of the area was a desert: blow sand formed travelling dunes and erosion was rampant. Because of its large stands of pine, the Bush Green property was spared that fate. Solutions to the desertification problem had begun to appear but were slow to have an effect.

Arthur worked the land his forebears had cleared, but he also branched out into a different business. He operated that portion of the Stanley property covered by red and jack pine as a woodlot. He had the same sense of good husbandry as his predecessors, and by then, Bush Green and the Stanley land around it had become a green gem in a raddled landscape. Arthur supplemented his income by working for the railways, which were booming at the time. He also had a natural talent as a carpenter. Arthur raised a large family, and to accommodate this, he had built a new and much larger cabin. That cabin, subsequently expanded twice, was where John and I were seated, drinking our Poire Williams.

I had always known that there was friction between the Stanley and Ballantyre families, but the sudden intrusion of the past, in the form of the skeleton, had lent a new urgency to this in my mind. For some reason, suddenly I wanted to know more.

"Tell me a bit about the Ballantyre family. What was the overlap in generations between them and your family?"

John leaned back and looked into the distance, collecting his thoughts.

"The Ballantyre family goes back at least as far my forebears here. I haven't tried to trace them back very far because, frankly, I'm not that interested in their distant past. They worked to build their timber business, but it wasn't until Lorne Ballantyre came on the scene that serious conflicts between our families arose. Obviously there were several generations ahead of Lorne, but Lorne was particularly hard-nosed and strong-willed, and, perhaps most importantly, he was long-lived. He took the reins of the family business when he was in his early twenties, and he retained absolute or almost absolute control until he was well into his nineties.

"And his son was Walter?" I asked.

John nodded. "Walter was one of his sons. But there were two others, Graham and Arnold, neither of them worth much."

"And then Walter had how many sons?" I prodded.

"Well, Walter certainly had a son David. It seems never to have been doubted back then that Charles was also Walter's son. But there was persistent speculation about Charles, nothing better than gossip when it comes right down to it. He was always seen to be Walter's son, but I've wondered…" John raised his hands in what looked like defeat. "But I need to come clean here. This is all just hearsay carried down through the generations. I really have no idea about Charles's true lineage. He might well have been a legitimate Ballantyre and maybe I'm maligning him unfairly."

I waited for more, but decided not to press further, that if John had more to say it would come out on its own.

"So", John said in what appeared to be a conclusion, "there was a long-standing animosity between Lorne on the Ballantyre side, and Cyrus's son Donald and grandson William." I knew the more recent history of the Stanleys. Arthur was John's father, and he encouraged John to move away from the land. John's response to his father's wishes was mixed. He took a forestry degree, but then became an accountant as well, and he took up a good accounting position in Cobourg. But he refused to turn his back on Bush Green. It was his home and he was rarely away from it for more than a few days. When John was in his early forties, an opportunity arose for him to take over a failing furniture manufacturing operation. He made that leap, brought the business back from the brink of insolvency, and ultimately made it a success.

"When was it you sold that business and retired? Was it 2008?" I asked.

"That's it", John said.

I asked John the occasional question as this family history scrolled again in my mind, and I agreed to join John in seeing off another glass each of Poire Williams.

"A fantastic story, even as an oral account. I can't wait to read it. You'll pass it to me as soon as it's in shape, won't you?"

"I certainly will", John said. "I'm expecting you to be my editor."

"Are you having to do much research, much digging?"

"I'm having to do a great deal. The diary my grandfather William kept is invaluable. He even recorded dates when he got parts of the story from his father. But I'm having to shore it up from more solid sources. It's become quite an experience."

A companionable silence followed, indicating that our particular topic of discussion had been exhausted. We sipped our digestifs. Looking surreptitiously across at John, I thought that some new distraction was weighing him down a bit. My guess was that it had to do with the skeleton. Something like that would certainly be an intrusion in anyone's life. But it struck me that John was trying to avoid something else.

We carried on talking about inconsequential things for some time, but the stress in my life just then, a long day, an excellent meal, and a generous amount of alcohol caused a reminder yawn to break the surface.

"Time to get you to bed", John said, rising and collecting bottle and glasses. "You're in your usual room and I've put your case on the bed."

I began thanking John for the evening, but he waved me off, shooing me to bed. As I walked to my room, although I was hoping for a quiet, pine-scented night, I didn't look forward at all either to lights out or to being on my own. My mind was still very much in a dark frame, the skull out under the tree having reminded me of loss and pain and loneliness. I was aware of being tired but expected that sleep would not come easily. Later, I recalled lifting the suitcase from the bed, and after what seemed like a magically restful twenty minutes, I awoke at half past five to a chorus of robins, lying between the sheets and wearing nothing but my underwear.

Dougie barked at something, signalling time to start a new day.

4

Visitors

I dozed for a while, then took stock of things. The apprehension that the skeleton seemed to have cast over me the previous afternoon and evening had been replaced by a driving urge to know. A body had been buried on John's land. It was John I needed to be concerned about, not myself. Those bones had opened my own personal wounds, but I was not threatened in any way. Somehow during the night the face of death that had appeared so powerfully before me yesterday had now been swept aside. In its place was a positive and rather urgent need to help John unveil the story behind those bones, to determine just what had happened, when, and why. With a new resolve, I rose, washed and shaved, pulled on trousers, and stumbled to the main room of the cabin. John's kitchen stretches along most of the west wall, and breakfast aromas that seem only utilitarian in the city were now enticing.

"Better get dressed", John said, standing at the stove and not bothering to turn around. "The coroner will be here in about half an hour. I want to make sure he focusses on the bones outside and not on your irresistible body."

Looking at my watch, I could scarcely believe that it was seven thirty. A good part of the day was gone already.

Fully dressed a few minutes later, I did penance for my urban lassitude by having only one piece of John's bacon and a cup of strong coffee. Hard on the heels of washing up our breakfast things, we were both outside with John's doghouse sketch, measuring and cutting lengths of wood. Having long since finished patrolling the limits of his property, Dougie sat nearby, supervising.

It was obvious that John could see in his mind the new doghouse and all the elements needed to make it. From our start at ten minutes to eight, we had half the wood cut to the lengths needed for the doghouse when the coroner's van pulled into John's drive. I waved John to go and look after him while I continued cutting.

In another fifteen minutes, I had all the remaining pieces of wood cut to length and sorted according to frame, floor, walls, and roof. At that point, wanting to let John decide exactly how to begin the assembly, I walked over to the fallen tree. John had placed a ladder in the hole on the side opposite the location of the bones, and the coroner, whose name, I learned, was Dr. Willis, descended into the hole and spent a good deal of time taking many pictures. At length, he climbed out and snapped off his latex gloves.

He pulled out his cellphone and quickly sent a text message, then looked up brightly to face John's questioning gaze.

"Been there a long time, would be my first guess. I've contacted the anthropologist, gave advance warning yesterday. Should be here in about forty-five minutes. Any chance of a cup of coffee?"

Without waiting for either an answer or an invitation, Willis began striding toward the door to the cabin. A busy man, it occurred to me. No time to waste. In a few minutes, we were seated at John's kitchen table, each of us nursing a cup of coffee.

"Will you wait for the anthropologist?" John asked.

"Yes. Good chance of rain tomorrow. I want all those bones out of there before that happens."

I asked Willis how one went about ticking all the boxes.

"Well defined process", he said, taking a sip of his coffee. "Anthropologist makes a determination. Matter of routine. Local

First Nations reserves are contacted. Sometimes they want to see the find. Mostly they just talk about it with the anthropologist. If the find has a First Nations link, the process goes in one direction. If not, we follow a slightly different path. Try to determine whether the death was natural or involved a criminal act. No matter which way it goes."

"And then?"

"Well, if the death was natural, we try to identify the person, locate any next of kin or near relative. If a criminal act was involved, then it's a police matter."

"In this case, do you know what—"

"Sorry, can't comment."

We chatted with the coroner a while longer, then he said he was returning to his van to make some phone calls and do some paperwork. John and I rose and went back to our doghouse construction.

Under John's expert lead, the doghouse took shape quickly. It would obviously be palatial, if only a one room palace. We were nailing on the sections of roof when a car pulled into John's drive.

The anthropologist.

She was about thirty and had shortish slightly curly black hair, was dressed in overalls, and looked like she was all business. Willis walked over to meet her, they shook hands, and held a brief conference. Then they both came over toward John.

"John. This is Glenda McGibbon. Anthropologist. John found the bones."

They shook hands; McGibbon smiled briefly, then inclined her head toward Willis.

"Yes", he said. "This way."

The three of them walked toward the hole. I followed almost out of earshot. By the time they reached the hole, McGibbon had pulled a notebook and camera out of her case and then stopped and spent about a minute examining the site.

"Okay", she said, gripped the ladder, and climbed down into the hole. Her investigation took about half an hour, then she climbed out again.

She addressed the coroner.

"No obvious signs that this was a First Nations burial. But that doesn't mean it isn't one."

"What's the next step?" I asked, a question which earned a frown from Willis.

McGibbon looked at me neutrally. "And you are?"

John briefly explained who I was and why I was present, and this seemed to satisfy McGibbon.

"The next step is a local First Nations consultation. I've already spoken to people at the Alderville reserve and told them what we know to date. Someone from that reserve will drop by." And, as if on cue, another car turned into John's drive. A man in slacks and a light shirt, who was neither obviously First Nations nor obviously not, stepped out and walked toward us.

McGibbon made the introduction somewhat formally, "John Stanley, this is James Paudash, First Nations Chief at Alderville."

"John", Paudash said, extending his hand. "Jim. Pleased to meet you." They smiled at one another.

"Well", Paudash continued, looking at Willis and McGibbon. "What have we got?"

McGibbon explained the situation to him and then they climbed down into the hole. They were down there only ten minutes when Paudash climbed out, thanked everyone for bringing him in at the beginning, smiled, shook hands again, and walked back to his car.

Then McGibbon climbed out of the hole once more.

"We have his agreement to collect the bones and start testing", she said, and I noticed that her clipboard held a form on which her signature and Paudash's appeared, as well as a date.

"Thanks, Glenda", Willis said. "That's me back to work. I'll keep you informed on what I find." The anthropologist smiled, shook hands with us, then returned to her car. Willis started back down the ladder. He was soon pulling bones from the soil, and he stopped every so often to take a few more pictures and make notes in his notebook.

Determined to subdue my apprehension, I moved to the edge of the hole and stood for a while to watch.

As Willis collected bones, he placed them in a series of plastic bags and also marked an image of a skeleton. It was quite clear that he was making sure he got the full complement of bones. It looked as though the body has been laid reasonably carefully and was buried deeply enough that no animals were able to detect it and dig it up. Within twenty minutes, Willis had six bags of bones, had done a final check on his skeleton diagram, and began climbing out of the hole.

He looked at me and offered a friendly nod.

"Out of curiosity", I began, "how long will it take to do the tests on those bones?"

"Not long", Willis said, evidently not interested in discussing the matter. I was curious to know the process from here but wasn't about to ask Willis. I could discover that easily from other sources.

Willis made a few final annotations and put away his notebook and pen.

"I believe I've seen you around before", he said to me, now in a more friendly, casual tone.

"Probably. I've been a friend of John's for many years."

"Is it your mother who lives in Gores Landing?"

"Yes. Do you know her?"

"No, not really. Met her a few times. I keep a boat there. Nice meeting you, Mr. Boscombe."

"Likewise, Dr. Willis."

Willis headed off to his car, and I returned to our doghouse project. Dougie followed me with his eyes; he seemed to be chastising me for idleness.

We finished the doghouse in less than a half hour, and it really did look grand. As we stood there looking at it, Dougie came over to make his own inspection. He looked less than delighted.

"His nose likely tells him that the wood reeks to high heaven", John offered. "A few days exposed to sun and air and then his old blanket inside on the floor should make it a lot more acceptable. In the meantime, he can sleep on some old cushions over on the porch."

John had a few other projects he wanted to do, but he suggested we stop for a few minutes for a cup of coffee. We trooped to the chairs on the porch, John continuing into the cabin to bring out mugs and coffee pot. Dougie looked a bit anxious until I took the chair furthest from the cabin door, at which point he relaxed and flopped down between the chairs. Keeper of his owner's chair, obviously, and a job he took seriously.

Coffee poured, we were both seated, gazing out at what looked like a perfect day. Grasshoppers leapt unpredictably into the air, crickets scratched away in tuneless monotony, several butterflies were performing a pheromonic dance in the sun-saturated air, the heady and hygienic scent of evergreen was everywhere, and an occasional burst of pine pollen would drift from the forest. If God was in Her heaven, then She was right here with us.

John outlined what he had in mind for the rest of the morning, which included some work in the vegetable garden, clearing some tree-pruning waste from the previous autumn, and installing an additional solar panel that had just been delivered. He asked me if I would like to join in, and I said yes without hesitation. Our languid coffee break floated on its own sea of space and time. Life was certainly good. At least, this part of it was good.

But I wondered what the next few days would bring. Willis had collected his bones in a matter-of-fact, professional way. For that operation, I forced myself to stand looking into the hole and watching. I had noticed it and he certainly wouldn't have missed it. When he had lifted the skull from the soil, several clods of earth had fallen from it, and I was quite sure that the story the skull had to tell would not be a happy one.

5

Ranleigh

We worked away quietly, but an active discussion was going on in my head. It was about the bones. The situation was giving me no rest.

How long would it take to get some information from the coroner? Would it involve just vaguely worded probabilities? Was there a chance that we would ever know just who had been buried there, when, and why? Or would it be wrapped up without any definitive conclusion? For John's sake, I hoped that whatever emerged would have enough finality to choke off the rumour mill before it got started. I wasn't at all sure why my mind kept circling this problem when there were no hard facts to work on at all. Was it just an obscure connection to my own loss and pain that kept me turning the thing over and over in my mind? Or was it my sense of impatience to have answers? And was this conflicting with my feeling that any answers, if indeed there ever would be any, would probably be a long time coming?

The chores John had lined up took about an hour and a half to complete, and when we finished the last of them, he suggested that we shunt quickly into Gores Landing for a spot of lunch. John had been glancing at me as we worked, and I suspected that he suggested lunch as a diversion, a change of scene, something to get me away from what had been so disturbing.

I had visited Gores Landing just two weeks earlier to see my mother. We wouldn't see her today since she was spending a few days with my aunt, her sister, in Ottawa. Nor would I be making any effort to see the man she was vaguely associated with, Lee Ackerman. He had an abrasive and sarcastic manner, entirely natural as far as I could tell, but I had taken a serious dislike to him. It seemed that the sentiment was mutual, which was okay by me. He and my mother had an on-again-off-again connection, something I didn't understand at all. She must have had her reasons, but we never discussed the matter.

On the way to Gores Landing, we drove through Ranleigh, my home village, just for old times' sake and at John's suggestion. I've always had the sense that John felt I was unfairly negative about Ranleigh. Maybe he hoped that the passage of time would help me see it in a different light. The place is essentially a main street dead-ending at the foot of a steep hill and four cross streets that, equally, go nowhere. The grass was well kept for all but two of the houses, and those two were vacant and staring. For most of the houses, flower beds and window boxes added nice touches of colour. But nothing could hide the place's wasting disease, a long economic decline similar to that experienced by many villages. It was visible in the main street, inexplicably named Ridge Street, where the shells of several former businesses now provided storage for items that had dubious provenance and no future. The ghosts of those former businesses peered out myopically through dust-coated windows. A single convenience store struggled on. Another frontage offered video games, cellphone repairs, and "confections". Stated baldly, the village was clinging to life somewhere far out in the long, low-value tail of the distribution that characterizes the municipal health of our society. Recognizing that people do live here, I struggled with that uncharitable thought which I considered, nevertheless, an undeniable reality. But I slammed the lid quickly on this image, since, otherwise, it would lead very soon to corrosive rhetorical questions about why people choose to live like this. They would have their reasons, and it wasn't my job to question those reasons.

"I'm guessing you're not finding this pretty", John said, evidently reading my thoughts.

I was about to try an answer, but John beat me to it.

"It's only one face", he said.

And it was true that the village itself, Ranleigh, represented probably the least appealing of my memories of the region.

John turned down Rice Street and drove slowly past the house where I had lived to the age of twelve. It was familiar, of course, and I expected to be depressed, but the place looked cheerful: it had been painted recently, the roof was in good repair, and a nicely edged bed of flowers and the ancient but familiar and now well-pruned lilac bush gave it all a smile. We left the village and headed toward Gores Landing, none too soon for me. During part of the drive, I questioned the feeling I experienced in Ranleigh. It wasn't the first time I had been back. It was the first time since Joyce had died, but that couldn't have... Reluctantly, and just why "reluctantly" I'm not sure, I said to myself that, unless our early years are truly horrific, we tend to be nostalgic about them, even though they might have been unappetizing. In my case, I'd had to live in a cold and draughty house, being acutely aware of prying by the village's two vitriolic gossips and feeling the sense of being a frog in completely the wrong puddle. On the one or two occasions I tried to explain this to my mother, her reply stuck with me: mental growing pains. In other words, or rather in terms of my own harsh interpretation, life hasn't beaten you into submission yet and made you accept your lot.

"A bit quiet, Steven", John said without taking his eyes off the road.

"Yeah. Still adjusting, I guess."

"Anything you'd like to talk about?"

"Maybe. But it will come out in its own time."

There wasn't the opportunity to drag this shred of conversation out any further because, without warning, and as was always the case for me, Rice Lake suddenly came into view. And the vista pumped me full of positive energy. At each encounter, Rice Lake looked a bit different, but was always just another variation on the same vision, a large and placid haven cradled lovingly in the arms of its many surrounding hills and providing sanctuary for a brood of islands. Shallow and warm in the summer, it's much different than other lakes further north, because of its size, because of the hills that surround it, because of the islands that seem to float on it.

We drove straight down toward the lake, John found a place to park, and we got out. The very distributed nature of Gores Landing might make it hard for a first-timer to believe that it really is a settlement at all. But one doesn't need to spend much time there to realize that the local spirit is alive and well.

We walked down Plank Road toward the fishing pier. We passed the short Lampman Lane, which rose slightly to our left, reminding me that one of the Confederation poets, Archibald Lampman, had spent some of his childhood years here in Gores Landing. I guess I always felt some connection to Lampman, given that I had spent about the same amount of time here as he did, in my case from age twelve to seventeen. I still felt attracted to and had some bond with the location, if not the village, in contrast to the unease I always felt when I thought about, and particularly when I visited, Ranleigh.

Lampman had lived here for about ten years. His poetry had always appealed, and it seemed clear enough that he had been inspired by the area around Rice Lake. Looking out at what lay unrolled before me now — the lake, itself a study in aquarelle mysticism, the islands floating in the haze of a waking dream, the whole brooding self-contained nature of the scene, almost like a world unto itself — I felt similarly affected, and some of Lampman's verse from "April in the Hills" floated naturally to the surface:

> I break the spirit's cloudy bands,
> A wanderer in enchanted lands,
> I feel the sun upon my hands;

And far from care and strife
The broad earth bids me forth. I rise
With lifted brow and upward eyes.
I bathe my spirit in blue skies,
And taste the springs of life.

"Very peaceful", John said softly. "I remember you saying that you enjoyed your time here", he added, after a delay.

"Yes."

I knew that, although John had been raised in his family's cabin, he had attended school here in Gores Landing and also had some feeling for the place. Then he had gone off to university at the age of eighteen. He was a forester in his blood and by education, but his formal parallel training in accounting ensured that he could always find steady work and have a good income. Secretly, however, he had surrendered to his first and only love: his several hundred special acres, sanctified by the sweat of his forebears, and the larger expanse of the Northumberland County Forest. He spent as much time there as he could, and within just a few years he was better informed about the forest, its history, and what was in it than pretty much any professional forester.

"But", John continued, still gazing out over the lake, "I wish only that I could have seen this place when it had its old-growth forests."

"Must have been impressive", I offered.

"Impressive would hardly be the word. Enchanted doesn't even capture it. A fantastic mixed forest, huge white pine, oak, maple, elm trees. What we've lost!"

It never did take much to get John talking about our forests, especially our forests past. "If only they could have left just some of it", he would lament. And I knew that he had strong views about past logging practices, about the attitudes that underlay those practices, and about the politics that just stood aside and let it all happen. His views brought him into conflict more than once with other foresters, those he considered to be secret apologists for those silvicultural rapists whose claim to forestry as a profession John regarded as nothing more than protective colouration. They tried to walk the superficial talk, but they had no chance against John, whose knowledge of forests and all the history surrounding them was complete, intact, and subject to instant total recall.

There were many occasions when I considered that John's interest and commitment might have rubbed off on me, and there were times when I wished that had happened. A bachelor's degree in general science, then a master's in physics seemed an unlikely prelude to my now more than twenty years career leading to the position of manager of warehousing for a large chain of pharmacies. Sounds dull, although it's anything but that. However, in some way I've always had the feeling that something was missing. The countryside? A job that would have been compatible with a rural or village life?

Something to do with a forest?

I was always pretty much convinced that this was all just the grass being greener somewhere else, or that peculiar human perversity, to chafe at the reality of all other doors slamming shut and locking when one is opened. This sort of conversation was heard on occasion among colleagues at work, when people would gripe about traffic or pollution or noise and yearn for a simpler life. It was all brought into sharper focus when one of our number at the warehouse announced he was leaving, had bought a delightful property in Janetville. The reasons for his tail-between-legs return just eight months later became known gradually.

"The library there wasn't good at all."

"Anything more refined than bread, eggs, or milk involved a half-hour drive."

"There were just too many nosy people."

***

In that regard, John was my hero. He had immersed himself in his own world, something that, I admit, likely would suit very few people. But I would need to go a long way to find more interesting, more informed, and more challenging company than John. One look at his library was enough to have that come through loud and clear.

And now? For me? Without Joyce? What would I...? Well, we would have to see.

"Let's eat", John said, and I could tell from his expression that both lunch and several more projects were dancing before his eyes. Back in the car, we drove up the hill out of Gores Landing, and John made the turn that I knew would take us to Sarah's Kitchen. Our meal was a light, simple affair, and John took us home via a slightly roundabout route in order to have a few more views of Rice Lake as it basked in the sun.

John received not much mail, mainly because that's the way he wanted it. He had a community mailbox in Ranleigh, and we stopped there now. There were three letters which John placed in the compartment between our seats, a wave of his hand indicating that they could wait until later.

Back at John's place, Dougie welcomed us as though we had just returned from a five-week absence, and John fussed him and gave him a small handful of kibble.

"Next job the tree?" I asked John.

"Yes. That's the priority for the rest of the day."

I helped John bring out from the storage area at the back of the garage two pairs of heavy work gloves, two sets of safety goggles, his chainsaw, a handsaw, a sawhorse, two axes, and a rake. We set to work. Somehow, the visit by the coroner and anthropologist and, especially, the removal of the bones had robbed the scene of all its negative portent.

"Let's strip off as many branches as we can, then we'll start cutting up the trunk beginning at the crown end."

"How much of it will be firewood?" I asked. "Which sections do you want to save for woodworking? Furniture?"

"We'll cut it into firewood except for the last twenty-five feet next to the root."

And so we began. The large branches were cut from the trunk, and from these the smaller branches carrying the foliage were stripped off and placed on a large square of tarpaulin that we had laid out on the grass. The large and now denuded branches were then cut to one-foot lengths and piled in John's wheelbarrow. When the barrow filled, I wheeled it to the woodshed, part of the large lean-to structure, which also included the garage and John's workshop. The woodshed could be accessed through entrances outside and inside the house. It took an hour and a half to separate those branches carrying foliage and to cut the large branches and stack them in the shed. Another hour was sufficient to cut the upper section of the trunk to the required one-foot lengths and to lug these sections to the chopping area next to the woodshed. In another forty minutes, we had the last twenty-five feet of the trunk cut into six four-foot sections, and we rolled these to the side of the house next to the workshop. By six o'clock, we had dragged the tarpaulin and its load of small branches, twigs, and foliage to a spot next to the woodshed, covered it with a second, slightly larger piece of tarpaulin, and weighted down all the edges.

I watched John as we worked. The sinews in his arms stood out as he sawed and chopped, but he moved with ease and economy. Although he wore a neutral expression, I was quite sure that he regretted, as I certainly did, seeing such a large, magnificent being meet its sad end. But I knew as well that John understood nature's ways of trimming and rejuvenating forests. This was one of them. Naturally occurring fires was another. It seemed random and wasteful, but over the long term it made sense and resulted in vigorous and dynamic forests.

"What will you do with the roots?"

"Let's see if we can tip the roots and the stump back into the hole. We probably can't, but if that's the case I'll ask a neighbor to come by with his tractor."

We couldn't.

I grabbed the rake, and over John's objections began raking the debris back toward the tree stump.

"Okay! I think that's it, John."

"Yes. Thank you. That's a good job. We'll just put away the tools and then we can have our reward."

Despite the care we took, our jeans were now marked by patches of sticky pine gum. John waved that off, a problem easily solved later, not a priority at the moment, and then he vanished inside the house. Less than a minute later he re-emerged carrying a tray that held cans of Pub House Ale and two mugs. We smiled at each other and John waved toward the chairs on the porch. With Dougie's help once more, I managed to find the right chair. The first long glug awoke in me the realization that I was not only thirsty, I was also famished. But rushing the consumption of a good ale is a sign of incompetence. We drank, watched ripples of pine pollen drift through golden bars of sunlight, and listened to birds and the breeze communing in the boughs.

Putting down my empty mug after its second filling, I stretched out my legs and sighed.

"I love visiting this place."

"Well, you've known it a long time. You used to ride here from Ranleigh on your bike almost every day in summer."

And I could remember many of those occasions, until a year after my father died. By then, my sister had moved away, and there were only two of us in the house in Ranleigh, me and my mother. After a year of struggle, she said we were moving to Gores Landing, that she had found a job there at a marina. It took my mother a long time to sell the house, and that just added to the struggle. But looking back later, I think there was more to it even than that.

When my father died, a hole appeared in my mother's life, one that she couldn't heal and that wouldn't be filled. I have since reached the conclusion that my mother is not a naturally happy person, that she has a large fatalistic streak, and that somewhere along the line she became convinced that life, and not she, was calling the shots. She's not happy now, I know. I think she doesn't understand, at some basic level, what real happiness is, and nothing I have ever said or done seems to have changed that for her.

There was also a hole in my life after my father died, but at age ten, I really didn't know what was going on. In some sense, my dad had been my best friend, and there was pain there. But transitioning from boy to man isn't easy, even under favourable circumstances. It was much later that I could see the hole, but by then John had become a kind of surrogate. It was all clearer, sort of, and just a matter of history, by the time I was thirty-five.

"And then after you and your mother moved to Gores Landing…"

John's placid comment drew me out of my jumbled recollections, placed me once more next to Dougie, surrounded by a cohort of reassuring protective pines. Mentally and emotionally, I slid back and into the present, my familiar here and now cameo, its edges smudged in Bacchic artistry.

And after we had moved to Gores Landing, how could I forget the many occasions when John had driven there, picked me up, and taken me back to his place? That was really the golden age of my childhood and adolescence. Of course, we don't know a golden age when we're in it, but it didn't take too many years before I was able to look back and see what had been happening: I was old enough to start being my own person, old enough to feel the awakening of a powerful natural curiosity, old enough to take an interest in and to soak up all the things that John told me, about the forest, about trees, about grasses, flowers, birds, insects, about…

"I guess you know that I hoped you would study forestry."

I smiled at John. "Yes. I guessed that. And maybe I should have done."

"No. I think you did the right thing, following your own nose."

John looked around contentedly.

"I'm glad those bones have been removed", he said.

"Oh!" I responded, a bit surprised. "Were they bothering you, or…?"

"No, not at all", John said. "It will just limit what the gossips can spin stories about."

I just looked at John, willing him to say more.

"Oh, everybody knows or soon will know about the bones. And people will talk about them in an idle way. It's the oddly specific questions that have already come my way that I find irritating."

"What kind of questions?" I asked.

"Before you arrived yesterday, somebody claiming to be a reporter came here with a lot of questions, wanting to know what I knew about it."

"What, that soon?" I asked.

"Yes. Too quick off the mark, I thought. And I have my doubts on whether he really is a reporter." John looked into the distance and shook his head.

I glanced at my watch.

"You're right", John said, springing into action. "We need to change, put some rubbing alcohol to work on these patches of pine gum, and then get the whole lot in the laundry. Is steak okay tonight?"

Steak was more than okay. By seven thirty, we had showered, got into fresh duds, sent the pine gum packing, fired up the barbecue, made a large Caesar salad, and were seated again with more Pub House Ale.

Dinner was accompanied by desultory conversation, bats began their aeronautic chase after bugs, and John indicated what he wanted to do the next day. At some point John had wandered inside and came back with one of the pieces of mail. He opened it, read it through, folded it again, and set it down on the table.

"Another ale?"

"Sure. Why not", I said, and I rose to get them. John waved me back to my seat, saying that he would do it, and then went into the house.

After three minutes, I wondered and eventually put two and two together. There had been something about the way John had looked at the letter, and from experience I knew that John could be subtle but at the same time make his meaning entirely clear.

I reached over, picked up the letter, and read it. Given the nature of the letter, and the events of early that morning, there was little doubt that I would need to make a phone call first thing the next day.

6

The Intruder

Peace and quiet reigned supreme. There was no breeze and the silence was pretty much absolute. Through my bedroom window, a patch of sky revealed a swarm of stars. The silhouettes of many pines were motionless sentinels. From the way things were illuminated outside, I could tell that the moon was low in the sky, indicating that morning was not far off.

But my feeling was not one of rural relaxation.

For no good reason I could put my finger on, it was one of foreboding.

I climbed out of bed and pulled on my jeans. When I stepped outside through the front door, I could see John, naked from the waist up, standing out on the grass and looking around.

Dougie growled deep in his throat, and I realized suddenly that I had been awakened by a sound like that.

I was about to say something to John when Dougie began barking ferociously. There was the snap of a twig, and John's large flashlight cast a flood of illumination onto a patch of nearby forest.

"Who's there?" John shouted in a commanding voice.

All at once we could see movement. Dougie was transformed instantly from a lap dog spaniel to an enraged Doberman, and he ran out onto the grass, howling ferociously. There was the sound of someone crashing through undergrowth, then a figure appeared at the edge of the forest, sprinting toward the road about a hundred metres distant.

My wits returned abruptly and I grabbed at the form in the front pocket of my jeans.

My cellphone.

Ambient light was low but the running figure was being captured intermittently by the beam from John's lamp. A strong-looking athletic figure. Light-brown brush cut. Black jeans. A black sweater. I managed to take six pictures before the figure disappeared around the corner of John's lane, and then there was just the receding metronomic crunch as the figure sprinted along the gravel road. Less than a minute later, we heard a car engine start and the sound of someone speeding away.

Dougie continued to bark, combining the satisfaction of a vigilant sentry and the regret at not having sunk his teeth into the leg of some varlet. The fur on the back of his neck was still raised. His challenging stance seemed to say, "just come back and try that again you cowardly bastard, I dare you." John walked over to Dougie, patted him vigorously on the flank, "good dogged" him generously, went back into the cabin, and emerged with a liberal reward of kibble.

We trooped back inside and, as part of his reward, Dougie came with us.

It was ten minutes to four. Morning light would begin to diffuse upward from the east in less than an hour.

"Cup of coffee?" John asked.

"No. Thanks."

But I took a seat at the kitchen table while John set about making a cup of instant for himself.

"Did you recognize the swine?" I asked.

John shook his head.

"No", he said without turning away from his task.

Coffee made, John came over to the table and sat across from me.

"Did you get anything?" he asked, watching me work my cellphone.

"I had time to try for six pictures. Three of them are just forms. Could be anybody. Two caught a good profile in mid-stride. One has a fair impression of the left side of his face."

I showed the image to John. He looked carefully, but eventually just shook his head.

"Don't know him", he said.

"What do you think he was after?" I asked.

"No idea", John said, sounding genuinely perplexed. "He was nowhere near the house, or the workshop, or my car. I don't keep anything of real value here. I often don't lock the door, but then…"

I realized that I didn't really know much about John's day-to-day life.

"Are you around a lot of the day? Do you leave for long periods?" John shook his head.

"No. It's more likely that people will come here. I go into Gores Landing or Cobourg occasionally, but not often, and just for a half hour of shopping or to pick up the odd thing. I'm rarely away for more than an hour. Much of the time I'm in the workshop. And anybody coming onto the property likely would hear the machines."

John sipped his coffee.

"But this Charlie was nowhere near the house. And do you think he didn't know about Dougie before he tried to do whatever he was trying to do? And what was he trying to do anyway?" This was just me thinking idly aloud. But I had a feeling about what had been happening.

"He could only have been looking at the fallen tree", John said.

"In the middle of the night?" I asked incredulously. "What is there to see?"

But John was ahead of me. "It does seem odd. Also odd and maybe arrogant not to think about the possibility of a dog, or motion sensors. But perhaps he was just starting. Maybe we interrupted what was planned to be a more thorough search."

We sat quietly, John gazing into his coffee, me willing my cellphone to tell me what this was all about.

"Okay", John said, draining his coffee mug, "we have time for another hour or so of shut-eye", and he rose and headed toward his bedroom. Partway across the room, he stopped and turned, a smile on his face.

Dougie stood in the middle of the room, evidently expecting something, his tail offering a slow and uncertain wag.

"Okay then!" John said to him. "Come on!"

Dougie pranced, gave a short, happy bark, and the two of them headed toward John's bedroom and a non-kibble reward that Dougie evidently earned only rarely and by going above and beyond.

I went to my bedroom, looked through the pictures on my cellphone again, found no new inspiration, stripped off my jeans, and climbed back into bed.

What had he been looking for? I asked myself. *In the middle of the night.* Well, maybe it was the middle of the night because he didn't want to risk being seen on John's property during the day. And if he, or somebody, knew that John was home almost all of most days...

I looked again at the pictures on my cellphone, finally emailed them to myself, then just lay there for a while, thinking that if I was going to extract any intelligence from these pictures, I would need some specialist help.

Finally, I set my cellphone on the night table. There was still no hint of the light of morning, and although I expected further sleep to elude me, it came as a surprise when I suddenly heard sounds coming from the kitchen. I checked my watch. It told me accusingly that the time was now almost seven o'clock.

7

Private Investigator

Emerging from the bed was no trouble. The recollection of the intruder of a few hours earlier now had that same odd character as a rapidly dissolving dream. But it also had that feeling of unreality that can attach to an event occurring after nightfall. Now, daytime had ushered in once more the real world, a place where intruders are no longer faceless, fantastical, and elusive, but can be cornered and hauled off to the slammer.

The day beckoned, I was well-rested, and I wanted to get on with things. Pulling on just jeans once more, I was surprised not to find John in the kitchen, so I walked directly outside into a delightful Friday morning. An avian serenade surrounded me. The flagstones outside the front door felt wonderfully cool and damp on my bare feet, but I couldn't decide whether the goose bumps and raised nipples were due to the chill air or the generous welcome of the sound and light show. Robins warbled their distributed woodland chorus, ruffs of breeze fluttered everywhere, but the main feature, once more, was the pines. Still wearing the last of their misty night garments, they stood around waiting for the day's developments. Their needles were laden with moisture, the grass shouldered a heavy load of dew, and somewhere the sun was rubbing sleep from the morning's eyes.

The business at hand was completed by one email, which I sent from my cellphone. I related the events of the past two days cryptically: I told Mark about the skeleton, gave him the names of the coroner and the anthropologist, mentioned the letter John had received, and noted the intruder's visit.

Just an alert and a request at this stage. Saying that it looked as though I would need Mark's help. Background could come later, when I had a chance to sit down with my tablet and type out more detail. Having greeted the morning, I went back inside and found John preparing breakfast.

"Ah! There you are. Eggs on toast?"

"Perfect!" I replied and went to get dressed. I returned a few minutes later, in time to help John carry coffee and plates of breakfast outside to the picnic table. As we ate, I was aware of being in a favoured spot.

"I thought we would start off by visiting the forest this morning", John began. "A proper visit, I mean."

I nodded agreement as I scoured that last bit of egg from my plate using the last bit of toast.

Taking another sip of coffee, I made to collect the breakfast things and carry them inside.

"No rush", John said, gesturing me back in my seat. "We can just enjoy the morning. No traffic light here to race through ahead of the guy in the car beside you."

I looked at John in some surprise, but then just laughed when I saw his sly smile and wink.

"It's not really a matter of slowing down to a country pace", John began, before I had a chance to say anything. "It's more a question of being economical and having purpose. There's nothing lazy about the woodland. All those plants and animals are trying to survive, and that's a serious full-time job. It just looks laid back to many people. But really, it's not laid back at all."

The morning was advancing. I looked out over the familiar line of trees against the sky, a scape that I had known for decades, since my boyhood. It was a view that appeared immutable simply because it was more than a few centuries old.

We sat in companionable silence for some time, then I stirred on my bench.

"The agenda for today?" I asked.

"Well, I want to walk down the road, and see where our intruder parked his car. And we should investigate where we heard him over there in the underbrush. Likely won't find anything, but we might be able to see what he was aiming at."

"What about the rest of the property?"

"Well", John began, "I did a check earlier this morning. Nobody tried to break into my car or shop, at least as far as I can see. Nothing's been damaged. Nothing's missing. So unless we did interrupt him, I'm at something of a loss."

I began collecting the breakfast things.

"Then we'll go into the forest. Let you say hello."

It rarely took more than that to remind me of so many tours through the forest with John over the years. We carried the plates inside, I washed them up quickly, overriding all objections, and then we set off to check for traces from the previous evening. But my mind was ranging through the past. As often happened when I visited John, many past conversations respooled in my mind. And this was something that returned with particular urgency since I had lost Joyce.

My memorable time with John had begun in a serious way when I was about fourteen. The loss of my father, my sister leaving home under a familial dark cloud, our move, my mother and me, to Gores Landing, these were all serious derailments. And on top of that, fourteen is an unsettling time in a boy's life. The unfamiliar hormonal turmoil that most men probably recall clearly from that age had been upon me. But, fortunately, a few other powerful compensating interests had been ignited. These came back to mind now, likely prompted by recalling a question John had pulled from the air over dinner the previous evening.

"Do you remember the first book on science that really made an impression on you?"

"I certainly do", I said, without hesitation. "It was *Crystals, Diamonds, and Transistors*, by, uh, by…"

"Marrison", John said. "L. W. Marrison."

"Yes. I think you loaned it to me."

"I did."

It had all come back clearly.

Back then, reading the book hadn't so much opened the door to a great world of learning, it had blown the door off its hinges. That book had raised a froth of questions in my mind. John had answered them all, but in John's way. He would never hand anything to me on a plate, except when we were right at the beginning of some topic on which I knew nothing whatever. When he thought it was appropriate, he would give me part of the answer to a question I had asked, invite me to guess what was missing, and either ask additional specific questions or suggest that I think about it a bit more. Often he would indicate something in his library and invite me to go looking for the rest myself.

There was general knowledge, certainly, and things linked to my burgeoning interest in physics. But pride of place was occupied by those things I learned about the forest and what was in it. And for that, the forest itself was our classroom.

"Ready to go?" John asked.

I glanced around the kitchen, checking that I had put everything away, and nodded before we set off down the drive and out onto the road. It took only a few minutes to find where the intruder's car had churned up the gravel as he made off. Pulling out my cellphone, I took several pictures. We returned to John's place to investigate the area where the snapping twigs had captured our attention early that morning. We found the spot where two tracks met. Fallen leaves, churned-up needles, and bent and broken live branches indicated someone evidently unused to moving quietly or carefully through the bush. One track led away deeper into the forest. The other moved toward the edge of the trees, showing signs of someone in haste.

"This looks like the direction he took when we challenged him. And it looks like he made his approach from there." John pointed along the track leading further into the forest. "Probably came off the road just beyond my place then tried to sneak in from there."

"So he must have known something about the layout and location of your property", I offered.

"Could have got that from any map", John said, shaking his head. "Didn't know about Dougie, though. That, or he thought he could sneak in without Dougie hearing him. Either way, poorly informed. Or maybe just arrogance born of ignorance."

During this investigation, I had taken several more pictures.

"Okay. Enough of this shit", John said, atypical vehemence in his voice. "Let's go say hello to the forest."

And so began a ramble that recalled so many others we had taken over many years. And our ramble also became for me a vivid reverie, a recollection of so many other visits to the forest that often seemed to blend together.

Those early forest visits had changed in nature over time. Early on, we were a teenage student and a teacher. Later we became just two students being taught by the forest. And as students, we regarded everything.

Birds.

Evidence of small ground animals.

Occasionally some bear scat.

"...and there's a bracket fungus." The sort of comment that would lead to extended studies of fungi, moulds, and lichens.

"...and the pines. Here's a jack pine", John had said on one of our first outings, reaching out, drawing his hand along the length of one of the twigs, and caressing the needles. I remembered the look on his face: soft, deferring, humble, smiling slightly as if in approval or as a supplicant asking to be informed, to be led out of his own ignorance. Years later I knew that what I had seen then was the regard of a lover.

"You can tell this one partly by the fact that the needles are in pairs. We won't pick a pair off the tree, there are probably, yes, here we are." And he'd stooped to pick up a pair of brown needles from the ground.

"Over here, now this one is a red pine. See? Its needles are also in pairs, but compare the length. The jack pine needles are a lot shorter and tend to be thicker. Compare the two against your palm, and you'll always be able to distinguish them."

I smiled now at this great store of memories. We walked on further. The trees enclosed spaces that were shaded, cool, resinous, and quiet because of the sound-dampening bed of needles on the ground. Perhaps not a savage place, but certainly holy and enchanted. A cathedral. A place where one would expect to find magic, but good magic, white magic.

My reveries resumed.

"And here", I recalled John saying, his voice taking on a tone of reverence. "This is the eastern white pine. We can't touch its needles. The branches begin way too high off the ground, but we can find, I'm sure ... yes, here." He stooped. "See? The needles are in groups of five. And look at the long, straight trunk", he said, and we craned, looking upwards to where the first branches appeared at what seemed an impossible height.

And now, back in the present, we stood for some time, perhaps at the same spot as back then, gazing upward.

My knowledge of the forest had come gradually, naturally one might say, triggered by things we saw or by questions that occurred to me. And it had been my realization that the large trees in John's forest were different from those around my home village, around Ranleigh.

"There are pine trees near Ranleigh", I had said one day back then, "but I don't think they're like this. Is there something different about your land here?"

"No. There's nothing different about the land."

And that was the day I began to learn the whole story, mostly depressing, sometimes infuriating, depending on my mood, but in this particular place, inspiring.

That was when John had begun relating the long story of his family, of their connection to these great mature trees, trees that had been standing hundreds of years before his family's arrival, and how that connection had developed. It was a story whose details I learned over a period of months and years, and I recalled it clearly.

On many occasions back then, we walked through the forest. John looked around at the trees, always wearing the same soft expression. I recalled the day he expanded on something he had described only fleetingly up to then.

"Donald's father could read and write, something that wasn't common then. He taught his son, and that learning came on down through the family, long before there were public schools or any laws about attendance. I've been lucky. Donald's father, then Donald, and all my relatives after them, they all could read and write, and they all kept journals. Not all of those journals survived, but many did. That's how I can tell you so much about the past."

"Do you keep a journal too?" I had asked.

"I certainly do", John had replied.

We drifted on among the trees. I still had been wondering about the difference between the pines here and those near Ranleigh, but I knew that John hadn't forgotten.

"You're right", John had said. "There is a difference between the pines here and those at Ranleigh. It wasn't just land clearing. Something else happened. Something that's still hard to understand."

John had stopped here, abruptly it seemed to me, and I remember looking over at him and seeing a different person. His face now wore a hardened expression, showing distaste, regret, loss.

He looked at me and his face relaxed.

"What happened?" I asked.

"Commercial logging. That's what happened. All the land around Ranleigh and, in fact, this whole area was logged out, stripped bare.

Except for my family's land here." And that's when I had learned the story about the Stanleys facing down the Ballantyres' logging crews.

"All the members of my family, and down through generations, developed an almost mystical attachment to the pine forests. All around here. Where my cabin stands now. And that was odd, in a way, because my family were all farmers. They acquired hundreds of acres, a lot of it very good, arable land."

"Could one family farm all that land?"

John shook his head. "No. Today, if one had a lot of equipment, it wouldn't be difficult. But back then… They needed hired help. And when I look back through their journals and the financial information they kept, it's pretty clear they were able to do it only because they were good managers and planners. Even then…"

"But they were interested in the forest. Why?"

"Good question", John said. "When I look through their journals, I see reverence. It just seems that they saw something exceptional in these big trees. Something worth keeping."

"So then, what did they do with the forest?"

"That's the interesting thing. They didn't do anything with it."

"Nothing at all?" I asked, but I had also sensed that something important was coming.

"As far as I can tell, Cyrus had come to love his forest, placed great value on it. Aesthetic value, that is. And that seems to have been passed on to his son Donald. But they both had become alarmed at the scale and the nature of the logging that was taking place. And as the land all around was being stripped bare of anything valuable, that seemed only to harden their resolve. There are statements pretty much to that effect in Cyrus's journal. So it became known throughout the area that no logging would take place in their woods. In Bush Green. None at all."

"Bush Green? That's the sign on your—"

"Yes. They called this wood Bush Green, after an area near Harlesden in Norfolk, the place Clifford's family left in England to come here. So, after I finished at university and decided that I would come back here, I made that sign, gave my house a name."

Our house in Ranleigh didn't have a name. In fact, I knew of no other house back then that had a name. But it seemed to me a perfectly natural thing to do.

"So now you have this forest", I said, feeling that I was just confirming an outcome, that it had been an interesting story.

"Yes. But it wasn't that easy. Nothing like that easy. There were a few families who became very big in the timber business in the nineteenth century. The Booths, the Bronsons, the Prices, the Boyds. The Ballantyres were the family that produced most of the timber in this area. They seemed to think they had the right to cut any tree they came across. And they looked at the Stanley property. They even began cutting here. But Cyrus and his sons turned up. Told them to clear off. That this was private land. Well, the logging crew pretty much ignored them, until Cyrus and his boys hauled out their rifles and fired a few shots into the air. That was the end of that felling operation."

We carried on walking through the forest and were now in a large stand of very big old trees. I had been here many times before. And John rarely missed an opportunity to check that I was still aware of what was around me.

"Do you know what these trees are, Steven?" John had asked me on one such past occasion.

I looked up at them, looked down at the ground, picked up some of the pine needles.

"They look like white pine."

"That's exactly what they are. Eastern white pine."

I remember moving away from John's side, into this great stand of trees. I had never seen trees so large. I looked up at them, and I was convinced that they looked down at me, that they were speaking to me.

There must have been more than a hundred of these giants, and I continued walking through them, could hear John walking behind. One of the trees was particularly large. I walked up to it, felt its rough bark, tried to wrap my arms around it, couldn't reach even a quarter way.

"Big White."

I turned to look at John.

"Big White. This tree has been known as Big White in my family for at least a hundred years."

"Is this what the loggers were after?"

"This is exactly the sort of tree they were after."

"So your great-great-whatever, he won."

"Yes. He won. But it was a long fight. The Ballantyres absolutely hated to lose, and one of them, Lorne Ballantyre, took it personally. There was very bad blood between him and both Cyrus and Donald. Lorne Ballantyre and, in fact, the whole Ballantyre family were an argumentative bunch of bastards. They were involved in a lot of court cases. But they had money. They could afford it. They didn't seem to care."

"So they just gave up?"

"Oh no! They didn't give up. They tried everything they could think of to get at these trees."

"They're worth a lot then, these trees."

"To someone like you or me, yes. Each of these trees would have been worth quite a bit, cut down and converted to squared timber. But to the Ballantyres, compared to the money they made from their bigger operations, what they would get from this stand would have been tiny, trivial."

"So then, why?

"They just couldn't stand the thought of losing."

"How did it all end?"

"It all ended when the timber boom ended. All the trees worth having had been cut, the logging crews disappeared, sawmills closed, and the glory days of the Ballantyre logging operations came to an end."

"And that was it."

"Well, that was it as far as the timber business went, but all the other consequences were still to come. And they were terrible."

And so John then explained to me how large parts of Southern Ontario were well on the way to becoming a desert, and how a few far-sighted people stepped in just in time.

That was my introduction to the Northumberland County Forest, and how it came to be.

Today we walked again through the forest on John's land, and although I recalled with pleasure many earlier days, there was still the contagion of our intruder the night before at the back of my mind. What had he been after?

Back at John's cabin, just before noon, we sketched out the rest of the day. There was a small amount of shopping to do. We agreed to miss lunch and have dinner slightly earlier.

"Is there anything you need to do?" I asked.

John hesitated.

"I should spend about two hours doing some woodwork. Do you mind?"

"No! Not at all! Go ahead. I'll finish raking and gathering up the debris from the tree."

So we went off, did the shopping, collected John's single item of mail, had another look at Rice Lake, returned to John's cabin, then separated to do our individual chores.

The raking was really an excuse. There was little left to rake, and when I had finished, I went inside, collected my tablet, transferred the photos from my cellphone, and sent a longish follow-up message to Mark Whelan. It took me a while to get the wording right so that the picture I painted was both complete and coherent, and then I sent it off.

From John's workshop, I could hear the sound of a router, then a sander, and, at intervals, John whistling, which I took as confirmation of work moving forward as planned.

Mark replied in less than half an hour.

How have you been? The developments at John's sound interesting. Should we get together when you're back in Toronto?

I replied: *Yes, let's get together. I'd like to hire you formally. If you're happy to go ahead on an informal basis for a few days, we can sign a contract when we get together.*

Are you still out there now? Mark asked in his next email.

He knew about Joyce. In fact, he and Andrea were pillars that I had leaned on regularly. I had known them for three years, had used Mark once professionally to provide arm's length investigation of some losses from the warehouse, we got along well, and the four of us, Andrea and Mark, and Joyce and I, became occasional social friends.

Yes. Needed a bit of country healing. In case questions come up, I'd like to be just "a client" for the time being. And, if possible, try to deflect any focus away from John.

Mark replied: *No problem. See you in a few days.*

8

Eye in the Sky

Over the years, right up to the time I went off to university, I spent a lot of time at John's place, and many days in his forest.

I learned about almost everything that was in the forest, or at least some of everything that John knew, and it seemed that there wasn't much he didn't know. There were the trees, of course; the pines, spruces, and larches, but also the big deciduous trees: Carolina poplars, maples, oaks, beeches, elms, ash, hornbeam, black walnut, birch, and others. Down in the low areas I learned about willows. There were a few plane trees. And we found black locust and several incomers.

And I recall being pleased with myself, knowing so much about so many trees, only to be somewhat deflated when we started on shrubs. And then grasses, wild flowers, herbs, mosses, lichens, and fungi. I was soaking it up like a sponge. There could be no such thing as "too much". I had never dreamed that there was so much in a forest, that it was so complex.

And then, once again, when I thought we were almost finished, we started on mammals, birds, reptiles, amphibians, annelids, insects, and it went on and on. By the time I was sixteen, when I walked into the forest with John, what I saw around me caused hundreds of names to fly up from memory.

I had other interests. Of course I did. There were girls, but I learned quickly enough that they had zero interest in bugs, snakes, frogs, and salamanders; they just didn't want to know. But it wasn't just the girls. It seemed that nobody my age wanted to know. So I learned very soon to keep my knowledge to myself, to avoid being branded a weirdo. And I didn't like doing that; it made me feel as though I were betraying John somehow. My interest in physics was becoming strong then, and I followed that interest all the way through to my master's degree.

During my university years I continued to visit John, but rarely. Then I met Joyce. Within five months we were engaged. And in April of the year that I received my master's degree, we were married. Looking back, it was a dream. We were delirious. Joyce settled into her career as an industrial photographer. She was good technically and good socially, and she was always asked to do more work than she could accept.

We visited John. Joyce wasn't a country girl, and John's house in the forest really wasn't to her taste. But John can work magic with people. She came to like him, then to love him. We visited as often as we could.

***

It was not yet six o'clock on the third morning of my visit to John. I was in front of John's stove, cooking breakfast. Being in this place, hearing the sounds and smelling the aromas of eggs and bacon cooking, the distinctive scent of homemade bread being toasted, it all merged in an odd surrealistic way with so many similar occasions in the past, including my last visit here with Joyce, before the diagnosis. And I suddenly felt so vividly that Joyce really was there again, that I could reach out and touch her...

"You're up early!" John said, having entered the kitchen silently.

"Slept enough", I responded. "Can't just lie around. Shall we eat outside?"

"Sure", John said with enthusiasm.

Judging by their volume and tunefulness, the birds agreed. There was broken overcast above us, and it was already clearing fast.

We assembled plates of food, cutlery, mugs of coffee, napkins, and trays and stepped out into the day. Even though it was still May, the morning air had that luscious feel of summer, and as we seated ourselves at the picnic table, a silent but extravagant cataract of sunlight broke through the retreating clouds, slanted in from the east, and splashed over everything.

We could hear birds all around us, but the only ones bold enough to drop in for a closer look were sparrows. Two of them landed at the end of the table and stood, looking at us like cheeky little ruffians, their heads always on the move, on the lookout for things good or bad.

One of them chirped.

John looked at me. "He's saying to his friend 'You take the one on the left'."

I tossed them two small pieces of toast. The ruffians fell upon them, and two seconds later had resumed their vigil as though nothing had happened.

"I know what they're thinking", I said. "'Not a bad start, even if it was meagre. Maybe the guy on the right is more generous.'"

John broke off two sizeable pieces of crust and tossed them down the table, but not very far down — about a foot short of the end, so only a bit more than two feet from where we were sitting. We could see the two sparrows calculating.

The more forward of the two hopped to the nearest piece of toast, grabbed it, then hopped back to safety. The other sparrow, realizing he had only a few seconds to act, took his courage in both feet, hopped to the other piece, snatched it up, and hopped away.

We watched them consume their feasts.

John reached into his shirt pocket, extracted a piece of paper, smoothed it out, examined it briefly, then looked up.

"I'm still pondering this letter I received the other day", he said, and he placed it on the table facing me.

John can be quite oblique. He often approaches things in a subtle way when he considers it best to avoid direct questions, to feel the way forward. I was sure that he had expected me to look at the letter a couple of days ago, when he made no effort to hide his facial expression as he read it, then deliberately left it on the table and went inside, taking far too long to retrieve just a couple more cans of Pub House Ale. He was asking my opinion now, confident that I actually had seen it, had had time to think about it. At the same time, he was making room for the polite fiction that perhaps I really was seeing it for the first time. I picked it up and scanned it, although I knew exactly what was in it.

It was signed *Gary Ballantyre* and was written in business letter format but had personal letter wording. In what I had thought was a long-abandoned affectation, the salutation "Dear Mr. Stanley" had been crossed out in pen and was replaced by a handwritten "Dear John". John Stanley and Gary Ballantyre knew each other on sight, and John gave him the polite deference that civility expects, but beyond that John would have nothing to do with him. Normally this sort of inter-family hatchet would have been buried long ago, and the present crop of Ballantyres were prepared to act out the cool pretension that it was all in the past. But everyone in the region knew the history, knew that the Ballantyres had failed in their bid to log out the Stanley land. The Ballantyres of the past hadn't been able to find a way to deal with that. And the present Ballantyres, it seemed, couldn't forget. A past defeat had been unavenged, and although it was kept out of sight, still it remained an open wound.

The letter read:

It was a surprise and a concern to hear that human remains had been found on your property. I am aware that this sort of thing can translate into some expense, and I want to offer my support to you. If you wish for any assistance, financial or otherwise, in having this matter resolved, please don't hesitate to contact me.

On the face of it, this wasn't an unusual offer. The Ballantyres could honestly be considered pillars of the community. They had been generous indeed in recent cases involving flooding, they made substantial contributions to support the local food bank, they had financed the construction of a new medical centre, and Ballantyre money had been converted into local scholarships for post-secondary education, support for an Indigenous women's shelter, an annual financial gift to the public library, and a whole raft of prizes in nearby schools.

And when I first read the letter, I had a warm sense of approval, which was followed almost immediately by the questions, *Why this specific event involving John? Why so soon after the discovery?*

I looked up at John.

"Any thoughts?" he asked.

"It's a nice gesture", I replied. "But a bit puzzling."

John just nodded.

"Any suggestions?" he asked.

"I would respond in writing. Thank him for a nice gesture, or something like that. But make or imply no commitment."

John nodded some more, and I sensed that this was pretty much what he had already decided to do. Privately I spent a moment longer reading the letter again. I was memorizing it, at least until I had a chance to write it out in my room. This was something I wanted to talk to Mark about.

We had begun the day early, and it was still shy of seven in the morning. We sat back and listened to the voices of the world around us. Mostly it was birds, but in the background was the quiet voice of the wind, the periodic creak of trees, the occasional chatter of squirrels, and the sounds of small animals moving through dead leaves and undergrowth.

I believe that I heard it first. It sounded like a large dragonfly, and I looked around to see where it was.

Nothing.

But then I realized that what I was hearing couldn't be coming from an insect. I stood and began scanning more widely. John had now heard it as well, and he was on his feet.

Then I saw it. It was an insect. A huge one. But it moved in the strangest way. Suddenly, recognition arrived.

I drew my cellphone from my pocket and began taking pictures.

John could see it now too.

"What is it?" he asked.

"It's a drone."

It was hovering over the hole left by the fallen pine tree.

Half a dozen thoughts flashed through my mind: Throw something at it. Ask John to run inside and collect his shotgun. But then inspiration hit, and I rose and began running down John's drive. In thirty seconds I was approaching the road. The thing was now on the move. I could hear it.

I galloped onto the road, looked both ways, and saw a car parked to the left, about fifty metres away. I began running toward it. The drone drifted in over the treetops, descended, and was collected by a man who emerged from behind the car. He tossed the drone and his controller into the car through an open back window and jumped into the driver's seat. The car engine roared. By then I had taken seven or eight pictures of the car using my cellphone.

Gravel flew out from the car's rear wheels. It lurched and accelerated forward.

It was coming right at me. Fast.

The car was now less than thirty metres away and closing at increasing speed. He had no intention of stopping, maybe not even swerving to avoid me.

The ditch was too wide for me to leap across it. I had no choice. I slid down into the ditch, sank up to my knees in slimy water, and marvelled later that I had recognized newts as the two small animals that leapt away from me in surprise.

The car roared past.

Oh shit! No!

It sounded like it was slowing.

Hanging around to confront the driver was the last thing on my mind.

I scrambled up the other side of the ditch and vanished into the thick undergrowth. Twenty metres into the bush left me with no sight of the road, which meant that chappie in the car wouldn't be able to see me either.

When I stopped to listen, I could hear the car, already distant, and receding quickly.

I have rarely seen John angry.

But when I emerged from the bush a sorry and sodden mess, walked across to where he was still standing, and explained what had happened, his face hardened in quiet rage.

9

Discussions

My time with John came to a close, but it had been another memorable visit. Our walks in John's forest had revived for me memories of the idyllic part of my youth, and I felt that I had communed once more with the unbelievable variety that makes up a mature forest.

Back in Toronto, I was ready to dig into my work again, but the first priority had been something else. Contact Mark Whelan. We had established by email an outline of what Mark would do on watching over John Stanley, but it was time to get into the details. When I spoke to Mark, it was no surprise that he had already started on the "case".

"Hello Steve. I was going to call you. When did you get back?" Mark said when I phoned him.

"Just this afternoon. I want to stay abreast of what you're doing on the John Stanley case. What's the story?"

"Well, it's early days, but I've spoken to the anthropologist and the medical examiner, voiced my interest, said that I want to be kept up to date."

"Did they ask who you represent?"

"No. But I'm pretty sure it's got their interest."

"Do you think there'll be any trouble getting information from them?"

"No. I don't think so. They're both paid from the public purse, and at this stage there's no confidentiality problems, since we don't know who the skeleton belonged to. For the moment, it's just a waiting game. But in the meantime, I'm doing a bit of digging in local records. Some of this stuff has been digitized, so searching it is fairly straightforward. Did you find out anything new over the past few days?"

"Not really. But the discovery of that skeleton seems to have awakened some creepy crawlies. Good reason for wanting to keep an eye on John."

"Does John know that you've retained me?"

"No. Not yet. And with any luck, he won't need to know for now. But I will tell him eventually."

"Sooner rather than later, I suggest", Mark said. "My digging around can't help but attract attention. People will talk. It'll get back to John. Better that it comes from you first."

"You're right", I said, kicking myself for not thinking of something so obvious. "I'll tell him tonight."

"That would be the simplest thing. Not that I expect anything earth-shaking. Frankly, at the moment, it looks as though we'll end up at the default option. Unknown person who died under unknown circumstances. Likely it will make its way quickly to the cold files."

There was a pause.

"Anything else?" Mark asked.

"Yes." And I told him about the drone.

"The drone pilot. What did he look like?"

"I got a picture of him as he was climbing back into his car. A bit blurry. But I also got a half dozen pictures of his car. The licence plate is clear in three of them."

"Good. Send them to me."

"Will do", I said.

"Also", Mark began, "I'd like to meet John, see his place. It helps to have a mental picture."

"No problem as far as I can see", I said, then changed the subject after a short gap. "How about a drink sometime?" I asked.

"Sure, any time. Are you free on Thursday evening?"

"Yes. Somewhere over your way? C'est What would be a good choice."

"Perfect. Shall we say seven thirty?"

"Good!" I said. "Done. See you then."

As it turned out, I didn't need to wait that long.

***

At one time, my job involved me having to supervise nine people quite closely. This made my job awkward and difficult, unnecessarily so. Our work was basically straightforward. There was no reason those people should need day-to-day direction. So I proposed changes to streamline things. These suggestions were repeatedly resisted until the day I told my boss that I was going to leave because I didn't have his confidence.

The problem really was just pointless but entrenched bureaucracy. But me leaving would have upset the bureaucratic basket and dumped some warm steamy stuff into my boss's lap. Suddenly, my questions about the value added by positions and functions seemed entirely reasonable. The end result was that the bureaucracy was seen for what it was, and it began to be stripped away. Responsibilities and decision-making roles began to be placed where they would sit most efficiently. Making the changes for this was not easy; change never is. But this was all done at a level above me.

Within just a week or so, lines of reporting were modified. My boss started checking regularly on my level of job satisfaction. My direct report staff dropped from nine to five, then to three, and then to just one. And I found that even that one could be given his head on most things.

So now the function I oversee is well oiled and my work hums along nicely, mostly under its own steam, without the need for my continuous hand-holding of staff. Indeed, most of my time is spent dealing with novel situations, problems, and irregularities, pinching these things off, corralling them, hacking off the rough edges. This delivers far more novelty and variety than does grunt work, and I find that my days pass quickly.

But there are also dark times. The times when I'm very much aware Joyce is no longer with me. I just have to get through them.

It was Wednesday evening when Mark called me. After brief preliminaries, he came right to the nub.

"Have you heard from John?"

"No. Why?"

"Could we get together? There's been a development."

Since Mark and I live reasonably close to each other, I invited him to come to my place. Twenty minutes later, I buzzed him up.

Mark is in his mid- to late-thirties and has an open face, a ready smile, and grey eyes that miss very little. I had warmed to him as a person the first time I met him and now we shook hands as established friends.

Judging from what I know of his and Andrea's condo and their place at Largs on Balsam Lake, Mark likes rustic things. I have a few items of that sort, not many. My condo is quite large and has three bedrooms, one of which I converted to my office at Joyce's insistence. I haven't changed much in the condo since Joyce died, and I'm getting used to the things that remind me so strongly of her. Mark scanned the living space quickly then followed me into the office. There, I have my desk, bookcases, a large leather sofa, and two wing chairs that murmur "gentlemen's club". I had a bowl of nuts laid out and cans of beer and a bottle of wine in a cooler on the low end table.

Mark chose a can of Flying Monkeys, I followed suit. We poured, clinked glasses, and enjoyed that first mouthful.

"How are you doing?" Mark asked.

"Okay. It's an ongoing effort. But let's talk about the development",
I said, wanting to stay away from my own past.

Mark took another glug of beer, crunched a handful of nuts, then
set down his glass.

"There's been an accusation made, of sorts", he began. "One of
the Ballantyres has been saying that, way back when, there was an
argument between one of theirs and one of John's, and the one of
theirs went missing."

"Would that be Ted Ballantyre who's saying this?"

"Yes."

"And is Gary Ballantyre saying anything?"

"He certainly is", Mark replied. "He's denying it all. On behalf of
the family."

"Is that it?" I asked.

"Not quite", Mark said. "Gary Ballantyre contacted me. Apologized
on behalf of Ted, but said I should be aware that Ted's a hothead, that
he's made wild statements in the past, and has been taken to court
several times."

"Gary came to you? How does he think you're involved?"

"Well, I've been asking around about things, talking to the
anthropologist, the medical examiner. I'm sure that word about me
has got out."

"Who does he think you're working for?"

"No idea. But he probably suspects that I'm working for John."

"Do you know whether Gary has spoken to John?"

Mark shook his head. "Don't know. I doubt it. I don't suppose
John has spoken to you."

It was my turn to shake my head. "No, he hasn't."

I grabbed a handful of nuts and pondered all this.

"What's your take on it?" I asked.

"It's pretty straightforward, I'd say. The Ballantyres are upstanding
citizens. They don't want Ted's wild innuendo swirling around them.
And it's probably just that: off the wall and without any obvious basis.
But all the same, when I see smoke, I always itch to check for fire."

I focussed more sharply in response to this statement. "You mean there might actually be something behind it?"

"Who knows? But better to check than assume."

"Has anything appeared in the local press?"

"Not yet", Mark said. "And probably not ever. I expect that Gary has taken steps to make sure of that."

"Anything online?"

"Haven't found anything yet. But I didn't look too carefully."

"So…"

"So", Mark began. "Before I go off checking for fire, I want to clear it with you."

"Sure, but … wait, though! Do you think there's something funny here?"

"Well, your observation that the skull was fractured … no, I think you said 'bashed in'. That could indicate an accident, or it could point toward a homicide, or, and don't take this wrongly, it might be that you were mistaken. But whether or not homicide is ruled out, Ted's statements are floating around out there. At the very least, I would recommend letting it be known that something more than scuttlebutt will be needed to settle this. But the decision is up to you."

"And if I say leave it? If we just do nothing?"

"It might all work out fine. The whole thing might just fade away. But suppose that the medical examiner concludes that that person was turned into a body by a blow to the head. That means somebody murdered somebody else, and that somebody else was found buried next to John's house. John might end up fighting an uphill public opinion battle. Oh, nobody could accuse him of doing it. It's almost certain the skeleton has been there far too long for that. But someone a few generations earlier in his family would be a good candidate for the rumour mill."

"Has the medical examiner made any statement on the skeleton?" I asked.

"No. Not yet. The word I hear is that the priority on the skeleton is low. Even if he does conclude that there was a homicide, there's no path forward for the police. A perpetrator would almost certainly be dead by now, and even if he or she isn't dead, a police investigation to determine who, how, and when would pretty much be pointless. No real trail to follow. So I expect that every other case coming to the medical examiner takes priority. We'll just need to wait."

I nodded.

"But whatever the medical examiner comes up with", Mark continued, "you might want to consider the independent action we could take, or that I could take on your behalf."

"I don't follow", I said.

"It could be days, weeks even, before the medical examiner states his findings. What's going to happen during that time? Probably nothing, but statements like those just made by Ted Ballantyre invite speculation. It might be hard for the rumour mill to resist an opportunity like that. But, on the other hand, it will become common knowledge that whatever happened occurred a long time ago. Maybe people will just say that it's a ghost from the distant past and move on. We don't know what the rumour mill will say."

I was nodding agreement thus far.

"Suppose that the medical examiner does conclude, days or weeks or even months later, that a homicide was involved. There will probably be a minimal investigation, but I would expect the police to conclude that there are much more important things to spend their time on."

"I see", I said. "So either way it could just end up in limbo."

"Yes. And this is just the sort of thing the rumour mill loves."

"Do I detect that you have a suggestion?"

Mark smiled. "Yes."

I waved him to continue.

"Okay. We can start off by assuming the worst, by supposing that it actually was one of John's forebears who did the deed, and the skeleton really does belong to a past Ballantyre."

"What?" I said, incredulous. "And bury the body on his own property? That would be insane!"

"Probably", Mark replied. "But there might be a perverse logic to it, doing exactly what nobody would expect. But don't get too exercised here. We're looking at what might be a worst case. And we're doing that just to put a tick in a box and see if that path might lead anywhere useful. I've worked through a rough logic, and it looks as though this is just an unlikely 'what if'."

I pondered that for a moment, not being all that familiar with trees of possibilities.

"Another case is more likely. Probably the body isn't that of a Ballantyre, that it was the result of some crime of passion, or even that it was some kind of straightforward farming accident and somebody brought the matter to an end by a quiet, informal, private burial. There will still be questions, though, because the skeleton was found on John's land, and that land has been in the family for generations. And so I think we need to be looking at something like our worst-case scenario, if only to be prepared."

I pondered this and the two general possibilities that suggested themselves: something done in the heat of the moment or something involving premeditation.

"Do you have any idea why Ted would make the statements he's made, why he'd say these things just now?" I asked.

"That, Steve, is the question of the hour."

I waited for Mark to continue.

"He probably has no idea whose body was unearthed. If he's just a hothead and likes the attention, then maybe he's made a story up just for fun. If he has a score to settle with Gary or others in the family, maybe he just wants to embarrass them. And then there's the other possibility."

I tossed Mark a quizzical expression.

"Maybe there's something behind it."

"You mean that maybe one of John's ancestors really did kill a Ballantyre?"

"Think of it in more general terms. Maybe somebody really did kill a Ballantyre."

"And what if that's true?" I asked.

"Well, then we need to proceed with great care. But we'll need to do that anyway. However, let's keep things in focus. At the moment we have no idea at all who that skeleton belonged to or how or why the person came to be dead. We might never know."

I asked Mark what he thought we might do. He outlined a few possibilities then suggested the one he preferred. We talked it over a bit and I agreed.

"What about the pictures I took at John's place? Any luck with them?"

I had sent Mark my cellphone shots of the intruder and of the car driven by the drone pilot.

"I have someone working on it."

"Any idea?" I asked.

"No", Mark said, and I detected some annoyance in his voice. "Taking longer than I wanted."

I just looked at him and made an impatient gesture.

"Well, you know, the mills of the gods and so forth."

It was evident that asking any more questions wouldn't help.

"There is one thing I wanted to ask", Mark said.

"Ask away."

"About a visit to John's place, just to take a look around. It sometimes helps to be able to picture a scene in my mind."

"When?" I asked.

"Things are nicely slow just now, so sometime during the next few days would be convenient for me."

"I'll find out", I said and reached for my phone.

John answered almost immediately. I explained what I was looking for, and he said to come anytime, to use my own key if he wasn't there.

"Is tomorrow or the day after okay?" I asked.

It was and the arrangement was made.

"That was easy enough", Mark said, and we spent a couple of minutes talking about what he wanted to do out there.

It was clear that we had pretty much got to the end of our agenda.

"Have you eaten?" I asked.

"Yes. Thanks. But … what did you have in mind?"

"Well, I've got some nice ice cream sandwiches in the freezer."

"Aha! Now you're talking!"

We had some more beer, ate the ice cream sandwiches, and caught up on each other's lives.

As Mark was leaving, I asked belatedly after Andrea.

"She's fine. She asked me to say hello, and she wants you to email her tomorrow and pick a date when you can come around for dinner."

That sounded just like Andrea, and although a threesome would be awkward for me initially, I found that I was really looking forward to sharing a meal with them.

Mark's strong handshake and his open and friendly grey eyes gave me a lift to offset the awareness that I would be alone for the rest of the evening.

10

Willis

A window came open in Mark's schedule, I freed up a half day, and we drove down to John's place. He wasn't there but had left a note saying he expected us to visit when it was convenient and to help ourselves to anything.

I showed Mark around. He looked at the upturned root of the fallen tree. I showed him where the intruder and the drone pilot had been. We looked at John's garage and workshop. Mark checked all the doors carefully. We took a few more pictures. And then Mark said he was satisfied and we returned to town.

After that, the weeks began to pass. We followed events through the occasional communication from Dr. Willis, the coroner, but most of our information began coming via Mark's contacts. The police had evidently used the same logic Mark had followed and concluded that the skeleton was pretty much doomed to be a cold case no matter what they found and that they would let the work advance only when time for it became available. Mark stayed in touch with Willis, who confirmed that "our" body was definitely on the back burner in terms of priority. Willis apparently wasn't under any particular constraint to keep to himself anything he found, provided that it went first to the police officer in charge.

"They fully expect the case to go nowhere." Mark relayed the message he got from Willis.

But Mark had noted to me that he sensed there was a subtext.

"Oh? What was that?" I had asked.

"Willis is a pretty straight-up guy. Once he was confident that I would be discreet, he opened up a bit. He said he was asked just to push the work forward whenever the other priorities allowed."

"Why would that be surprising?" I asked.

"Well, I really would have expected that they wouldn't waste any time or money on it, that they would just close the case and move on. Cases have been closed before when there were more loose ends flapping than in this one."

"So why haven't they just closed it?"

Mark smiled. "I skated around that one a bit with Willis. He didn't make any direct statement, but my impression was that since it's the Ballantyres who are involved, a bit more than nominal effort is seen to be prudent."

"So Willis is plugging along. How long will that continue?"

"No idea", Mark said. "But I expect that somewhere a decision will be made to close the case when nothing new has emerged and it's obvious that an 'appropriate' amount of effort has been made."

"So. Behind-the-scenes politics."

Mark nodded.

"But we'll be able to have access to any results?" I asked.

"Yes. I think that Willis and I are pretty much attuned. My sense, anyway. I think he'll pass me anything he finds as soon as it's clear nobody will object."

"All on an informal basis?" I asked.

"Oh, yes. All nod and wink."

I paused, wondering how to put what I wanted to say.

"Isn't this an odd way for a medical examiner to operate? Having sidebar discussions with people who are just members of the public?"

"Yes. It is", Mark said. "And there is something going on here. I don't know what, but we might find out eventually. In the meantime we probably should just treat this gift horse appropriately."

I pondered this for a moment, wondering if we were wasting our time. Even with a connection to Willis, we might find ourselves after some weeks or months holding a small handful of unconnected facts, a jigsaw puzzle missing three-quarters of the pieces and the picture.

"Has Willis found anything at all?"

"Yes", Mark said, rather brightly, I thought. "He said he had recovered a viable tissue sample from a bone and a tooth, degraded, he said, but probably good enough to get a DNA result."

"What about the damage to the skull?" I asked.

Mark was shaking his head.

"I asked about that. Willis said he's waiting for some information he requested."

"What does that mean?"

"Don't know. But it sounded straight up. Didn't seem like he was trying to hold back anything."

"And is he going ahead with a DNA test?" I asked.

"Yes", Mark said. "I think so. He was a bit cagey. It's a grey area. The cost probably can't be justified. But he indicated that the decision was his on whether to proceed or not."

Mark paused here. I waited.

"My sense is", Mark continued, "that there are two things in play here. First, I think there is a fair bit of official pressure from the Ballantyres to get the case to a point where it can be closed and the whole matter buried. But at the same time, somebody appears to want a particular outcome. There'll be some push through the police for Willis to make all this happen."

"Ted Ballantyre?"

"Yes. That's my guess."

"You said two things were in play", I prompted.

"Yes. And the more important of the two is that Willis's curiosity has been roused. My opinion."

"So we wait."

"Yes. Mostly", Mark said.

"Mostly? What's 'mostly' mean?"

Mark's rather conspiratorial smile surprised me.

"We have our worst-case scenario", he began. "I'd like to keep working on that. We don't want to miss anything. There will always be variants to consider. But this is really your choice. You're the paymaster."

I had already decided how this should go.

"This is about John. And this situation gives me an unaccountable bad feeling. So I'm not prepared just to hope for the best. Unless someone has had a man like John as a mentor and friend over decades, I think it would be impossible to explain the felt obligation. I'll do whatever it takes to make sure that this thing, whatever it might be, doesn't cast any sort of shadow over John. To a very great extent, he's made me who I am."

But there was something else I realized I wasn't sure of.

"Suppose there is a DNA test done. How will that make any difference?"

"Well", Mark began, "one result that Willis has already passed on to me is that the skeleton is that of a man. So I would expect Willis to specify a Y-chromosome test."

"What will that tell us?"

"On its own, nothing."

"So…"

"So, we'll need another piece of information, and that's where you and I need to be a bit devious."

"Okay", I said. "Just lay it out for me."

Mark was nodding, and he stopped a moment to collect his thoughts.

"The result here will be immediately important if the body turns out to be that of a Ballantyre. That would really fire up the rumour mill and could put one of John's ancestors under a cloud. But the test result itself won't help there, at least not on its own. Once we have the

DNA result from the skeleton, we — and by that I mean you and I — need to have a way to determine whether we're dealing with a Ballantyre or a non-Ballantyre."

"Won't the Ballantyres want to know that too?"

"One of them might", Mark replied without hesitation. "The rest of them, probably not."

"So, you think Ted will want to know, but Gary and the others won't."

"Yes. Gary and the others are nervous. If there's enough information on the table to say with certainty that the skeleton was either that of a Ballantyre or a non-Ballantyre, then it won't go away. If it is a Ballantyre, Ted will be able to raise all sorts of merry hell. If it's not a Ballantyre, then who was it? So, better to have complete uncertainty rather than enough information to say 'either-or' with certainty. From what I've seen so far, Ted wouldn't miss a chance to stir up old animosities. Gary wants the whole thing just to quiet down and fade away."

"What do you propose then? You said something just now about being devious."

"What I propose is that we get our hands on some DNA from a living Ballantyre male, and we have that tested. Comparing that result and the skeleton result should tell us whether or not the remains are those of a Ballantyre."

"But how will we get hold of Willis's DNA results?"

"We'll just need to rely on his goodwill that he'll pass them on to us."

"Is that a realistic expectation?" My doubts must have been quite evident.

"I think it's reasonable", Mark said. "At that point, the results will just be a lab report. Without a reference sample to compare them to, nobody will be able to conclude anything."

"But Willis would have been able to get through that same logic easily. Why would he even do the test?"

Mark was nodding again, and I could see that he was about to express a judgment.

"If he does request the test, he'll just be carrying out his duties as a medical examiner, even though he might be bowing to some pressure from the Ballantyres to assemble enough non-conclusive information that the police will be able to close and bury the case in good conscience. If he doesn't request the test, maybe there would be concerns over evidence being suppressed. I'm not sure. But my sense is that he would do the test and turn the results over to the police, and the matter would then be out of his hands. The police could then close the case when they saw fit. End of story."

"That would leave us operating on our own."

"Yes", Mark said.

"So, then…?"

"Yes. So then", Mark picked up the thread, "we would be able to confirm for ourselves either that we're dealing with a Ballantyre or a stranger. If it's a Ballantyre, we can decide what to do next, and that next thing would be either something or nothing. If we do nothing, chances are that it would all fade away. It's deciding what a 'something' might be that's the problem."

"But this seems to be going nowhere?" I complained. "What would be the point?"

"If nothing else, it would leave us holding positive information and some means to decide what to do no matter what possibilities might emerge."

I sat there looking into space.

"I'm lost", I said at length. "Do you have a recommendation?"

"Yes, I do. My recommendation is that we do some detailed scenario work. What options would be open to us if we go ahead with our own DNA test and the results confirm that the remains are those of a Ballantyre. There might be more than one option, and we need to know how any of them might go wrong, possibly blow up in our faces. That would also help us decide whether we even want to go down that road in the first place."

"You mean, whether we want to try to confirm that we're dealing with the skeleton of a Ballantyre?"

"Yes."

"And if we don't do anything", I continued, "if we don't go down that road at all, as you put it, isn't that the safest course?"

"It could be", Mark said. "But there's always Ted, the loose cannon, the maverick. If he somehow goes ahead on his own and shows that the skeleton is indeed that of a Ballantyre…"

"We could just deny it. It would be his word against—" Then I stopped, backed up a little, tried to see a larger picture. "Ah, yes", I said. "I see the problem. If anybody is in the crosshairs, it'll be John. Yes. We, or more likely just me, can't suddenly pop up and start making statements."

"And then there's the other side. Ted might be a hothead, but I doubt that he's stupid. If he went ahead, had his own test done, was able to conclude that the remains belonged to a Ballantyre, he wouldn't just stand in the village square and say so. He'd keep his cards close. He'd have a plan. He'd cook up a plot. That would mean we would have no idea what to expect, would always be on the defensive. John could be a sitting duck for whatever rumours Ted might want to hatch implicating his ancestors, and there might be little or nothing we could do to shield him."

I ran my hand through my hair in exasperation. Mark looked on, apparently waiting for me to say something.

"So…" I began, then stalled.

"I agree. It's far from being a transparent situation. We need to work through as many possibilities as we can, and we need to do that fairly soon. Willis won't be in a rush to send off for the DNA test, but that doesn't mean that we necessarily have a luxury of time."

Mark stopped here for a moment.

"There is one other thing", he began.

I returned a questioning glance.

"When we visited John's place, the day he wasn't there, it was clear to me that someone had picked the locks on the doors to John's house and workshop."

"Picked the… Why is this coming up only now?"

"I wanted to do some background digging", Mark said, "and I'm sorry I kept this from you. But if either of those places had been burgled, I'm sure we would have heard of it by now. And the background digging involved searching to see whether anyone was active in the area, if there had been a spate of break-ins."

"And?" I demanded.

"Nothing."

"So what does this mean?"

"I think it means that someone has been looking for something specific. They're not interested in burgling. They're searching."

"What? All this based on just some evidence of locks having been picked?"

"No", Mark said, and now his voice became cold and official. "I think that the intruder, the drone pilot, and our picklock all are aspects of the same search."

This was definitely food for thought.

"So…" I said, not knowing even what to ask.

"We have parts of a picture", Mark said. "We don't know what it means. But I suggest that I go away and think. There's a logic behind all this, somewhere. I need to try and find it. It won't take me more than a couple of days. Then we get together again and decide what to do. Do you agree?"

I gave it another moment's thought.

"Yes. I agree."

"Good", Mark said, smiling and reaching for another beer. "Now tell me a bit about what John's been up to lately. How's he doing?"

Five minutes later, I had to smile in some admiration at the way Mark had nudged the discussion away from intruders, snoopers, the whole fraught DNA topic, and all its risks and unknowns and glided into a pleasant conversation about a man and his forest and the years I had spent with both of them.

11

Bold Claim

For the next few days, I buried myself in work. There were a couple of longer-term projects that could be started at my convenience, and I began working my way through them. Work is indeed a diversion, and as a diversion it was something positive. At least for me. It's creative, and it demands, and receives, my full attention. As a result, I find that I'm quite often in an upbeat mood when I head for home.

That upbeat mood can help to balance the impact, at least in part, when I see once again all the things that remind me of Joyce.

About half a dozen friends keep in contact with me, and I go out with them, or visit them at their places, fairly regularly, on a sort of rotation basis. They're all good and close friends, and I know what they're doing and really do appreciate it. And those evenings always are enjoyable and relaxing. But in an odd way, they somehow serve also to underline my status and remind me both that my time is being filled, even if very companionably, and of the reason why the time needs to be filled. It all sounds ungrateful on my part. It's certainly not that, and I would never say anything to any of those friends.

But something else had happened recently. I found that I was spending more and more time thinking about John. His family's past as successful farmers and stalwart landowners, and the way they had stared down the Ballantyres, kept coming back to my thoughts. The discovery of the skeleton, the involvement of Mark, our initial discussion of the possibilities that might unfold all provided a new focus for my energy but also gave me a new awareness of how intimately John's present was entwined in a past going back generations. It came as something of a surprise to see that that past was still having an impact today. And it was a past that I found I knew too little about. Despite having spent so much of my youth with John, still I had blind spots concerning him. This just amplified, rather than diminished in any way, the residue gained from my years with John. There was something now that stood out more clearly from the background, and that was how I viewed those stands of old growth white pine on his land.

During my recent visit, our discussion of the nineteenth-century rape of the white pines in Ontario brought the reality home to me in what now seemed a rather surprising personal and urgent sense, as opposed to my "intellectual" understanding of it all up to now. The differential here was the gap in my appreciation of how large a shadow the Ballantyre family had cast back then. And I decided that if Mark and I were going to pursue what had begun, I would need to fill that gap. It wasn't enough to know just John's past. I needed to know the Ballantyre family past as well, and the lumbering industry in general that dominated that past.

I began searching for information. It didn't take long for the titles of books and articles to start turning up. I managed to find a copy of the book *Two Billion Trees and Counting*, and it arrived in the mail a few days later. I read the whole thing over a single weekend, practically at a sitting.

The story of all that frenetic logging, the subsequent mad attempts at farming by people who weren't farmers, on land that was entirely unsuited to what they were trying to do, and then the failures, the broken dreams, the details of the resulting desertification of large stretches of Ontario, and the uplifting story of E. J. Zavitz and his work — well, I was hooked. I recalled Zavitz's name and the situation he struggled with in general from discussions with John, but I was now filling in a lot of detail that was new to me.

And this was also the beginning of something else.

A vague and unfocussed sense of outrage.

The accounts John had related about his forebears in Northumberland County, and their resistance to the Ballantyres logging juggernaut, now were coming into sharper focus. It was more than just an arid historical account of no current importance. It was living history, and I thought for a moment that people might find it engaging in a real way in their lives today. That might well colour our outlook on the skeleton problem, mine and Mark's. And ultimately John's. I entered the titles of more books and papers into my notebook, material that I had to acquire and study, essential background to whatever might be coming.

On Monday evening I called Mark.

"How far has your thinking advanced? When can we get together and carry on our discussion about the skeleton?"

"Well, hello Steve. Yes, I'm fine. How are you?"

The humour in his voice made the taking of offence impossible and caused me both to laugh and to stumble like a social novice.

"I was going to phone you this evening", Mark said. "Obviously you've spent some time thinking about all this. Me too. I've now worked my way through quite a few possibilities, and I agree that we should get together and decide what to do next and when. What's your schedule look like?"

"Well", I began, trying to recover some aplomb, "I'm free any evening this week. If you have time, take your pick."

"Good! How about getting together tonight? We could take a first stab at things. Why don't you come over here. I assume you've eaten. Yes? I took some time off today and made a pecan pie, so if a bit of dessert works, we could have a sociable hour or so with Andrea, then get down to business."

Remembering what a good cook Mark is left me no practical option but to say yes, and forty-five minutes later the door opened to my knock, putting me face to face with the beautiful, smiling Andrea.

"Well, hello gorgeous!" I said in reflex, surprising and slightly embarrassing myself.

"Get in here, you big oaf", Andrea said, putting her arms around my neck.

I'm not sure how Andrea and Mark do it, but it seems they are always able to be the perfect welcoming hosts, no matter what the occasion. Within minutes, I fell into the hot tub of love that is their home, not feeling in the least an intruder or out of place. Soon we were seated before glasses of wine and laughing about I can't remember what.

I asked about Andrea's work, and she launched into an animated discussion of her current pet project. Mark rolled his eyes indulgently but without sufficient circumspection.

"Now Mark Whelan", she retorted in mock rebuke, "you know damn well that what I do is Renaissance high art compared to what you drag out of your daily cesspool."

"How about some pie?" Mark countered smoothly, not missing a beat.

"I don't know how he does it", Andrea said to me. "But you will have some pie, won't you? And a scoop of ice cream?"

From there, the conversation cruised forward effortlessly. Andrea asked about my visit to John, having evidently been primed by Mark. I found myself smiling as I spoke about the forest, John, and what a refreshing several days it had been, almost not noticing Mark slip out to return bearing pie, plates, a tub of ice cream, a scoop, and utensils. Generous wedges of pie were served and we tucked in.

"Mark, this is fantastic. I'll give you fair warning that I might just pig out and ask for seconds."

We ate pie, talked, laughed, and sipped wine. Mark offered coffee and went off to prepare it, returning a short time later carrying three mugs. I sat back, full of pie and at ease, and sipped my coffee. There was companionable silence, punctuated by a short commentary on a play Andrea had seen recently and Mark's account of several books he had failed to read. As she finished her coffee, Andrea glanced at her watch.

"You'll excuse me, Steven. I have a client meeting first thing tomorrow, and I need to get ready. It was lovely to see you again. You owe me an email on coming over for dinner soon."

And she rose and left.

"Well", Mark began, clearly about to change gears. "I'd offer you more pie, but I see that you've vacuumed it all down to the last crumb. So now, to work?"

We moved into Mark's den, where his large oak desk and thick, rustic coffee table set the mood. There was a small pile of paper on the coffee table, and two chairs were drawn up next to it, a sign that this would be action central for the next hour or so.

"Here's a chart I've drawn up of the possibilities I foresee", Mark said as we sat. He handed me a sheet of A4. "I'll walk you through it. But just take a minute to study it."

There were two main branches in Mark's chart, quite a few boxes recording possibilities, and many marginal notes printed in Mark's small, neat hand.

"So, you can see the general outline", Mark said. "I won't go through everything, but let me just hit the main points. Overall, I think we really have no practical option but to go ahead with our own DNA test. Don't worry about how we get a sample", he added quickly, evidently seeing the question in my face. "I'll look after that. I'm just an investigator who has an undefined role, as far as any outsider is concerned, and we need to keep it that way. No basis in fact or deed for any suspicion that you or John are up to anything."

Mark waited for an indication that I agreed. I nodded and he carried on.

"The basic idea is for us always to have the maximum information, to know whatever it is that Ted might know. We can speculate on what he might do based on what he might know, and that'll help us be prepared."

"So, if the skeleton isn't that of a Ballantyre…" I began.

"Then as far as I can see, that's the end of the road. Most likely it will be a case of unidentified remains henceforth and forever."

"And if it is that of a Ballantyre…?"

"Then", Mark said, "we'll have our work cut out. And we can't afford to wait. Doing that work should be our priority, starting now."

"What work is that? Trying to figure out which Ballantyre? Doing whatever historical research we can?"

"Yes. That's exactly it. I would guess that we have anywhere from a few days to a few weeks. So let's assume it's a few days. There must be some good records on the history of the Ballantyre family."

"Yes", I said. "There are. Although if there's anything to hide, I expect the Ballantyres would have made sure it's hidden."

"Anything else?" Mark asked.

"Well. Newspaper records. And John's family journals."

Mark's quizzical expression made me realize that I hadn't related any of the journal story to him, so I explained it.

Mark leaned back and thought a bit.

"Okay, let's walk through the whole thing again in detail, make sure we haven't missed anything." That exercise took another fifty minutes.

"Good. You look after John's family journals. I'll do everything else. But right now", Mark said, reaching for a fresh sheet of paper, "I'm going to list the actions we need to undertake. Read them as I write. Let me know if you don't agree with anything or if you think I've missed something."

At the end of another forty minutes, we had a list of actions, all but one of them assigned to Mark. Given our most limiting situation, that we had only a few days, it looked tight. But Mark sat back with a smile.

"We can do it", he said. "We're on the way."

12

Voices from the Past

And then things appeared to go quiet.

Mark went quiet as well, but I expected he was working on other cases. More than a week went past. Then on Tuesday evening John and I had a long telephone conversation, during which I recounted how much my recent visit to him meant to me. In telling John that that visit had awakened old interests, I was gilding the lily only slightly. In fact, I had been doing a fair bit of reading, and I suppose some of what I had learned must have come through in my words. We didn't need to speak for long before I was reminded how good John is at seeing what's between the lines, hearing unspoken messages.

"Well", John said, as our conversation changed gears subtly, "I'm delighted you enjoyed being here. I certainly enjoyed your company. We've been too long out of the habit of spending time together."

I mumbled something about good friends and that I had been reminded of the need to spend more time in the forest.

"You're welcome any time, Steven. And it sounds as though you're doing more reading along those lines, I mean related to forests and whatnot."

It was the "whatnot" that indicated John was on the scent. He said he had no real idea where my interests were. "But I can make a few suggestions."

He then began listing the titles of books and papers, asking if I was familiar with them. Many of them were the items I had acquired only recently and begun reading. I'm pretty sure that John suspected this, but he carried on as though these were just suggestions from the blue on some of the material I might want to check. I said "Mmmm" a few times in acknowledgement. I knew that my playing ignorant wasn't fooling him, but he's too much a gentleman to give me any sign that I'd been second-guessed.

But then I asked him if he thought the formal histories might be supplemented by the material in his forebears' journals.

"My family's journals? Well, you know that they need to be read from a different perspective. They're accounts written entirely from within their own times, and the times from some of those accounts go back almost two hundred years. To read them properly requires an act of considerable interpretation."

I didn't know quite how to respond to that. So I asked him some specific questions about the journals.

"Yes, I've read them quite a few times. And on many occasions I've realized that I had to question myself on what I thought the words meant. These people weren't skilled writers. Or grammarians. But they were describing their world."

John paused here.

"It sounds as though you've begun trying to peel back the layers of the onion", he said, his words having the same impact as would be the case if he were actually here physically and regarding me closely.

Maybe it was my recent reading. Maybe it was something flowing from my boyhood years spent with John and his forest. Maybe it was my personal loss causing me to dredge my own past for meaning. But it was certainly the case that I was acknowledging my years spent with John as a mentor and what I had learned from him. And what I had learned about forests was complex and subtle. My recent reading had widened this knowledge to include a good deal of additional cultural and conceptual freight. I was developing a somewhat different view now on what "forests" mean. Different from the received views people in the street might hold. Certainly different from nineteenth-century views. Back then, people might have held simplistic ideas about forests, that they were just annoying barriers to agriculture or that they were a one-time source of great wealth, something over which "we" had been given dominion. *One of the more pernicious biblical ideas*, I thought, not for the first time.

"It's a demanding job, reading those journal entries", John said, "but I'm sure you know that."

Not sure whether my own thoughts had blocked out something John had said just before this, I simply waited for him to continue.

"I've studied those journals for many years. I continue to learn from the forest, every day. And I can say that the physical complexity, and indeed the spiritual complexity, of the forest is far greater than a few simple words can convey. The people who wrote those journal entries saw essentially the same forests. So although they reflect things seen through a different lens, they are important primary sources of information. The people who produced those journals were writing from within a conceptual world that doesn't exist now. But they were documenting what they saw."

This was far more than John had ever said about his family's journals. It was becoming clear that he saw the discussion going someplace specific.

"Can you give me an example of something in the journals that might be puzzling? Or easy to misinterpret?"

John moved effortlessly into summarizing items from the journals.

"A lot of what they wrote reflected elements of their world that we might have trouble understanding today. They sometimes refer to things like 'the Lord's master plan'. Although they knew almost no detail about forest complexity, they did seem to see the forest as some great living, but not well-defined, entity. And they were imbued with the notion of moderation, and this might have been what incensed some of them so much about the greed and profligacy displayed by the Ballantyres and their loggers." Having said this, John went quiet, as though he was gazing into some far distant place.

"You might have guessed this already", I said, "but I would like to look through your family's journals. But if you have any reservations about this…"

Even over the telephone, I could tell that John was already shaking his head, dismissing my concerns. "There are quite a few bits of family history in them. So I don't want to see any of the material published verbatim. It's hard to understand why, but there are still active antipathies at work out there, and I don't want to see that situation aggravated. I know that's not what you have in mind. Of course. I have no problem whatever in you reading them."

He paused.

"As I said, those journals are voices in time. When I read them in parallel with historical accounts, well, those journals just make it all come to life."

At that moment, I wished I was there with him again.

"And", John added, "those accounts are full of anecdotal history, a lot of small details, especially on anything local to the forest here." He hesitated a moment. "I didn't have the chance to know anybody further back than my grandfather, but when I read those journals, I can hear people speaking."

John then offered all his family's journals formally for me to examine.

"But I do want that to happen here. I don't want the journals to leave my house."

I agreed without hesitation, and we set a time late on the coming Friday when I could arrive at John's place and spend all or part of the weekend there. We said our goodbyes. I was very much upbeat, and that probably came over the line to John. But he also sounded at least intrigued, if not excited. We had such a long common background, but here I was about to look into something that had been, thus far, available only to John and went back much further than either of us. Was this okay? Would John really be comfortable with this?

When we met on Friday, and before we took this thing any further, I would make very sure that there would be no problems.

It was now eight thirty. My conversation with John had lasted almost an hour, and I decided to go for a short walk, partly as a change in pace, partly to mull over some of the things John had said. But as I was heading for the door, the phone rang.

"Steve. Mark here. Is this a good time?"

"Yes. What's up?"

"A development. I've lined up a lab to do a test on Ballantyre DNA. That test will give us a reference file. All we need now is the sample."

"Will that be hard to get?" I asked.

"No. Not hard. But it has to be legitimate, and we'll need to be able to show its provenance."

This wasn't something I expected so soon, and I wondered whether maybe we were going a little too fast. But then I remembered how careful Mark had been about marking out the general course we would pursue, the specific tasks needed, and getting my agreement on it all beforehand.

"Steve? You still there?"

"Yes. Sorry. I just had a long conversation with John so my head's in a different space."

"Are we still on track for the DNA plan?"

"Yes. Yes, of course." I paused here, examining my own feelings of hesitation. "What's the schedule on this, on the reference test, I mean?"

"Once the lab has the sample, we should have the results in about three days. It could have been sooner, but I told them I wanted the full slate of QA measures on this result."

"How will you—"

"Now Steve. I'm not going to tell you anything about obtaining the sample. The less you know at this point, the better."

We talked a little about possibilities and next steps.

"How do our lab's procedures compare with what the medical examiner's lab will be doing?"

"They're comparable", Mark said.

"I'm assuming that the Ballantyres will know in advance if Willis decides to go ahead with a DNA test on a sample from the skeleton?" I asked.

"Hard to imagine that they wouldn't, given how well connected they are."

"And when that DNA result comes in, Willis will just turn it over to the police?" I asked.

"That's what I expect."

"What will they do with it?"

"Good question. They might decide to check it against whatever DNA evidence they have on missing persons, although they won't find anything going back to the date of that skeleton. My guess is that they'll just write a quick report and close the case."

"What about the Ballantyres?" I asked.

"What about them? I spent quite a bit of time going through old records looking for missing Ballantyres. None was ever reported. Although there was a Ballantyre who fell out with the family and decamped to Australia. At least that's the story that was put out."

"I suppose you looked for him in Australia."

"Yes", Mark said. "Found nothing. But that could mean anything. That he didn't go to Australia. That he changed his name. That he just deliberately went underground."

"Was that about the same time as someone who became our skeleton was buried on John's land?"

"No way of knowing", Mark said. "We won't get anything more than an approximate date on the skeleton. Probably will be something like 'mid-nineteenth-century', but that could be anywhere within a span of forty years or so. So, yes, the skeleton could be the missing Ballantyre, but would the Ballantyres want that possibility to be kicked around in public? I doubt it very much. But it's a possible outcome, and that's one of the cases we looked at. The reference sample will be just insurance for John."

We talked a bit more. Mark indicated what he would be doing next, then we ended the call. The change in pace had been as good as a walk, so I just cued up some Erik Satie music, flopped in my chair, and thought about how things around me had started to become interesting, complicated, and potentially a little threatening.

13

First Peek

For the next three days, things went quiet. I busied myself at work, collected more of the titles John had suggested, and read way too late every evening. The history of what had happened in Northumberland County was interesting, if depressing, and the background to it was potentially enormous. A big part of the story forming in my mind was not only the physical extent of the rape of the eastern white pine, but also the mental outlook behind that activity and, particularly, the various social and zeitgeist factors that might have driven it all. I had to keep reminding myself that this wasn't just a local violation of nature, but something that had happened throughout eastern North America at roughly the same time. It was just that the local assault seemed to be so much more painful. Why this feeling of localized offence was so strong intrigued me and was something needing to be explained. But I had also to keep reminding myself that a first priority was to see those events within the context of their time, before trying to pass any judgments on them, indignant or otherwise.

Thursday night found me reading until 1:00 a.m., simply unable to break off even though I knew that the next day would be hell as a result. I would be travelling to John's place the next day for what I now suspected would be just my first walk through his family's journals.

The morning rolled around far too early. Red eyes glared back at me accusingly from the bathroom mirror and informed me caustically that no overnight sandstorm had been responsible for my current condition of gritty discomfort.

Despite that, things looked up once I arrived at work. Not only did the day go quickly, but I also found that by quitting time I had accomplished quite a bit.

I arrived home at just before six o'clock. My case had been packed and stowed in the car that morning. I changed quickly, sent John a cryptic email message saying that I was leaving, and headed down to the car, even though rush hour traffic would still be brutal.

It was brutal. But I think it was the lure of spending more time with John and in his forest that made me ignore all that.

More than three hours later, at twenty past nine, and after repeated and frustrating bouts of stop-and-go traffic, I pulled into John's forest oasis, having stopped earlier for fuel and to call John to let him know when I would arrive.

"We'll eat when you get here", he had said as we ended the call.

The porch light at John's place burned in invitation, the great silent trees all around offered their generous welcome to the returned prodigal, and Dougie was already outside my car, tail wagging fiercely. John crossed the grass toward me, smiling, hand stretched out in greeting, took my case, and ushered me into his home.

The luscious scents in the air as I crossed the threshold told me everything I needed to know about what had been happening in John's kitchen over the past several hours. A tray of scalloped potatoes sat on a rack next to the stove, and a pot on the front burner had saturated the room with the aroma of pork ragout, while a small heap of mint leaves was almost certainly destined to join the peas that were about to be tipped into boiling water.

"Leave the case here", John said, setting it down just inside the door. "You look bushed. Come." He laid a welcoming arm over my shoulder and led me toward the table. "Have a seat and let's share a drink. We'll be eating very shortly."

Two bottles of a good gamay were lined up to accompany the meal, and in just fifteen minutes, before we moved to the stove to help ourselves, we had already half emptied the first bottle. The wine, the food, that unique sense of relaxation offered by a Friday night, and the prospect of another weekend with John and his forest all combined to lift my mood into the clouds.

"John, this is excellent. Thank you."

"There's more. Help yourself to seconds."

I did. We both did.

Gamay provided both the introduction to and the valediction for the meal. We had moved to John's large comfortable sitting room chairs, and I almost wished it had been a few months earlier so that we could have enjoyed a fire. But, as usual, John and I had plenty of companionable talk to exchange and the level of wine in the second bottle supplied rearguard flow to the culinary part of the evening which had already left the field.

We both carried dishes to the sink, and I insisted on helping wash them. John dried the plates and utensils and put them away. We chatted while doing this, John asking about my books and reading, me making it clear that my teeth were now sinking into something promising. We finished and hung the tea towel to dry.

"Tomorrow morning. A walk before breakfast?" John proposed. "You probably need to clear mind and lungs. And since you've evidently been doing some reading, you likely will want to recalibrate the forest."

I just nodded, recognizing that tiredness was now gaining the upper hand. But, I thought, it would more likely be the forest recalibrating me.

"Six thirty?" I asked.

"Yes. Perfect. The weather's expected to be fine."

I thanked John once again for dinner, picked up my case, headed to "my" room, and said good night just before closing the door.

Seated on the bed, I spent some time just enjoying the peacefulness of the place. I must have remained there, contemplating in a kind of stream of consciousness way, for at least fifteen minutes. The house was enfolded in the forest's deep and primeval quiet. Outside, Dougie gave a muted bark, probably in response to some animal moving about. A healing scent of pine pervaded the air. It was all about as close to heaven as I could imagine. Apart from having Joyce...

From my case, I pulled pyjama top, sponge bag, and a copy of Robert Harrison's book *Forests*. I placed the book on the night table, alongside watch, wallet, and cellphone. A winking blue light on the phone told me there was some kind of notification to be looked at. I almost ignored it, but then decided to check. I activated the phone and went to email.

It was a message from Mark.

Interesting development. Could be important. Call me when you're able to talk. The message had been sent a little over an hour earlier.

Opening the door to my room, I looked out into the main living area of John's place. There was a night light by the bathroom door on my immediate right and another off to the left near the vestibule at the front door. There was no light showing beneath the door that led off the living area further into the house and to John's room.

I moved quietly toward the front door, opened it carefully, and stepped outside. The night was a pine cloister. A delicate gauze of faint stars, tacked in place by hundreds of bright points of light, was draped across the sky. Dougie came up to me, tail wagging in query. I scratched his ears and patted a flank, and he seemed to understand that I was acting out yet another absurd nocturnal human ritual, nothing that intelligent life needed to worry about. As Dougie strolled back to his doghouse, which still looked spanking new but had now, evidently, been brought to olfactory acceptability, I moved off toward the trees, to be far enough from the house not to have John hear me or become worried.

Even though it was very late, I knew that Mark was not an early-to-bed type, and I dialled his number, knowing that if he didn't want to answer, he wouldn't.

"Whelan."

"Hi Mark. Sorry to call so late. But there might be few chances to call you tomorrow. Got your email. What's up?"

"Willis's forensic DNA test results came back. The claim being made is that it's a match for a Ballantyre."

It took me a moment to get my head around this.

"Hang on, Mark. How could they know that it's a match for a Ballantyre?"

"Well, *they* don't necessarily know it. This information is coming from Ted Ballantyre."

"From Ted? How is he involved?"

"Very good question."

"How old is this information, Mark?"

"I heard it less than two hours ago. Passed it on to you right away."

"What happens now?" I asked.

"Not sure. I expect that Gary Ballantyre might have something to say in the morning. What else might happen here, I don't know. But there's something you should be doing pretty much right away, well, first thing tomorrow that is. You need to bring John Stanley up to speed. There's no way he should be hearing about this from anyone but you."

We spoke for just a few minutes more, but there was really little else to say. This news would loosen tongues, and a number of metaphorical pigeons would now be quite restless, fearing the imminent arrival of the metaphorical cat. We ended the call and I went back inside and to my room.

This outcome was one possibility on the chart of outcomes that Mark and I had constructed. We had thought a bit about how to respond to it, so I wasn't floundering in a panic, but it was something we considered unlikely. I got ready for bed, but then sat there thinking of what I had to do first thing in the morning. Sliding between the covers, I lay there for another twenty minutes or so as many different thoughts chased each other through my mind. In the end, I formed a mental outline of what to say to John, turned out the light, and eventually slipped into an odd tangle of chromosomal dreams.

I heard the robins begin tuning up at about four thirty, and then I dozed lightly but luxuriously for the next hour and a half. When I was dressed and ready for the day, I opened the front door to John's house to welcome a dew-laden morning emerging from a sky streaked in pink and purple high clouds. John was slowly quartering his property, and I moved off toward him.

"Sleep well?" he asked.

"Yes. As I always do here. Can we go and take a look at Big White?"

John smiled and nodded agreement and off we went. There was no breeze. The pines were resinous, their bark darker than usual from the dew. Dainty droplets clung to the ends of the conifer needles. Dougie snuffled around, becoming thoroughly wet as he shook water from the branches he disturbed. A squirrel scolded us roundly for the offence our presence offered to the morning.

From John's house to the stand of pines that included Big White is about four hundred metres, and we moved slowly and soundlessly over grass and patches of fallen needles. As we approached the grove of the largest pines, the wood gradually closed in on us, and I knew once more the exquisite and ineffable mystery of the place.

"I suppose by now that you've learned quite a bit about Zavitz, and what he did, and why he did it."

This was an opening I hadn't expected, but it seemed an invitation for me to begin talking about my recent interest in the forest and what had prompted it. I took my time.

"I'm not sure exactly how I came to this. I think it might have been something that made me realize just what we've lost in terms of old-growth forest. And I think that 'something' was the book *The Golden Spruce* and an article I read just a few weeks ago about what different people mean when they use the terms 'forest' and 'wilderness'."

John looked at me for a long moment as we continued moving through the forest.

"And where do you think this will take you?" he asked.

"I'm not sure at all. But I feel that I'm coming to a different understanding, an understanding of forests at a different level. Does that make any sense?"

John just nodded, but I could see that he was secretly pleased at how this conversation was unfolding.

"I need to do more reading. That's why I wanted to take a look at your family's journals."

Big White was now less than fifty metres away. We approached the tree without saying anything, and then I walked up to it, touched the rough bark of its massive trunk, and, well, basically uttered a silent 'hello'. We stood looking at the tree and at the several dozen others that surrounded it in their grove.

"Let's take a seat", John said, moving toward the bole of a fallen tree about thirty metres away. We could hear Dougie's energetic exploration somewhere out of sight.

The lines I had constructed carefully a few hours earlier, about the comments Ted Ballantyre was broadcasting, now seemed to be deserting me. But I had to raise the matter with John. I could think of no nice, suave intro, so I just jumped in.

"I'm keeping an eye on what's happening about the skeleton that you found under that uprooted tree a couple of weeks ago. I know you didn't ask me to do that, but I'm doing it. I hope you don't mind."

"No", John said, after a short delay. "I don't mind. It might be useful to compare notes."

"Compare notes? I'm not sure I—"

"I'm keeping a fairly close watch on that myself. I don't suppose you're about to tell me what Ted Ballantyre has been up to?"

I must have signalled the most gauche double-take, because John began to chuckle.

"Ted has been putting it about that the skeleton is that of a Ballantyre. Is that what you've heard?"

"Yes", I said, "but ... how...?"

John smiled.

"I'm a little surprised, Steven. Quite a few people know me around here. And I do keep in touch with many of them. Add to that the general disapproval most folks have of Ted and, well, it's not that hard to keep abreast of things."

It took me a while to regain some composure.

"What are you going to do about it?" I asked.

"Do about it? Well, nothing. What can I do about it? I have no reason to believe that it's true, and because it's Ted putting out the story, I have good reason to believe that it's not true. I think I'll just wait. The truth will out."

We talked about it a little more, but it soon became clear that John was not interested in dwelling on the thing at all.

John rose, looked around for a moment, then stooped and picked up something.

"I'm sure you remember what this is", he said, smiling and holding before me the stem of a plant and its curious swelling.

"It's an insect gall."

"Yes. So now let's go and see what the forest can teach us today."

We rose from our log, I spent a few minutes more gazing up at Big White, then we moved on what turned out to be a leisurely ramble that lasted almost an hour.

Back at John's place, we prepared toast, jam, and coffee.

"Okay", John said as we cleared away the breakfast things. "Let's plan the day. We'll do a bit of shopping first, but that won't take long. After that, there are things I need to do around here. I have two woodworking projects I'd like to finish. There's a commission for a set of four cereal bowls and a large cutting board for meat. Those will take about four hours. So I suggest that you settle in with the family journals this morning, then when I've finished in the shop we can break for some lunch. Will that do you?"

"Yes, indeed", I said. "But I would love to take a quick look at your bowls and cutting board."

"Fine", John said. "We'll finish the dishes and head out to the shop for a few minutes. Now, in the afternoon I need to sweep the chimney. It's not a big job, but the cleanup means that it will take at least three hours. You can busy yourself again then with the journals."

Before our shopping expedition, while John was feeding Dougie, I spent a few minutes in my room sending a quick text message to Mark, relating my discussion with John about the DNA test results.

14

Into the Past

John and I didn't mention Ted Ballantyre and his DNA story again, and the weekend was another languorous delight deep in the woods. Dougie was in his element, having two humans to look after in a universe where he was at the centre, making it a worthwhile three-body problem. We had several more walks in the forest and a long post-prandial evening on the porch, and I had two sessions bent over the journals from John's family. I was not surprised to see that John had taken the trouble to make copies of all the pages of the journals, and these copies filled three binders. John walked me through the lives and the generations that were reflected in those entries. The handwriting varied from elegant at one extreme to scratch on the edge of legibility at the other, and the grammar and spelling showed similar ranges of capability. But the ideas, the sentiments, the threads that stretched and changed across two centuries really caught my attention. John had already done a fair bit of work trying to link newsy statements in the journals to actual recorded events in newspapers. It was from these connections that I began to see a past world through eyes that were not my own.

I filled the notebook I'd brought with observations, questions, and comments well before the weekend was out, and also before I had

completed even a first pass through the journals. More than once, I
noticed John looking at me as I scribbled yet another note or flipped
back through the journal pages to check a previous item against what
had currently caught my attention. There was anecdotal family
material here, and comments on crops and what a difficult or
bounteous year it had been. But there were also items that would
easily qualify as local history and more than a few character sketches,
not penned explicitly, but woven into some passing note about a
neighbour's illness, a marriage, a death, or some comment on a
community. The development of the logging industry was here, as
was the arrival of the railway, the fortunes of shipping on Lake
Ontario, the improvements in roads, and the seemingly inexorable
rise of the Ballantyre family empire. There were hints, growing
stronger as the decades marched at me from the pages of the journals,
of the animosity between John's family and the Ballantyres. There
were also hints of despair, as the land around the Stanley properties
was logged bare and the desert conditions that Zavitz would need to
deal with later began to appear.

What struck me full in the face, however, was the connection
between the Stanleys and the great pine forests that were initially all
around them, the reverence they obviously felt for these quiet giants,
and the Stanleys' increasing resistance to what seemed the
Ballantyres' implacable urge to log out all the forests on the Stanley
lands. Here were the accounts of those armed stand-offs John had
told me about, between Stanley men and Ballantyre logging crews. At
one point there was a fairly detailed summary, written by someone
who had been in attendance, of a tense meeting between Stanley men
and the man who at the time was head of the Ballantyre clan, a bent
and crippled but intransigent figure. The account was written in a
here-and-now style and had been transcribed, one assumes verbatim,
into the journal. The author of the account wasn't identified.

Knowing both the Stanleys and the Ballantyres, it was hard to say
what would happen. Neither group was going to give way. The logging
crew seemed to think that they had a free hand, since the Ballantyres

were determined to carry the day. But the Stanleys just told them to leave. "It's not your land. You won't be cutting trees here today." It was when old man Ballantyre waved his arm to have the loggers start work, that's when the action began. There were shouts of "Stay Back!" from the Stanleys. When the loggers kept coming, five rifles were raised into the air and discharged. I ran for cover. Didn't know what might happen next. But the loggers fell back. The Stanleys stepped forward. Their rifles were still aimed at the sky. The Stanleys shouted again. "Get off our land! Leave now! Before someone gets hurt!" Half an hour later it was all over.

I sat back thinking. Those guys had balls.

"It's four thirty, Steven", John said, intruding into my thoughts. "You've been at this for more than five hours. Time to knock off for today. Here", John said, placing a can of Pub House Ale and a glass in front of me, "time to celebrate a hell of a good day's work."

I nodded and smiled, suddenly realizing that I was tired, thirsty, and hungry.

"Okay", I said. "But I'm going back at it tomorrow. I can hardly believe what I'm reading. This stuff is gold dust."

We snapped the cans, poured, raised our glasses, and that first glug had me almost ready to believe that God does love us and wants us to be happy. John looked at the binders, my notebook, now fairly battle-worn, and various loose sheets spread across the table.

"I think you'd better take these binders home with you."

"No, John, I really do think they need to stay here, with you."

John was shaking his head.

"When I said that to you, I realize I was being possessive. As far as I'm concerned, these documents are priceless. But now that I see how you're devouring this stuff, I'm sure my ancestors would send me horrible nightmares if I sent you back to town without their stories."

I wasn't going to argue with that. I thanked John and was happy to put away the binders, pack up my sheets, and start getting ready for a Saturday evening meal.

"I thought we could have barbecued chicken tonight. Would that suit you?"

"Your barbecue sauce?" I asked hopefully.

"Well, yes. Most of the commercial ones I've come across are half salt."

"Perfect. I'll just clean up and then come back to help."

"No, no need. It's all in hand. You go and clean up, then we can sit and enjoy our beer. Sound like a plan?"

I smiled and headed off to my room. There was just time to send another quick text message to Mark, telling him there would be nothing more to report while I was here but arranging a time to get together after I was back.

Our meal that evening was another delicious Stanley feast. John had paired the chicken perfectly with a smooth cabernet franc, and at ten o'clock we were still seated at the table. We talked about the day just passed, and I began making enthusiastic plans on how to fill the last day of my visit. I prodded John until he came up with a list of odd jobs that needed doing and then bullied him into fitting as many of them into the day as possible.

Having an agenda going forward, we settled back to quiet enjoyment of the wine. John was busy asking me about my work, my life, and, more subtly, my future. It was during this conversation that I took a close look at him, perhaps the first close but guarded study I had made of him in a couple of years. I'm not sure what prompted it, perhaps just an idea that had unexpectedly ripened, but I was suddenly seeing John in a different light. He didn't look older, or tired in any specific way, but he did look like a different person. John was now seventy, although his general condition, his vivacity, and his mental acuity were typical of someone much younger. What was John's future, I wondered. John had brought in money through his accounting jobs and, later, the woodworking business he had taken on to rejuvenate, and I doubted that in retirement he was short of funds. John had never married, and I knew that he had never stated or shown any regrets. For quite some time, his work and his life really had been his house here in the forest and all that was around it. Evidently he was still very active with woodworking, and it seemed likely that would continue for a while at least. His interest in reserving quite a lot of the fallen pine tree appeared to confirm that. But what about later? What would come next for John? He was someone who was going to be moving into a new phase, but what would that be?

I must have pondered this for several minutes before a clear answer came: John likely had a quite clear idea on what would come next, and although that wouldn't be some vaguely defined "feet up and smell the roses" lark, several ideas began to tease the edge of my consciousness. Would he finish writing his story of the forest and of his life? Even more interesting, would he produce some account of his family and how they had loved and worked and protected and lived on this land? Through his career, John had written a good deal of technical material, and his writing style was clean and clear. Casting surreptitious glances at him now, I couldn't see beyond his placid but impassive face, couldn't really get a hint of his thoughts. It was then that another notion claimed my attention front and centre.

During almost all my boyhood and adolescence, my time with John could be seen as a close and detailed history. Inevitably, we had disengaged and moved apart. But now? Were we moving back toward each other? Was some future vaguely suggesting itself here, one that needed to be defined and honed? A couple of wild possibilities arose suddenly, coming at me out of nowhere, and I was caught totally off guard.

"Everything all right?" John asked.

I looked up, surprised, befuddled, as though I'd just been unwillingly teleported to a strange new planet.

"Is everything all right?" he repeated.

"Yes. Of course. Why wouldn't it be?"

"It's just that your expression changed so abruptly that I thought something had gone wrong."

"No", I said. "I just… It seems… Okay. I just realized that the focus of my life has changed a lot over just the past few weeks. I'm reading stuff that I never touched before. I'm digging out the history of this place, a place I thought I knew intimately, but now I'm seeing it in a very different light."

John was nodding. "And your personal life has changed massively", he added.

I nodded in turn.

"Do you want to talk about it?" he asked.

And I found suddenly that I did.

So John and I talked for the best part of two hours. And I think that, during those two hours, both our lives turned something of a corner.

Sunday was a day of working together on chores that I suspected John was saving but that I insisted we clear away. There was another long walk in the forest, three more hours spent working through John's binders, and a delicious meal of spaghetti Bolognese at four thirty that afternoon, covering the lunch we had skipped and setting me up for the trip home. John accompanied me to my car, I loaded my suitcase and the three binders, we both smiled in amusement at Dougie, who seemed crestfallen that I was leaving, and then we exchanged a firm and very warm handshake, while John looked straight into my eyes.

"This has been a great weekend, Steven. Thank you for coming. And I'm so pleased that you're finding my family's journals interesting."

There was a subtext here that I'm sure we were both very much aware of, and I gave John a long and brotherly hug.

The drive back to Toronto was uneventful. Many elements of my discussion with John replayed in my head. But the view into the past that was unfolding for me took precedence. I was eager to get back to the material in the binders, sink my teeth into it again. At ten thirty, I pulled into my underground parking slot, and fifteen minutes later I had sent a longish thank-you email to John, along with a promise to keep him informed on my study of his family's journals. I then called

Mark, let him know that I was back from a very enjoyable weekend, and arranged a time when we could get together.

Even though I knew I would regret it in the morning, I lugged the binders and my notes to my office, switched on the computer, and began transcribing, reorganizing, and expanding my notes. At just after one thirty, I saved the Word file I had created, closed notebook and binders, and went to bed.

Somehow my alarm clock managed to compress a little more than five hours into what seemed like about twelve minutes, but I climbed out of bed feeling energized. A quick shower washed the sand from my eyes, and an hour later I was at my office desk at work but already anticipating my arrival home at day's end.

15

The Sample

The day couldn't pass quickly enough, although I had plenty to do and no time to fret impatiently. Some of my colleagues likely were surprised to find my desk clean and locked and me absent at four thirty that afternoon. At just past five o'clock I was back home, doing more work transcribing notes, reading a little further into John's family journals, and getting ready to meet Mark at seven. We had decided on dinner at his place. Neither the timing nor the fact that we would be huddled most of the evening would be inconvenient for Andrea because she was out of town for two days.

I wasn't sure whether Mark would have found out anything new, but there was no doubt that he would have done a good deal of follow-up on Ted's bombshell. The significance of Ted's comments, whatever Mark might have turned up in pursuing them, and where to go next would likely be a central part of our discussions.

By six thirty, I had begun reading the third and final binder of the Stanley journals. My notes were proliferating, and as I had already found, the effort at transcribing, collating, making linkages within the journal entries across years and decades was yielding a rich and generous reward. It occurred to me that John probably had done something similar, although most likely just in his head, and that at least another weekend would be needed before we could get together and compare what we had found through our independent and different approaches. At six forty-five, I bookmarked my place, closed the binder reluctantly, and headed off to Mark's condo, about a twenty-five-minute walk from where I live, but a trip that would be done by taxi on this occasion.

"Come in", Mark said, smiling as he held the door to their delightful condo unit open wide. We shook hands, but my focus was hijacked almost immediately by the rich and inviting aroma of lasagna. Among the group of people both Mark and I knew, all of them agreed on his accomplished and sometimes fearless style of cooking. I was already looking forward to a full evening.

"But to avoid any chance of being sidetracked", Mark said as he ushered me in and closed the door, apparently anticipating my imminent derailment due to gastronomy, "I think we should just run through what we'll be discussing tonight and where we want to end up." We moved into the sitting room, where a bottle of wine and glasses shared table space with two neat piles of paper.

"I'll summarize what I've found and what I think will happen next, and then I'll outline where our focus should be for the next few days. Okay?"

But then, as if to contradict that, Mark poured two glasses of wine. Interpreting what must have been my questioning expression, Mark offered a short clarification.

"Truth serum. To keep us focussed."

Mark's walk-through took only about three minutes, and at the end of it, I was almost reluctant to head toward the dining table. But only almost. It was quite clear that an excellent meal would kick off the full evening that lay ahead of us.

We helped ourselves to Mark's superb lasagna, and I left the salad for a second round. At length, we raised our glasses in a silent toast, took a first sip, then turned our attention to the food. After only a few mouthfuls, and after I had offered compliments on the food, our attention began being diverted.

"Yes, I did some digging today", Mark said in response to my rather open-ended question. "I actually went out to Peterborough, did a bit of archive searching, had a meeting with Gary Ballantyre, did a bit—"

"You spoke to Gary?"

"Yeah. Wanted the chance to ask him a few things while I could look him in the eye."

I said nothing, just kept on chewing my mouthful, set down my fork, and waited for Mark to continue.

"He seems to be straight up. He made it clear that he's really annoyed at Ted for churning things up. I caught Gary just after he'd finished his lunch. He found out about Ted's comments from a third party, apparently. He flared up again even as he told me that."

"Did he confront Ted?" I asked.

"I don't know", Mark said. "I didn't ask him directly, but after we'd been speaking for a few minutes, and it looked like Gary was going to wrap things up, I suggested that I might talk to Ted myself."

"And?"

"Well, then Gary said, quite adamantly, that he would take care of his brother."

"So you didn't go to see Ted?" I asked.

"No. I went to see Dr. Willis."

I had to smile, both at the turns this discussion was taking and at how the pace of events seemed now to be gaining speed. But I just waited for Mark to pick up the thread of the account again.

He told me that it had been his intention to see Willis, but that some greater purpose and urgency was attached to that visit by what happened during the last few minutes of his discussion with Gary Ballantyre.

"I mentioned earlier that Gary had just finished his lunch", Mark said, after taking another sip of wine. "He led me into what looked like a small dining room, and we sat on opposite sides of a table for six. This was where our fifteen-minute discussion took place. Toward the end of that time, and when Gary had become quite steamed up, he selected a toothpick from a small container on the table and began picking his teeth impatiently, almost angrily. When he told me that he would deal with Ted, he tossed the toothpick in frustration onto a small decorative plate on the table. But then his expression softened and he apologized and asked if I would like anything to drink. I suggested coffee and he rose and left the room to get it."

I guess I looked a bit obtuse; it seemed Mark expected me to say something and I didn't.

"So that toothpick went with me to Dr. Willis."

Enlightenment dawned and I was pleased that I had Mark's help on this problem.

"The meeting with Willis, then. I suppose it was a bit calmer."

"Not at all", Mark said. "As soon as I asked about the story Ted had put about, Willis flew into a rage. Said that the whole Ballantyre family was insane. That he had phoned Gary and chewed his ear off, shouted at him over the phone. Said he was going to have a long discussion with the officer in the OPP who was investigating the case, distance himself completely from Ted and his absurd story, that it had no basis in fact, and that he had related nothing to either of the Ballantyres about the DNA test results."

"So the results didn't show that the skeleton was that of a Ballantyre?" I asked.

Here Mark smiled and shook his head.

"I asked Willis that. He erupted all over again. Went red in the face. Cursed Ted roundly. Asked how he, Willis, could have tested a sample of Ballantyre DNA that he didn't have and compared it to the test results from the skeleton. Of course he had done no such test! Of course he hadn't confirmed that the skeleton had belonged to a Ballantyre! It was all invented by Ted, that moronic hothead!"

Mark smiled and shook his head once more, but he evidently relished passing on the dramatic emphasis Willis had projected at him.

"I just let Willis blow himself out. I presume I might have been among the first people Willis had vented to, because his internal store of lava seemed to be still white hot. In due course, Willis calmed down, and he asked me whether I'd like something to drink. Except he didn't wait for an answer, but just poured us two generous doubles."

There was another pause here. Mark was evidently relishing the theatricality of the whole business.

"When I saw the brand name of the scotch Willis had poured, I just had to laugh. Willis smiled too, but the kind of smile you might allow yourself when you're casting a pox on someone."

"And?" I asked.

"The scotch was Ballantine's."

Mark laughed again.

"So we drank, and Willis drifted into a more relaxed mood. He eventually said that he understood I was looking out for John Stanley in all this, and was there anything I could tell him. I said 'not much', but then passed on a bit of harmless background. Pretty soon, it seemed that we both regarded ourselves as co-conspirators against the Ballantyres. That's when I pulled out the toothpick, unwrapped the Kleenex that had protected it, and set it down in front of him."

By then, I was up to speed. Mark said it took Willis less than five seconds to start asking questions. What's this? How did you get it? The Kleenex — is it unused?

"So, Willis is going to test it?" I asked, incredulous.

"Yes. Or in his words, 'Damn right I am!' And it was clear that he was delighted to have a sample of guaranteed Ballantyre DNA. But he said that the test results would be only for his own information. That he would share the results with me on the same basis — no further disclosure whatsoever. He said he had already sent a demand to the investigating OPP officer to formally obtain a sample of DNA from either Gary or Ted, suggesting that Ted's actions constituted interference in an ongoing investigation, and that if he didn't get his sample that way, he was quite prepared to go above all their heads as the independent medical examiner."

"The DNA on that toothpick", I began, "it doesn't have any provenance. We can't prove it's Gary's."

"No", Mark said, shaking his head. "Willis now has the perfect reason to demand a sample of genuine Ballantyre DNA. The test of what's on the toothpick is just personal fireproofing for him in the event he takes an opportunity to blow Ted out of the water."

I nodded and had to smile at this turn of events.

"Do you think he'll get his sample?" I asked.

"Yes. Eventually. But Gary will put up resistance, and it will be effective at least for a little while, given how well he's connected. But I suspect nobody doubts that Willis will carry out his threat if his formal request is blocked. And I'm sure that nobody wants to have to explain away the implications of any public statement that Willis might make."

This information gave our discussion an entirely new direction. We began thinking about what to do when we got Willis's confirmation that the skeleton was not that of a Ballantyre. I had dug out, from various archives, information indicating with near certainty that, prior to the Stanleys, there had been no previous registered owner of the land on which John's cottage sat and where the skeleton had been unearthed. So it looked as though the body had been buried for reasons that were shady at best. We worked through some scenarios and their implications, plotted out some next steps that would maximize the value of time we might invest, and agreed that I would let John know, in confidence, the conclusions from Willis's toothpick test results as soon as we had them. We then leaned back to do justice to the rest of Mark's excellent wine, partly in relaxation, partly in celebration.

At ten forty, I said good night to Mark and walked home through a warm windless night. Even scrolling through the events that had unfolded thus far, I had to admit that they were strange and puzzling and that any eventual explanation of them was likely to be peculiar. For some reason, I couldn't shake from my mind the old mantra that truth is stranger than fiction.

16

DNA

The next four days took me through to the weekend, but I hardly noticed it. My first job was to make my own copy of the journals. I needed to be able to mark them up and annotate them, and I didn't want to do that to John's copies. A day later my copies were in their set of red binders, sporting more than 150 coloured flags, each flag marking an item that I had noted for subsequent review, collation, and analysis. I had had some vague notion of spending the coming weekend with John again, but the need to finish my first pass through the Stanley family journals, and comb out what I could, took precedence. I did speak to John — he was quite interested in how my reading was going, and we agreed that I would spend the following weekend with him. I would take his copies of the family journals back to him then.

I now had a rather fierce regimen at work: arrive very early, slog like hell for eight hours, then head off home for another four hours or more working on John's journals. I'm not sure what my work colleagues thought. I deliberately piled a mass of stuff on my visitor's chair, a pile that said "Don't even think about it!" to anyone who might have had an urge to park and shoot the breeze. I blew off meetings, kept work discussions to the absolute minimum, and cut off at the knees anybody who proposed broaching a subject that wasn't lined up dead centre on a current work priority.

So, every day around five o'clock, I arrived home carrying a takeout meal, and by five twenty, I was back into my Northumberland County Forest paperwork. Saturday morning, I was seated in my den before six thirty. At just shy of two o'clock that afternoon, I sighed as I made my last note from the last binder. The rest of Saturday, until almost ten o'clock that evening, and all day Sunday, I spent sifting, collating, and consolidating my notes.

The days spent on the journals indicated that there would be significant follow-up work. I had identified more than 160 references, statements, and hints in the Stanley journals that might well be confirmed, expanded upon, or given greater focus by articles in contemporary newspapers. I had no particular expectations there. In the middle of the nineteenth century, the number of local papers in rural Ontario was limited, the population was small, and that population wasn't distinguished especially by its literacy. What I had already looked like a gold strike. But I couldn't regard it as being really anything more than hearsay, although even hearsay can be useful. But finding independent corroborating material could put solid legs under this stuff. It appeared that the following week would be a continuation of much the same work regime. And more than just looking forward to it, I relished it.

Identifying the relevant newspapers wasn't straightforward, but it wasn't all that difficult either. I wasn't going for completeness. What I intended was just to troll through the newspapers, looking for items that appeared to match the comments I had flagged from the Stanley family journals. Most of the newspapers had been digitized so the search was far quicker than sitting in front of a microfilm machine and going square-eyed. It also meant that I could do quick searches based on a limited number of keywords and use what I found as a basis for following up on specific journal items.

It surprised me that three days was enough to make a good pass through all the available electronic files on newspapers. By the end of that time, I had located thirty-six news items that corresponded with, and corroborated, what seemed significant entries in the Stanley journals, and a further fifty-two items that provided useful background to notes in the journals. Although there were instances where the journals and newspapers didn't agree entirely, there were no outright contradictions. What this confirmed for me, at least to first order, was that the journals appeared to be reliable sources. Not a good reason for blind faith in everything the journals contained, but enough to banish any urge to discount or doubt their contents out of hand and to justify cautious credulity.

Collecting all these minor discoveries into a spreadsheet was the next exercise. I had no particular expectations that something clear and definitive would emerge. But even so, I was disappointed when all I found was an assortment of local history details — interesting in their own right and showing that there were many real events arising from ongoing strife between the Stanley and Ballantyre families — but nothing that could be linked even remotely to the skeleton.

"What did you expect, Boscombe?" I said to myself. "Did you think the answer would just fall into your lap, a nice little package tied up in ribbons?"

I tried to dismiss this negative view. Solid details had been teased out, I assured myself. They could, and probably would, be important as further information came to light. But as upbeat as I might try to be, I did have to admit that the skeleton, how it got there, and who it had belonged to might just be details that were now behind a permanently closed door.

As part of this effort of combing through journals and newspapers, I had decided to produce separate tracks for some of the main characters in the piece, particularly among the Ballantyres. These were timelines showing the charmed lives of a series of successful Victorian gentlemen.

Except for one person.

Charles Ballantyre.

This was the single remaining thread that begged to be pursued, although there was no indication that it would lead anywhere other than the satisfaction of personal curiosity, probably irrelevant to any larger picture, and almost certainly having no connection to the mystery of the skeleton.

I spent another two hours nailing down the last of the news items I had found that were of interest, documenting everything, and filing it all away. After that, I turned once more to my short timeline for Charles Ballantyre.

Born in 1848, nine years younger than the youngest of three preceding sisters and one preceding brother, Charles had taken over the helm of the family in 1870, at the age of 22, after the sudden death of his father, Walter Ballantyre. The Stanley family journals contained a good deal of commentary on the apparently turbulent affairs of the Ballantyre family, and there seemed to erupt at intervals an endless series of disputes and disagreements among the Ballantyre fathers, sons, brothers, cousins, and uncles. One of these disagreements appeared in 1874. There was no detail on why it arose, but on the ultimate consequence there was no doubt. It was reported, and probably discussed widely, that Charles Ballantyre relinquished the position of head of the family, and there was some hint that he had emigrated to Australia. End of the story. Or so it seemed. But there was a good deal of action elsewhere.

In 1874, the stand-off between the Stanleys and the Ballantyres was as fierce as it ever became. But there were also some high-profile legal dust-ups between the Ballantyres and other lumber barons and a short-lived but rather public disagreement between Charles's successor, David, and a local businessman, Malcolm Smithers, who later became a local blowhard politician. I found several references to this row in news items, and there was a good deal of commentary in the journals, but it seemed to be a sideshow of no real significance. Maybe it was just another display of Ballantyre pugnacity.

At quarter to eleven, I decided to pack it in. I had found hints and loose ends, none of which might be significant, just more fine brush strokes on the canvas of a well-to-do but perennially unsettled family. I had pretty much decided to give the whole thing a rest for a couple of days and coast toward another good weekend of John's company, now just two days away.

My cellphone vibrated on the desk. It was a text message from Mark.

DNA result in from Willis. Skeleton not that of a Ballantyre. Remember, your eyes only for now. Talk later. It looked like my couple of days' rest would be postponed.

Mark and I had discussed the possibility of the skeleton not being that of a Ballantyre. The DNA result likely would be definitive, and Willis wouldn't have passed it on unless he had checked it thoroughly and was convinced it was correct. Our expectation was that such a result would signal the end of the road. The skeleton of an unknown person, dead probably more than a hundred years. We expected that the chance of determining the identity of that person would be essentially zero, and the driver for putting in the effort needed to try to make that identification simply wasn't there. Any event linked to the skeleton was beyond all living memory, so anything called *closure* was meaningless. It looked, indeed, like the end of the road.

In a way, this news came as something of a relief, despite being a rather unsatisfying non-event outcome. The body of our unknown could have become a body for reasons natural or otherwise, although I was fairly sure that Willis knew which it was. It might have been buried on Stanley land out of simple convenience, financial expedience, religious disagreement, or for any of several personal motives. I looked at the pile of file folders and binders I had amassed over the past while and sought out the positive. I had learned a good deal of interesting local history from John's family journals, and that alone seemed to have been worth the effort. I had learned more about the long-standing strife between the Stanley and Ballantyre families. Viewed today, the unconstrained and febrile nineteenth-century pace set by the lumber barons for clearing land was both horrifying and intriguing, and I found myself curious to know more about the mindset and the local and global factors that had driven it. Thinking of the stand of great white pines still on John's property, and trying to imagine what an entire primeval forest of them spread over Ontario might have looked like, I could easily see myself giving it all closer study. But that, if undertaken at all, would be just a spinoff.

In terms of wrapping up the immediate problem of the skeleton and any present-day fallout from it, all that remained was to discuss with John, Willis, and Mark the best way forward that would also leave little or nothing for the gossips to nibble on. But now I was already sensing the need and the desire to move on, and I looked forward to speaking to Mark very soon. I wanted also to speak to John, by telephone as soon as possible, and face-to-face during the coming weekend. In a way, it felt good to be about to give the whole matter a decent burial, so to speak.

I went to bed more relaxed than I had been for quite a few days, but also feeling just a little bit cheated that a situation which arose amid so much drama had now come to such an abrupt and undramatic end.

17

Mark, John, Willis, and Ted

Before heading off to work the next morning, I sent Mark an email saying that it looked as though we had no chance of determining whose skeleton had been found but that there were several loose ends that I wanted to try to tie off.

Can we get together this evening? I asked. Then I left for work.

I decided to keep what had become my current schedule and hours for work until it became clear that we really could wrap up this skeleton business. So, at about five o'clock that afternoon, Thursday, I arrived home. The reply I'd received from Mark late that morning suggested a time and place to meet. The spreadsheet I had created, containing dates and events related in some way to the skeleton, was a useful summary of where things stood, so I printed out two copies and relaxed over a beer for the forty minutes until I would leave to meet Mark.

Mark had suggested a cosy spot that I didn't frequent often, The Turner House, on Trinity Street just north of Eastern Avenue. It has space for about fifty people, and is always nicely full, but rarely jammed. The bare brick walls smile at patrons in that mature benevolence typical of well-aged and well-loved buildings. The food is unabashed pub fare, but the beer is excellent. As I entered I had to smile at the timeless atmosphere of the place and Mark's friendly wave from his spot at a corner table.

We were all relaxation and smiles, and that was due to more than just the expectation of good beer and pleasant company. Once orders had been placed for pints and grub, I looked across at Mark.

"So. It looks as though this venture will end in a blind canyon."

Mark nodded. "A bit unexpected", he said. "And, I have to say, somewhat disappointing. This case has been unique in my experience. I had hoped that our end point would turn out to be more, how should I say, definitive."

"Unique? How do you mean, unique?"

"Well, we've worked on a crime that took place about a century ago, and it seems to have had no real consequences. Apart from whoever the victim was, nobody in that time seems to have been affected. It was so long ago that even the victim would have remained in oblivion if it hadn't been for that windstorm. As far as we know, there have been no real impacts in the present either. What we have is an unknown victim and an unknown perpetrator, and we're at the end of the road. My wife would probably regard this as the perfect case. No possibility of risk to me. But it certainly hasn't been boring."

"No", I agreed. "Not boring. But we need to wrap it up. So, I'll want an invoice from you. But I think we do need to have some statement on where we stand as well. There are loose ends. I can't see that any of them will be a problem for John, but…"

Mark was nodding. "There are loose ends", he agreed, "but the only important ones are the ones in the present."

"Such as?" I asked.

"Well, the main one is Ted Ballantyre's puzzling insistence that the skeleton belonged to a Ballantyre when we now know for a fact, even if he doesn't, that that's not the case. And Willis has said, sort of publicly, that nothing points to that being the case. I'd like to know which Ballantyre Ted thinks that skeleton belonged to. Ted must know that his contention will now be tested. It's okay for him to have his opinion, but it's a very strong one, seeing that it appears to be based on nothing. Sure, he's a hothead and a stubborn sod, but he's not stupid. It's just, well, puzzling."

"As long as we've done everything reasonable to make sure there's no comeback on John."

Our beer and food arrived, and we both raised our glasses and took long swigs. I looked appreciatively at my now seriously inroaded pint.

"Things look better already", I muttered.

"Then there's Charles Ballantyre", Mark said, continuing with his summary. "What's the story with him and where did he go? I'm convinced that today's Ballantyres, Gary and Ted, know a lot of the details here. As far as we're aware, Charles is the only Ballantyre from that period who's missing. So since the skeleton can't be Charles's, I have to wonder why so much mystery surrounds him."

I shrugged, but then picked up knife and fork and began eating. We spent five minutes working our way through our helpings of excellent meatloaf. Then I downed tools, reached for my beer, and looked at Mark, hoping that my expression would signal the desire to come to a conclusion. He read my expression correctly.

"Okay", Mark began. "Here's my take. If we leave things as they are, I think there's a chance that John will need to deal with something, sooner or later. There's no denying that the skeleton was found on his property, and the rumour mill might try to make something of that. Probably John's just going to have to face whatever rumours do come up."

I had tried to think my way through a process that would tie all this up as tightly as possible but had come up with nothing that seemed fully satisfactory.

"I'm in your hands, Mark. You're the one with the experience here. Tell me what you think we should do. If anything."

Mark took another sip of beer, set down the glass, twirled it for a moment on its mat, then looked at me.

"How diligently have you looked into Charles Ballantyre?" he asked.

"How diligently? Well, the Stanley journals, a few newspaper items from the time. It's hardly what I'd call 'diligent', really just low-hanging fruit."

Mark looked at me silently, speculatively, for a moment.

"It seems to me there are several threads here. First, there's the Ballantyre dynasty, and I have to admit that I get lost in it sometimes. Then there's what always seems to me to be an irregularity: Charles Ballantyre. Then, of course, there's Ted, who probably knows all the family's back history and dark secrets but also seems to be pursuing his own agenda."

Mark halted here while continuing to regard me.

"Just give me a thumbnail genealogy of the Ballantyres", he said.

"Okay", I replied. "It's really quite straightforward. Way back when, a father and son, Jacob and Douglas, built up the lumber business from nothing to a sizeable local operation. Those two made no public splash, so their names are unknown today. Then there was Lorne, the real firebrand and slave driver, and he turned the business into a very large affair and kept sole control of the corporate reins for at least fifty years. Then there was his son Walter. Walter had two idiot wastrel brothers, Graham and Arnold, also unknowns, and a promising son David."

"And what about Charles?" Mark asked.

"When we come to Charles", I said, "we're in unmapped territory."

"So do you think Charles is a black sheep?"

"Don't know", I said, "but there are things about Charles that make him a somewhat irregular fit to the family. And that makes me wonder. The Ballantyre family wanted to appear as aristocrats. So, for them, and especially for someone like Lorne, any suspicion of a black sheep would be completely unacceptable. So, I wonder, even though I have no hard evidence."

"Suppose you go away and try to dig a little deeper. More newspaper files. Old police records, if there are any. City archives. See what you can come up with. Maybe talk to librarians and archivists, tell them what you're looking for. Word might get around."

"What do you think I might find? Why do you think we should pursue this?"

"I have no idea what you might find", Mark said, his hands and face speaking eloquently of puzzlement, doubt, and curiosity. "But it seems to me a glaring irregularity. It's the one outstanding thread we haven't followed to its end."

"It's not likely that I'll find much. At least I have no reason to expect I'll find much."

"That's okay", Mark said. He evidently had something else in mind as well. "Ted's position in all this seems to be deliberately provocative. But to just what purpose, I can't tell. Whatever he's trying to do, he's working in a current day context that we know nothing about. So maybe what we need to do is pull his chain a little."

I just waited for Mark to continue. We each had another sip of beer. Our waiter moved back and forth, busy but not rushed. Muted conversation all around indicated that the nearby patrons hadn't the least interest in what we were discussing.

"Let's give it another three days", Mark said, appearing to have resolved something. "I want to have a discussion with Willis, see if there's anything else he might be able to tell us. Then I think you should contact Ted, by email at first, then go and see him. Basically, tell him that we've hit a wall and we're going to wrap up what we're doing, but also to say that we're satisfied the skeleton belongs to a stranger, that we'll ask for a final statement from Willis, the anthropologist, and the police, and that will be that. I'll talk to Gary and say that we're satisfied this is a non-event."

"What are you expecting?" I asked.

"I don't know. But if Ted's claim of the skeleton being a Ballantyre is based on some present-day agenda he has, he probably won't back away just because we're throwing in the towel. Gary's role in all this is cloudy as well. I'm hoping to provoke them, and maybe we can read something from whatever their response is. It might all fall flat, but at least that would be consistent with a low probability of any comeback for John. It's the best I can think of."

We talked about it a bit more, trying to identify any specific items that this prodding and poking might unearth, then agreed on what each of us would do. After that we started into the evening's real work by ordering two more pints of beer.

The following morning, Friday, I was up early in order to think through, in more detail, the lists of tasks Mark and I had developed for ourselves the night before and to get ready for my trek east that afternoon for another weekend with John. After sending out emails to arrange the weekend's activity, I arrived at work before the normal start time, slogged like a madman until mid-afternoon, then sneaked off early at just after three o'clock. The Friday freeway traffic was about as bad as I expected, but a sigh of resignation and being tuned to a good classical radio station helped me ignore the driver idiocies that were occurring around me, rather than rise to the psychological bait they offered.

It was just before seven o'clock when I pulled into John's drive. Leaving my car, I leapt around in a way guaranteed to cause Dougie to jump and bark excitedly, but dragged my case from the car when John crossed the grass toward me, smiling in welcome.

"Steven! Looks like you're in good form. Welcome! Come on in!"

"Good form? Well, tired actually. But greatly relieved to be out of traffic and back here." I looked around at the stately pine forest and could almost feel its exhalations relieving my week's stress.

"Come in! Have a beer or a glass of wine. I hope you haven't eaten. I've made a nice pot of chili and some fresh baps."

I smiled at John in a way that I hoped would say "Yes, indeed! Thank you! How wonderful! You thoughtful old bugger!" Secretly I hoped that, at least in my case, there really was no balance in the universe, otherwise all the great and good things that came my way at John's place would be redressed by some overwhelming fresh hell that would soon bear down upon me.

We coasted through an evening of food, brown ale, conversation, laughter, and friendship until I was unable to suppress a huge yawn, at which we both laughed.

"Off to bed with you, I think", John said.

We had a short argument about the dishes, but then we both pitched in, and fifteen minutes later, I hung up my tea towel and we bade each other good night.

Sliding between the sheets and then having morning peer in at me above and below the curtains were events separated by a deep gulf into which I must have parachuted quietly. It was the gulf of a perfect night's sleep. I could hear Dougie outside mumbling about something, and likely that meant that John was up and about. Fifteen minutes later, at the luxuriously late hour of 7:45, I was outside with them. A mist had arrived during the night, and the great pines wore it like a suggestive gown.

"A walk before breakfast?" John suggested enthusiastically.

"With pleasure."

We headed off into the forest, along a firebreak, and walked in silence for about ten minutes. Some distance off to our right, a squirrel was scolding something. To the left, Dougie was busy snuffling. A couple of hundred metres ahead of us, the firebreak crested a hill. As always in this forest, I seemed to be aware of a life force that pervaded everything, vibrant and powerful but also gentle and quiet. And that life force always seemed to be present in me as well. The Great Spirit, perhaps? The mist was clearing slowly, the gentle kiss of its dampness giving way to the more vigorous embrace of the day's rising heat. I wondered once again, not at all idly, how it was that eager gangs of metaphors seemed to crowd around me in the forest, singing in whispers very like those of the pines themselves, waving for attention. I was reminded of tree DNA, the large numbers of genes trees possess, conferring on them, it seemed, the ability to meditate out of time, across ages, to know things in a way I could not, but being able, at the same time, to make me well aware that they did know. Sometimes, they seemed almost to embody or, perhaps more accurately, to inlignate, giving in to the quirky metaphor of something becoming real by virtue of being made of wood, a reconciliation of opposites, a sort of woodland Jungian contemplation. I doubted that I would ever try to explain this to anyone, but I felt no reticence, did not blush at these thoughts. I just let them unfold privately.

"Are there any projects you want to work on today?" I asked John.

"I've almost finished turning a lamp base for a customer. There's about another hour's work to do. But I'm not on a deadline. If there are things you'd like to do…"

"Well", I began, "there are things I wanted to talk to you about, some items in your family journals, where this whole project of the skeleton has got to. But I need about two hours first to talk to Dr. Willis and Ted Ballantyre. I have appointments with them at ten and eleven this morning, as you know, but after that…"

"That will work out well. We'll go back soon and have breakfast, then I'll go off to the workshop."

"Fine", I said. "A nice breakfast will be good." I looked around at the trees. "But there's no rush." And I noticed John's sly smile.

We finished our walk, and as soon as we turned to retrace our steps, Dougie loped back along the firebreak, turning to look back at us regularly, evidently wondering what the holdup was.

Breakfast was eaten outside at the picnic table and consisted of John's homemade bread, cut thick and toasted, lumps of cheese, and large cups of coffee. A clutch of sparrows fluttered down to get their share.

I met Dr. Willis first, and that meeting involved not much more than running through what I knew and having Willis confirm it. My objective was to find out whether there was anything further I should know about before visiting Ted Ballantyre.

There wasn't.

But Willis did pass on to me, almost in an offhand way, two final things about the skeleton, items that he personally wanted to complete.

"I'm quite confident that whoever owned this skeleton suffered from Paget's disease."

I must have looked puzzled.

"It's a wasting condition that can limit mobility severely and cause considerable pain."

"Is that important to know?" I asked.

"No. I don't think so. Although, in his case, it was fairly severe."

"And the second thing?" I prompted.

"Yes. I asked for, and have just received, an expert opinion on the skull injury. The specialist I consulted can't be entirely definitive, but she feels confident that the cranial damage resulted from a blow to the head, and that it most likely was the fatal injury. She also confirmed my suspicion that whoever the person was, if their death occurred today, it might well be judged taking into account the eggshell skull rule."

"So the person had an abnormally thin skull?" I asked.

"Yes", Willis said.

I had heard of this and decided to check on it later. My discussion with Willis was brief and businesslike. He had nodded to acknowledge, in no surprise whatever, that Mark and I considered we were at something of an impasse and we wouldn't be pursuing the skeleton business any further. He said he had nothing further to add, at which point he returned to his desk and sat.

He was becoming restive and evidently had a good deal of other work he wanted to get back to. I thanked him and we shook hands cordially.

It was clear that Willis had moved beyond his earlier frustration and irritation with the Ballantyres and had more important things to deal with. As I walked back to my car at ten forty, I called Ted to see if he objected to me turning up ten minutes early for our meeting. Ted was in a buoyant mood and told me to come right over.

Ted lived on his own in a generously sized house on the edge of Cobourg. He must have seen me drive up since he was waiting outside his front door as I walked toward his house.

"Good morning, Mr. Boscombe. Come in."

I turned down Ted's offer of coffee, there was a brief exchange of small talk, and then Ted asked how he could help me.

"Well, I'm not looking for any help, Mr. Ballantyre. I just wanted to bring you up to date on what Mark Whelan and I have concluded."

He cocked his head slightly, probably at the word *concluded*, but I carried on before he could ask a question.

"John Stanley and I have been friends for many years, and when the remains were found on his land, I wanted to satisfy myself, as a friend, that he would face no awkwardness."

"Awkwardness?"

"I think you know what I mean, Mr. Ballantyre. In any case, it does seem to us now that since there's no reason to believe that the skeleton recovered belonged to a Ballantyre, then no old wounds would be opened."

"Whoa! Didn't belong to a Ballantyre?"

"Well, Dr. Willis assures me that nothing he has found would justify believing otherwise."

"Well, I believe that's not the case", Ted said bluntly.

"I'm sorry. Does that mean you believe that Dr. Willis is holding back something?"

"I believe that the skeleton did belong to a Ballantyre."

I just stared at Ted for a moment, hoping that my gaze transmitted doubt and disbelief.

"I have no reason to believe that, sir, and none appears to be forthcoming. So, Mark Whelan and I will not spend any more time on the matter. The skeleton is likely more than a century old, and I doubt that we will ever know who it belonged to. That's the only message I wanted to leave with you, Mr. Ballantyre, so now I will say goodbye." I rose promptly, hoping to signal without doubt that our meeting was at an end.

Ballantyre raised one hand, obviously intending to carry on the conversation, but I turned and walked out the door. I heard only the first part of what Ballantyre began to say.

"This needs to be discussed, Mr. Boscombe. I think…"

None of this was really any different from what Mark or I had expected. I anticipated Mark's smile when I related my two conversations to him, and I smiled as well, being fairly sure that this was not the end of the matter and that now we were entering a waiting game of unknown duration.

18

Border Crossings

The rest of the weekend with John was peaceful and restful since I could set aside the matter of skeletons and Ballantyres and obscure intrigues. John and I did spend some time on points I had flagged in his family journals, but these turned out just to be filling in details. We had several more walks in the forest, some pottering in John's woodworking shop, and an excellent meal of lamb shanks.

But then the weekend closed behind me as I made the drive back to Toronto on Sunday afternoon. There were tugs in both directions here: I found myself increasingly reluctant to leave John's place in the forest, although I wasn't sure just what that might mean, but at the same time, I looked forward to a return to the city and a discussion with Mark on finally wrapping up this whole skeleton business.

"So", Mark began when I met him at his and Andrea's place that evening and we were settled in their den. "Did it go about as expected?"

I explained my odd conversation with Ted Ballantyre.

"He's insisting that the skeleton belonged to a Ballantyre", I said, "but he seems to have no real basis for being so dogmatic about it." I'm sure my puzzlement showed.

"Well, we can be sure he's doing that for some reason. He's not obtuse, but I'm very quickly coming to the view that there's something about his thought processes that's not entirely rational." Mark paused here. I gestured that I didn't understand what he was getting at.

He nodded. "You've probably come across people who have trouble finishing any sentence. They get partway through one and then start another, and sometimes there seems to be only the vaguest connection between them. I'm beginning to believe that there might be something similar going on with Ted. Oh, he finishes sentences all right, but there's something disjointed in his thinking. Either that, or..."

"Or what?"

"Or, he's taken a stance for reasons so firm that for him it's all fact, and his faith isn't shaken even when he isn't able to support his statements."

"So, you think the discovery of this skeleton has prompted him to make some connections that seem entirely obvious to him?"

"Possibly. But it might actually be the case that he knows something."

"I'm not sure I follow", I said.

"Let's say that there's a big ugly secret somewhere in the Ballantyre past, and that some serious actions have been taken to cover it up." Mark hesitated here. "I think that maybe Ted knows something."

"But is it important for us?"

"Probably not. Unless it has something to do with the skeleton."

"Does this point to anything we can do?"

"That's the problem", Mark said. "I really don't know. I think we have no other choice but to wait and see if anything else happens."

I must have looked lost.

"Well, either nothing will happen, and the whole business will just fade away, or something will happen and then we'll need to see what that might mean."

There was no point in trying to postulate outcomes. The odd gyrations that had taken place to this point had now just run down to a standstill. No new hypothesis came to mind, at least none that made any sense, so any attempt at further planning seemed to be just a waste of time.

"Well", I said, hoping I was sounding decisive, "just out of curiosity, I'm going to take a closer look at the one quite odd thing about the nineteenth-century Ballantyres."

"Charles Ballantyre", Mark said flatly.

"Yes, Charles Ballantyre. As you suggested. There is indeed something strange there. Why would the head of the family business just drop everything and vanish from sight?"

Mark shrugged. "Weird family? Too much in-fighting? Decided he'd had enough?"

I didn't reply.

"Okay", Mark said. "Go for it. Yes, it is odd, but then the whole family seems to be odd, was always odd."

By unspoken agreement, we then dropped any further discussion of all things Ballantyre and turned to the task of making sandwiches for ourselves from the sliced ham, fresh bread, lettuce, and various condiments that Mark had laid out on the coffee table.

"Too bad Andrea isn't here", I said as I bit into the generous sandwich I had just constructed. "Where is she?"

"Oh, she'll be here. She's on her way home from the office. Probably will arrive in just a few minutes."

"The office? On a Sunday?"

Mark smiled and nodded, and I remembered that Andrea was driven to do work that she loved, that every day was potentially a work day.

We munched happily, and about ten minutes later Andrea came in. From our spot in the den, Mark called out "We're in here. Come on through."

There were the sounds of keys being tossed onto the kitchen counter, shoes clattering on the floor, and a sigh that sounded as though it had come all the way from her ankles.

Andrea made her entrance, good-looking as ever in faded jeans and a pale caramel sweatshirt and made even better looking by being evidently tired and ready to collapse, but drawn to the attractive array of food on the table before us. Mark pulled up a seat for her and poured her a large glass of white wine.

"Can I make you a sandwich?"

"Do I look that helpless?" Andrea asked through a wan smile.

"Yes."

"Okay, then. Yes. Lots of ham, a good smear of mustard, two leaves of lettuce, and four fat dill pickles."

We munched in silence. Andrea set down a half-eaten sandwich on her plate and looked at it appreciatively.

"Oohh! I feel better already. So what trouble have you two been brewing?"

Mark gave a thumbnail sketch, but then deftly shifted the conversation onto Andrea's day. Although I was a fifth wheel in this gathering, it was an atmosphere so relaxed and generous that I just sat back, smiled, and enjoyed their company.

We finished our sandwiches and drained the last of the wine. Then, by wordless, simultaneous agreement, we began making ourselves each another sandwich. Mark left to find a second bottle of wine.

Andrea finished making her sandwich before me, took a generous bite from it, then looked at me as she set it on her plate.

"I've never met John", she began. "Mark has told me a little about him. He sounds interesting. How's he taking all this?"

"With great equanimity."

"How so? He's not worried?"

"Not in the least, or so it seems. I've no idea whether he's read any Seneca, but he's certainly a follower: no point in fretting about things you have no control over."

"But he must be concerned that a skeleton was found buried on his property."

"Concerned? I don't know. I think he considers it just an odd puzzle. He's spent so much time on his own in the forest that I think he no longer takes much account of what other people think of him. He has friends, of course. Many friends. Although I don't think he's talked to any of them about the skeleton. Just this weekend, when I was saying to him that it looked as though Mark and I were stymied, he seemed to wave it all off. He talked about past generations of his family, and the thing of most concern to him was how they were treated by the Ballantyres of the time. But then he just shrugged and said that some years ago he came across a quote attributed to Bernard Baruch that he said made a lot of sense and had stayed with him."

Andrea raised an eyebrow that quite clearly invited me to tell all.

"He told me that Baruch was reported to have said, or written, 'Be who you are and say what you feel, because those who mind don't matter and those who matter don't mind.' I asked him how he thought that applied to him, but he just suggested I think about it." I paused here for a second. "Seems to me that, in the matter of the skeleton, he feels there aren't many people he needs to discuss it with."

Andrea considered that for a moment but then decided to change course.

"So are you going to drop your inquiries, or let things slide, or...?"

"Well, we're going to wait and see", Mark said, having re-entered the room.

"But I'm going to dig into one of the Ballantyre characters", I said, retrieving the conversational reins. "Charles Ballantyre. He relinquished control of the family business in 1874 and just dropped out of sight."

"How does that figure in things?" Andrea asked.

"Possibly not at all. But it seems out of character to me. Giving up is something foreign to the Ballantyre nature."

More wine was poured, Mark finished making his second sandwich, and our meal resumed, taking its natural precedence over ancient family intrigues.

We finished eating and chatted some more about inconsequential things in general. The conversation reached a natural lull. As I drained my wine glass, I had the sense that the room was speaking to me, hinting at the desirability of two occupants rather than three. I rose and thanked them both for the food, wine, and company. There were protests for me to stay a bit longer, but within ten minutes the streetlights were drifting past and a mild humid evening was ushering me along the sidewalk toward home.

At work the next day, Monday, I went back to a more normal work pace, and when I arrived home at just before six, I was looking forward to a light meal and then a few hours of fairly laid-back digging into the mystery of Charles Ballantyre.

Without the frantic drivers that had pushed me so hard to get through John's family journals, I did settle down to more measured and systematic internet searches for anything having to do with Charles. The starting point was material I had dredged up in searching through newspaper accounts for items to match events I had found reported in the journals. There were news stories reporting Charles's "abdication" as head of the Ballantyre empire, but nowhere were there reports of any interviews on the subject with any Ballantyres. Old Man Lorne Ballantyre, then in his eighties, had erupted to the prodding of one journalist until other family members silenced him and led him away. That reporter had noted that Australia had been mentioned, but without specifics. That was presumably where the notion had arisen of Charles decamping to Oz. Apart from that, there was little family commentary.

I then spent more than two hours digging through the digitized passenger lists of ships bound for Australia. New York seemed most likely as a port of departure, so I checked digitized information on border crossings into the US. In the 1870s, Montreal was by far the dominant city in Canada and had the best train service to New York. If Ballantyre was headed for a ship in New York, he would likely go there through Montreal. But there was no record of a Ballantyre crossing into the US from Montreal at any time in 1874. Records incomplete? Travelled under a different name?

There was also a way to New York via Niagara Falls from Toronto, the trips from Toronto being dominated by visits to the falls themselves. With no expectations of success, I began looking.

It was tedious, probably a waste of time, and more than once I was tempted to give up.

And then, suddenly, there he was.

Charles Ballantyre. September 27, 1874. Crossed from Niagara Falls, Ontario, to Niagara Falls, New York.

This cut down the date range for passenger ships out of New York. And when I began looking, a world of interesting history associated with the settling of Australia opened before me. But there was no time to stop and graze. I scanned the passenger lists of ships bound for Sydney starting from September 28, 1874. There was a mixture of clippers, older sailing ships, ships having steam auxiliary power. But about forty minutes later, I had reached the end of the 1870s. No Charles Ballantyre. Once again, there was the possibility of incomplete records or travel under a different name. But why cross into the US as a Ballantyre but then sail away as someone else?

Another possibility was becoming likely.

That Charles never did go to Australia. That he just hopped over to the US and kept his head down.

I stopped at that point and pondered.

Had I been duped? Why did I adopt the possibility, without any real questioning, that Ballantyre had taken himself off to Australia? If all he needed to do was make himself scarce, there would have been plenty of options within Canada. He was hardly a nationally known figure. He could have hidden himself away comfortably in Montreal and nobody would ever have known. And yet, apparently, for some reason he had skipped off to the US.

There was something not right here. On a whim I began looking for other records of Charles's travels. It took the best part of an hour and was based on the speculations of a suspicious mind, so I could have been wildly off track. But I had sunk in my teeth and they were going to stay sunk.

In the end, my searching had become so mechanical that I almost missed it.

But there he was, once again.

Charles Ballantyre, entering Canada from Niagara Falls, New York, June 7, 1876.

What had he been doing?

Based on these findings, what should I be looking at next?

There were no obvious answers here. I wrestled with it for some time, at one point listing some possible rationales on a clean sheet of paper. But nothing on my list pointed to any obvious next steps. Apart, that is, from going over the Stanley family journals once more. But I did decide to dig a bit more.

I knew that the squared timber from Ontario's great white pines was almost all destined for England or the US. Because of their location further inland, most of the Ballantyre timber went to the US, and the family maintained an office in New York to look after paperwork, customer contacts, and handling the great flows of cash that were coming back to them. I did some further digging, looking for connections to that office, Ballantyre Holdings, and came up with a longish list of company names. Nothing seemed definitive.

Almost an hour into Tuesday, at 12:45 a.m., I saved the electronic files I had created, shut down my computer, shovelled various pages of notes into a manila folder, and called it a night.

19

Many Hints

Tuesday at work came and went in a disconnected blur as I worked my way mechanically through a range of tasks. In fact, it was almost relaxing, and at the back of my mind, the results of my searching the previous night, and their possible implications, percolated quietly. I knew that I would be back at the Charles Ballantyre problem once I arrived home.

And when I did arrive home at just after six o'clock, I changed gears in a leisurely way by finding a largish single portion of boeuf bourguignon in the freezer, giving it a quick partial thaw in the microwave, then transferring it to a casserole and letting it come to temperature. This would take a while, so I sat back with a glass of nice gamay and reflected calmly on what I had found the previous evening. The day's percolation had been productive, and a few possible paths forward now suggested themselves.

Having boiled some rice and added a few handfuls of frozen peas to the rice water, I served up my meal and took my time enjoying it, although my mind was already gearing up to another evening of digging and sieving information.

Starting where I had left off the previous evening, I took some care in going through the computer searches, because what I wanted to do now was expand the scope somewhat. I was looking for anything that might be linked to the Ballantyres but that involved anyone who wasn't a Ballantyre. Not easy to do, and a lot of net casting brought in no fish.

It wasn't that there were no names. There were names galore. I came across people called Jardine, Handley, Thickson, Brock, Toole, Smithers, Callan, Reesor, Davidson ... they just seemed to march endlessly across my screen. But I could see no connections. Some of them were nothing more than disembodied names, forlorn islands in a sea of undifferentiated history, having no links to any mainland. I tried digging further into those that seemed to come with some historical baggage, but the tracks all petered out, having led nowhere useful.

I sat back and let my mind drift. Maybe this really wasn't what I should be doing. It was like water sinking into desert sand, soon gone as though it had never been there. I cast around for other approaches, but none came to mind immediately. I peered at each name separately, hoping for some inspiration, but they remained obstinately uncommunicative. Three of the names I had seen before — Callan, Thickson, Brock — but closer examination brought me to an unconnected context in each case. I hesitated briefly over Smithers, but then moved on.

But I moved only a short distance.

A faint light of memory flickered.

Smithers. I had come across the name before.

Where?

Checking through my notes on the Stanley family journals yielded nothing. So it was unlikely I had seen the name there.

I then began working through my notes on newspaper accounts. An item dated October 1874 noted that David Ballantyre had taken over the family businesses, that he would be assisted by two other Ballantyre men, his uncles Graham and Arnold, and that the Ballantyres had refused all requests for comment. Comments were reported to have been made by several other businessmen in the Cobourg area, saying complimentary things about the family in general and David Ballantyre in particular. There was also an interview of a local politician, Malcolm Smithers, in which he made a rather lengthy pabulum statement about business continuity. It sounded tangential, hardly relevant. But I decided to invest a little more time to see if I could dig more deeply, having no other leads. Perhaps, in its turn, it would reveal something further.

But another twenty minutes of effort produced nothing.

I had shied away from a cover-to-cover reading of local newspapers, something that would have meant ploughing through years of issues, a task of unspeakable boredom. Thus far, I had used just items in the Stanley family journals to provide clues on what to look for in the press reports.

But that did give me another idea.

Where might I find other family journals, or equivalent, for the same time period?

It took a surprisingly short time to find a curious site called the Rural Diaries Archive. Could be promising. There were about a hundred family or personal journals on the site, all scanned. More than I had expected. I began looking through them. They were all of inherent interest, but as expected, there was great scatter among the diaries in terms of detail, time, place, and quality. Several were devoted to a single family or a single person. Most of them seemed to be pegged at or near population centres too far removed from Ballantyre home ground to be of any use.

But then there was one diarist from Cobourg. Her name was Sarah Milliken. Looking through the entries, some of which were quite extensive, I was surprised to see that the diary ran to more than four hundred pages. The entries began in 1840, when it appeared she was in her twenties, and stopped in mid-1889, presumably flagging her incapacity or death. Doing a quick check, I eventually found a death notice for Sarah Milliken of Cobourg, dated July 1889.

Okay. At that point there was nothing else but to dive in and start reading. The early entries, for the 1840s and 1850s, seemed to be of the "informed gossip" nature, but a comparison of specific items to contemporary news reports showed a fair congruence.

All right. I was now becoming cautiously optimistic.

Turning to the 1870s, I began looking for anything related to the Ballantyres. To my surprise, I found quite a bit. It was all just rather inconsequentially newsy, and it probably reflected the fact that local people talked about the pillars of the local society. Nothing new there. There was an entry in mid-1870 that included a couple of short paragraphs about the sudden and unexpected death of Walter Ballantyre and about Charles Ballantyre taking his place. There was a comment about Charles being *a pleasant man*, but also noting that he *moved with increasing difficulty*.

I skipped forward quickly and located an entry for September 1874 which recorded that David Ballantyre had taken over as head of the Ballantyre businesses and that little had been heard from Charles Ballantyre, along with Milliken's comment *perhaps because of his condition? Did Charles suffer from arthritis?*

It was clear now that I needed to read through the entire period from 1870 to 1874. This took less time than I expected, about an hour and a half, but it was worth the trouble.

Malcolm Smithers turned up four times in the diary during that period. In all instances, Smithers was reported to have something to say about the Ballantyres. There were no accusations, and no derogatory comments appeared to be attributed to Smithers. But there did seem to be something vaguely unsatisfactory that had inspired Milliken's entries. Or was I reading more into it than was there? Let's just say, I advised myself that, based on the diary entries, Smithers had some interest in the affairs of the Ballantyres.

I decided to read on.

There was nothing further about either Charles or Smithers. I worked my way through the last few months of 1874, then through 1875 and 1876, but then I came to a sudden stop.

September 18, 1876. The diarist had entered a cryptic note. *Malcolm Smithers, keen fisherman. Surprised to learn of his drowning death in Lake Ontario. Freak accident, I'm told.*

I struggled to interpret this. But then an inner voice said *Leave it, Boscombe. You're clutching at straws, maybe imaginary straws.*

And I had to admit that the voice was probably right.

But checking again in the newspaper reports, the drowning death of Smithers was indeed reported, the result of what was *probably a freak accident on either September 15 or 16*. There was one follow-up press report two days later, a brief note that was half news and half death notice, and it recounted Smithers's career as a local businessman and politician. And that was it.

Except for Milliken's comment four days later, on September 22, that Smithers *endeared himself to few people*.

I had to step back from all this. I had nothing definitive here and my view risked becoming distorted. These notes involving Smithers warranted nothing more than the judgment that they recorded someone's impressions of what might have been a series of local events that occurred independently of anything in Charles Ballantyre's life.

But this diary was a good find, and I would read more of it. At the moment, however, the most intriguing bits of information were the reported statement blurted out angrily by Lorne Ballantyre that Charles had gone to Australia, Charles's documented crossing from Canada to the US at Niagara Falls, and then his documented return to Canada a little less than two years later.

It was now almost eleven thirty. I hadn't nailed anything down, but I had found items of information that could be significant. Too late tonight to embark on another extensive set of searches, but half an hour spent carefully going over what I had found and making any notes that came to mind would be worthwhile. And for the next twenty minutes, that's what I did.

Files saved, notes arranged in folders, computer shut down, I treated myself to a generous armagnac and pondered what I would do on this tomorrow evening. There was no obvious direction forward. Maybe it was just the ragged and unsatisfactory end of the road. Maybe it was time just to shelve the whole matter and let it all die out quietly.

Somehow, I found myself strongly resisting that.

20

Unexpected

Wednesday morning.

Good night's sleep, surprisingly, since I had retired fairly late and expected to be kept awake by what I had uncovered during the evening's searching. Need to remember to round off more evenings with an armagnac.

Another day of solid but not very challenging work lay ahead in the office, and in the shower, I pondered the day that awaited me and how, or whether, I would continue chasing after more Ballantyre nuggets that evening.

The routines of shaving and getting dressed passed almost unnoticed as various threads connected to Ballantyre, Smithers, and Milliken waved in the cerebral breeze. Juice, vitamin pills, coffee, and a piece of toast. At 7:30, I began getting ready to head to the office.

My cellphone rang. It was Mark.

"Morning Mark. What's up? You going to ask me to go fishing?"

"Do you have important things at work today?"

Odd question to ask, I thought to myself in good humour, until I realized from Mark's flat expression that something was coming.

"Nothing special", I said. Short delay. "Something's happened, hasn't it?"

"I just had a call from Willis. You're right. Something has happened. Willis wouldn't say what over the phone. We need to go out there."

"When?"

"Immediately. I can feel that it's something important. I'm on my way to your place right now. Be there in less than five minutes. Meet me outside?"

"Yes. Okay."

The line went dead abruptly.

Walking quickly to my den, I grabbed two manila files, a notebook, and two pens and shoved them into my leather document folder. Scooping up keys from the kitchen table, I locked my condo and left the building just as Mark's car pulled up. He began driving off almost before I had the door fully closed.

"I've just texted Willis saying we're on our way."

Mark tapped the steering wheel with his thumb, a nervous habit I recognized, and one that told me he expected Willis's news to be significant.

"No hints from Willis?"

"No. None. But he hardly knows me. He wouldn't phone me, and not at this hour, if it was anything trivial."

"And not wanting to discuss it on the phone."

"That too."

Traffic was now heavy, well into morning rush hour, but Mark threaded through it expertly while I sent a text message to my boss warning of my absence for the day because of a personal emergency.

Soon we were on the parkway, and Mark cranked up the speed well beyond the modest limits laid down by our solicitous authorities. About fifteen minutes later, we joined the expressway, and Mark soon had us passing almost everything while we both watched for signs of the boys and girls in blue. Once we had cleared the eastern limit to the city, traffic became lighter.

"Why would Willis contact you?" I asked.

"Good question. Two reasons, I expect. First, I get the feeling he doesn't have complete faith that the local constabulary will hit the ground smartly, or that they'll be running when they do, or that they'll be running in the right direction. Second, he's aware of my PI status and he knows that we've got John Stanley's back as our main priority and that anything to do with John and the skeleton isn't part of an active investigation. We'll see just what he says."

"Did he ask you to come to him, or did you offer?"

"No. He asked. And he asked us. In fact, it was more a demand than a request."

"Well! Looks like we're about to learn something significant."

Mark just nodded. We rode in silence for a few minutes.

"Did you make any headway on the Charles Ballantyre angle yesterday?" Mark asked.

"I did. Some curious findings. But nothing really solid."

"Curious?"

"Yes. There's a speculation out there that when Charles left as head of the Ballantyre businesses, he went off to Australia. I couldn't find any record of him doing that. Yes, I know, might have looked in the wrong place, incomplete records, and all that, but I did find a record of him crossing into the US at Niagara Falls in September of 1874. But then, and this really surprised me, I found a record of him re-entering Canada at Niagara Falls a bit less than two years later. I came across some other stuff too. But I don't know where it fits in. Or if it fits in at all."

"Is there a way forward from there?"

"No", I said. "Not really. Not one that's obvious." I must have sounded a bit discouraged.

"Well, never mind. Maybe what Willis has to say will clear a logjam or two."

We rode on.

The countryside drifted westward past us, and as usual I was fascinated by the ranges of hills, sometimes green and close by, other times blue or purple and more distant, that form the great moraine stretching along the north shore of Lake Ontario. I have driven across that moraine and through it many times and at many locations, and I am always struck by the variety, the subtlety, and sometimes the intensity of the folds, valleys, and promontories. I watched them now idly, a sideshow remnant of the massive ice sheets that had their curtain call not that many thousand years ago. I was awakened from this reverie by a sound from the driver's seat.

"Sorry", I said to Mark.

"I just asked if you could text Willis and let him know we'll be with him in about fifteen minutes."

"Yes. Sure", I said, reaching for my cellphone and wondering where I must have been for the past forty minutes.

We took the Burnham Street exit to Cobourg. Mark found his way unerringly through the city's streets and soon pulled in to a visitor parking spot at the hospital where Willis had his office and autopsy space. As we entered the hospital, Willis rose from a chair near the door and waved us to go back outside with him.

"We can meet in your car", Willis said. "Lead the way."

Seated in Mark's car, Willis abandoned all preliminaries.

"It's a slow day today, but even on slow days I'm interrupted fairly often in my office. We won't be interrupted here, and we don't need to worry about being overheard."

After a brief pause, Willis continued.

"Thank you both for coming on very short notice. I'll get right to the point. Ted Ballantyre has been found dead. The initial determination by the police is suicide. I'm not accepting it without solid evidence. And even based on what I've been told is the physical evidence, the death is suspicious, so we'll see what he has to say once he's on my mortuary table."

"Where was he found? And when?" Mark had found his voice before I had.

"Late yesterday afternoon", Willis said. "I learned about it just past midnight. He was found in his home."

"What? How…" I began, not finding the words and trying to take it in.

"As it was told to me", Willis said ponderously, "Ted was expected at an afternoon meeting yesterday — don't ask me where. He was to meet his brother Gary and two others, but he didn't show. Apparently, this wasn't uncommon. It looks as though Gary then went to Ted's place yesterday evening sometime and found him. Gary then called the police."

"Why suicide?" Mark asked.

Willis was in the back seat, Mark and I in the front, and we were turned facing him. He looked for a few seconds as though he was gathering his thoughts, but his expression was almost a scowl.

"Let me start by saying that I find it distasteful to discuss a matter this serious based on hearsay. But that's all I have. For the moment, anyway. So you must consider that all I'm about to say might change."

Willis paused again for a moment.

"What I have comes from the police. And it seems to me that some of what they have comes from Gary Ballantyre. There'll be a full investigation, of course. And an autopsy. Gary went to the police yesterday, early evening, I suppose, and reported finding Ted. He then went back to Ted's place with the police. I was asked to be ready to perform an autopsy, and my police contact told me what the investigating sergeant had found. Ted was lying on his bed, his left shirtsleeve rolled up. On the night table next to him was a syringe and an almost empty vial of potassium chloride solution."

Willis stopped there, evidently feeling that we had all the information we needed. I could see his expression changing, most likely because of my look of incomprehension.

"Potassium chloride is the chemical used in the US, and elsewhere, for legal execution by lethal injection", Mark said, for my benefit. "I assume, Dr. Willis, that the vial contained enough that death would be a certainty when it was injected."

Willis's impatience showed.

"I don't have that information", he barked, "along with a lot of other information I don't have." He stopped and regained control.

"I'm sorry. I should keep my bad temper to myself. I expect to receive all those details and I'll share with you what I can when I can. For now, I must demand that you tell none of this to anybody, because officially I'm speaking out of turn. There's one exception to that", he added. "John Stanley." And he looked back and forth between us for an answer.

"Yes, absolutely", Mark said.

"Of course", I muttered.

"I'm telling you this out of respect for John."

"Thank you, Dr. Willis. Do you have any indication when the autopsy will take place?"

"Yes, Mr. Whelan. It will be this afternoon. The body was delivered to the hospital sometime last night and is now in my mortuary."

We thanked Willis, he nodded and smiled wanly, then said he had to get back. He climbed out of the car and strode purposefully toward the hospital main entrance.

21

More from Sarah

We watched Willis enter the hospital but then sat without saying anything for about thirty seconds.

"Well!" Mark began. "The plot thickens."

"Why would Ted kill himself?" I asked.

Mark shrugged. "Too deeply involved in something serious that we don't know anything about yet? I don't know."

"And if he didn't kill himself, who did kill him, and why?" I asked, continuing to snatch at shadows in the dark.

"Don't know that either", Mark said. "But I think we should drive out and speak to John. The rumour mill will be at warp nine, and he should have information that is as good and as current as possible, from us and not third or fourth hand."

"Yes", I agreed. "Good thinking. I'll call him." I pulled out my cellphone, got hold of John, and said that Mark and I were in Cobourg and we'd like to drop in.

"Let's go", I said.

"Okay", Mark replied. I directed him to John's place as we drove out of the hospital car park.

Each of us was evidently absorbed in his own thoughts during the short drive to John's place. But when we arrived, the welcoming committee (Dougie) raised everyone's spirits by showing his overflowing enthusiasm at having visitors, and we accepted John's offer of coffee. Seated again at the picnic table, I walked John through what we had learned that morning. It didn't really surprise me that he showed practically no reaction to our news.

"What's next?" John asked, almost as though inquiring idly and pointlessly about yesterday's weather.

"Not sure", I said. "We're going back to Toronto now. I need to sit and think about things. I'm not really sure there *is* a way forward. We'll see. And, of course, I'll keep you up to date."

We talked a bit more about things in general, John's face lit up when he told us about a new commission he had received for two end tables, and Dougie went from one to the other of us, the effervescent cheerleader.

Mark looked surreptitiously at his watch, and I realized that time was money for him. So we thanked John for the coffee, made our farewells, and soon were on our way back to town.

There was no real conversation for the first half hour of the journey. Eventually, Mark broke the silence.

"I don't see that there's much more I can do on this. I don't know whether you have something specific you want to follow up."

I scratched my head. "I need to update the table of events and facts", I said. "Not that I expect anything new to emerge from that exercise. And I want to go over the Milliken diary again. The first pass was fairly quick. I need to look at it closely now. Maybe there are things between the lines."

I saw Mark nodding out of the corner of my eye.

"The next possibility for some solid information", Mark said in a thinking out loud voice, "is likely to be the autopsy on Ted's body. Although we can't rely on Willis sharing everything with us. Or even anything. I'd say we've entered a slow phase. No doubt there'll be some investigation into Ted's death. Something might come from that. Or nothing."

"You can likely drop out now, Mark. I'm sure you have other work that needs doing."

"Yeah. Well. Let's just see what happens. Rather than drop out, whatever that might mean, I'll just shift into neutral."

The rest of the trip home was punctuated by desultory questions and answers about work, the weather, and a few choice political absurdities.

By the time we arrived back in Toronto, the day already felt like a downer. Mark dropped me at my place, I toyed with the idea of going in to work very late, but decided just to take the day. A day of vacation. No big deal. But then I just flopped around, unable to settle on anything, and reflected in an unstructured way on the day now almost gone and where we had got to in the skeleton business. It did occur to me, vaguely, that the skeleton now represented no real threat to John and that I should drop the whole matter. I was surprised at the internal resistance this thought met. Eventually, I made myself a scratch meal from things I found in the fridge and drifted through what seemed like an evening glide path ruffled by mild mental turbulence on the approach to bed.

Thursday and Friday at work fluttered past unfruitfully. Saturday's only accomplishment was a half-hearted cleaning of the condo. It took me all of Sunday to read just fifty pages of *Treasure Island*.

In the shower on Monday morning, I delivered myself a stern lecture, felt better for it, and, on arrival at my desk, threw myself into a full day of demonic work. At six thirty, I let a drained Steve Boscombe into his condo, changed into jeans and a scruffy sweatshirt, and headed off to The George, the best place in my area for fish. A delicious but light meal and a half litre of wine later, I headed home, batteries recharged.

I then started in on what I had told Mark I was going to do, and two hours later I had a table of events and facts compiled and checked. It was larger than I expected, and a success of that magnitude was a perfect start.

Sarah Milliken's diary came next, and since I had transferred a copy to my iPad, I settled into my favourite armchair and began going through it again, carefully and from the beginning. It really was rather gossipy in places, something that normally would put me right off, but I brushed aside my impatience and focussed on what might be behind the commentary. From earlier work on the diary, I had satisfied myself that enough of the entries could be confirmed against more factual material to convince me that all the entries likely were inspired by actual events, that the more breathless elements in the diary were just embellishments she had added out of sheer boredom, and that they were not invention. It was the things she was embellishing that I was after.

Scattered through the pages, and over a period of many years, there were entries on Lorne, Walter, and Charles Ballantyre, consisting of both personal family comments and snippets that had a business flavour. I found that these were scattered over many dozens of pages, and moving back to my desk, I began listing them by date order on a notepad. This exercise began to be interesting, since having these Ballantyre family commentaries all in one place painted a picture that hadn't come through from the scattered diary items. The family really seemed to have an outsized presence in the community. There were a few instances where individuals disputed what a Ballantyre had said about something. The diary left little doubt that none of the Ballantyres was shy about delivering strong and out-of-proportion responses.

There was a good deal of commentary about the Ballantyre mansion, Pine Lodge, which sat on 550 acres of land just north-east of Cobourg, a settlement that had been called Meyer's Creek back in the day. The Ballantyres were a closed family, virtually no townies ever saw the inside of Pine Lodge, and there was eager speculation about the mansion's expensive furniture, sumptuous drapes and wall hangings, silver trays and goblets, crystal chandeliers, and other absurdities that piled up without apparent limit. The Ballantyre men were seen about the town, the women much less frequently, but Claire

Ballantyre, Lorne's wife, not at all. According to word on the street, she had done the impossible by surviving practically every known malady and was reported variously to be reclusive, disabled, or mad.

I dutifully made a note of it all, and even this condensed version ran to over two pages. There was an odd note about the surprise birth of Charles in 1848, and there seemed to be a vigorous buzz over the fact that nobody realized that Walter's wife, Eleanor, had been pregnant. Why this should have caught the townsfolk unawares was puzzling, given that it seems Eleanor had no confidantes and no visitors. Perhaps the urge to know other people's business is equally insistent and unrelenting across all times and all space. Eleanor wasn't particularly old when Charles was born, considering the sometimes lengthy parenting years in those days. He was the youngest of that brood, and I detected Milliken's hidden desire to know more, given that he was the youngest child in the family by nine years. It looked as though the actual event prompting the entry was just the sudden announcement of Charles's birth, the bulk of the commentary being unsupported window dressing.

Move on.

Focussing on further entries involving the Ballantyre family members, I completed a pass through the entire diary by eleven thirty. By then I was becoming groggy, but I did go over everything I had culled from the diary, including going back to all the individual pages where I had found the comments to double-check the wording and my interpretations. At midnight, I packed it in, filed my handwritten notes in preparation for entering them electronically later, and headed off to bed, looking forward to another chapter or two of *Treasure Island*.

I think I managed only about a page and a half. At quarter to three, I awoke, the bedside light still burning and me feeling inflated by some weird idea that I was Jim Hawkins.

When the alarm woke me again at five forty-five, I was more than a little hazy but ready for a shower and another day at the office.

22

A Second Look

It didn't feel like a Monday. But I had no idea why I had this sense, because it was actually a Wednesday. It didn't feel like a Wednesday either, but then I had to wonder what a Wednesday ought to feel like. I shook my head, trying to clear the confusion, then just went through the usual morning ritual.

My work isn't particularly challenging, and I noticed that this thought was occurring to me more and more frequently. Never mind. I'm good at it, it pays reasonably well, and I get along with my colleagues, although I consider none of them to be close friends.

On this non-Monday that felt like neither a Monday nor a Wednesday, I attacked my work with energy, buoyed up by a sunny mood that I simply accepted without knowing its origin. Feeling perhaps that, through our efforts, Mark and I had converted "The Threat of the Skeleton" to "A Forgettable Anthropological Oddity". Shouldering all that aside, I steamed through my day's tasks, and was more than ready to lay down tools at five o'clock. On the way home, a vision of supper — ham and pineapple, a nice creamy pasta with bacon bits, and peas with mint — appeared before me like a genie out of a lamp. I picked up what I needed at the local supermarket, and at six thirty, I complimented myself on the meal I had begun to consume. Lingering over a further glass of wine at seven fifteen, I found that I was looking forward to attacking what I had mined the previous evening from the diary.

But not just yet, I said to myself, holding my glass up to the light, Jim Hawkins examining his…

No idea where this Jim Hawkins stuff is coming from. Sure, it's a fine tale, well told, but…

Ten minutes later, I was back at my desk, file folder open, a plan of work already forming. But when I had looked through my notes, I stopped short and looked up.

Jim Hawkins! My upbeat mood and sense of expectancy had nothing to do with *Treasure Island*. Jim Hawkins was just a sign. The real thing now leapt from the pages at me.

Smithers.

On a separate piece of paper, I jotted down, from yesterday's notes, all the instances where Milliken had referred to Smithers. But then — no, that wasn't true. What I had noted were the instances where there had been a reference to Smithers and a Ballantyre.

Going back to the diary, I managed to find a further four items where the name Smithers appeared. So, altogether, nine diary entries that mentioned Smithers. And a single Smithers: Malcolm.

I assembled all Milliken's references to Malcolm Smithers, then retreated to my armchair to ponder them.

When people are spoken of regularly, it occurred to me, it is either because they're popular or not popular. In Smithers's case, it was definitely the latter, based on the tone of Milliken's entries.

Malcolm had become a minor local businessman when he was still in his late teens. He began a small hardware store, but it seemed that he traded in anything anyone wanted to buy or sell, and his bargains were shrewd, although that wasn't the word Milliken used. By his late twenties, he was well off, and although unmarried, it seemed that he had never wanted for female company practically since his years of puberty. But in those activities, he had been discreet enough that any gossip about him hadn't gained any real foothold. He didn't shy away from public disputes, most of which it seems he won. And it was only a matter of time before he began crossing swords with members of the Ballantyre clan. For what reasons, Milliken didn't specify.

There was a short series of arguments, apparently fiery, between Smithers and Lorne Ballantyre, but these settled down when Smithers decided to go into local politics, where it pays handsomely to choose only and exactly the right battles. Malcolm Smithers had been born in 1824, and by the time he had become a local politician in the mid-1850s, his hair-trigger public aggression was a thing of the past.

One last entry by Milliken noted Smithers's death by drowning in Lake Ontario in 1876, and it included the neutral comment that he had been *an avid fisherman and a good swimmer.*

I sat back and looked at the full page of notes on Smithers that I had pulled from Milliken's diary.

Why? Why Smithers?

Two questions, really. Why had I focussed on Smithers, when my interest always had been the Ballantyres? And why had Milliken spent so much ink on him?

I made another quick pass through her diary, and a convincing answer to my first question suggested itself. Nobody but the Ballantyres had warranted as much comment as she had given Smithers. He had been, apparently, a focus for Milliken, and I had noticed that I had not been conscious of it initially, but now it was front and centre.

But then, my second question, why had he been a focus for her?

Because she hadn't liked him? From what Milliken reported, he sounded like someone easy to dislike.

Because he had been successful at practically everything he had turned his hand to, and she was jealous somehow?

Or because he had been a topic of regular and general discussion, and she was just reporting what she had heard?

Okay. Enough. I had satisfied myself that Smithers had been just a byway, a local who had attracted comment. There was then one more ore body to mine, and that was to dig through the local newspapers looking for any further references to the Ballantyres that I had missed. This looked like a large and boring job, but one that I felt I couldn't avoid any longer in order to be able to claim completeness. I started on it.

At half past midnight, I had found what seemed to be three distant items that referred to the Ballantyres, all of them well into the penumbra of my area of interest. Two involved minor land deals. A third reported the death, in 1907, of an aged servant, Mary Somerville, who had been employed by the Ballantyres from the age of fifteen.

None of this seemed to be of any importance, but I noted it all, placed the sheet into my file folder, and sat back to think where things stood.

The Smithers inquiry, while curious, shed no light on anything. And that left — what?

Only the business of Charles Ballantyre. He had taken over as head of the family business, had left that role a few years later, and had slipped across the border into the US. But then two years later he had returned to Canada and seemed to have faded immediately into obscurity. Had he returned again to the US without leaving any paper trail? Had he gone off to live in quiet seclusion somewhere in Canada? Although this was a loose end, I could think of no way to follow up on it. I fretted for a while.

But then, feeling I had learned at least something new and interesting, I poured myself a generous glass of armagnac and settled down with my now half-read copy of *Treasure Island*. By two fifteen, at least three hours after I would have gone to bed on a normal evening, I closed the book, pleased at having enjoyed the story far more than I expected, but annoyed at myself, knowing that I would be a basket case at the office. One final luscious sip of armagnac was all I remembered before dropping deep into the arms of Morpheus.

To my great surprise, I practically leapt from bed less than four hours later, at six o'clock, growling "Har Billy!" and looking forward to a day's work. In the shower, where it seems some of my best thinking is done, I wondered fleetingly whether some combination of armagnac and Robert Louis Stevenson was for me the key to a fountain of something.

At my desk in the office, the day passed, and although I did get quite a bit of work done, by three o'clock that afternoon, my ass had begun to drag. There had been a fairly glowing compliment from my supervisor on my "incredible productivity of late", and I decided that this could be considered as agreement to an unspoken request to leave for home at four fifteen. Something quick appealed for dinner, and Caesar salad with slices of herbed chicken breast won that lottery. The local deli has good prepared chicken breast and a pass through the supermarket gave me the wherewithal for the Caesar. At five thirty, I had consumed a very satisfying light meal and surrendered to the siren song of my bed.

Awake again at eight thirty that evening, I was oddly puzzled at my still buoyant mood. A bit of transcribing of notes to electronic form ought to be a decent interlude before returning to bed and pinching off what might easily become a slide into a life of nocturnal wakefulness. At ten o'clock, I poured myself another glass of armagnac, and then at six the next morning, I wondered what I had done with it.

And now here I was at Thursday. The day didn't have the appeal of the previous three, but I determined to be at my desk on time, make a good fist of it, and churn out product. This effort was intended to produce gentle zephyrs speeding my boss's continuing voyage on the Sea of Euphoria. Between shower and breakfast, I emailed Mark asking about a drink at The Turner House again. By nine o'clock that morning, an answer was on my cellphone: *Meet here at our place? Six thirty? Drinks? Then dinner at 8 with Andrea? Deal?*

Dinner with Mark and the fair Andrea. It was a no-brainer.

23

The Postulate

The evening with Mark, and then with Andrea and Mark, was as full and exhilarating and companionable as anyone could wish. Andrea and Mark are so relaxed with each other, and they entertain guests with such natural ease that you don't even notice it until you have occasion to think about what's actually happening. Before Andrea arrived home at just after eight, Mark and I avoided all things skeletal and talked about his work for a while, then we talked food while I helped him prepare dinner, or rather did little more than watch while he began putting together the main dish.

He had chosen moussaka but, by the time I arrived at six, he had done about half the background work and, apart from me playing sous-chef three times removed, I just watched the assembly operation. There was a schedule for this, timed such that the cooked moussaka could come out of the oven by about eight fifteen. Other ingredients were laid out for a Greek salad, and one that seemed guaranteed to satisfy the pickiest epicurean. When Andrea arrived, she took one look at us in our fatigues seeing off the last of the evening's first bottle of wine. Handbag and briefcase were dropped next to the hall closet.

"I see I'll need to dress for battle if I'm to join you two. Back in a minute." She headed down the hallway and returned almost immediately, having swapped her navy business suit and blouse for jeans, a University of Toronto sweatshirt that was well along the road to comfortable shapelessness, and bare feet.

"Assyrtiko!" she observed in evident approval, looking at the almost empty wine bottle. "I assume there's more. No! I'll get it!" she insisted, waving Mark back to his seat. Returning from the wine cooler to the large rustic coffee table where we were sitting, Andrea opened the bottle and poured herself a glass, almost in one fluid motion.

"Let me guess, then", she began. "Gyro? Or souvlaki?"

"No, moussaka."

"Didn't we have that last time?"

"No", Mark responded. "Last time we had kleftiko. But if you don't want moussaka, I can order in a cheap rogan josh. Or make you a plate of peanut butter sandwiches."

Andrea looked at me, smiling and shaking her head.

"What do you do with a guy who always remembers the right thing at the wrong time?"

"Don't answer that!" Mark ordered, rising from his seat. "It's a trick question! I'll be right back." And he strode toward the kitchen, shutting out any reply.

"Here we are", Mark said a few seconds later, setting down a bowl of marinated octopus, forks, small plates, and napkins.

Wine and seafood mingled companionably, but that thought had no sooner arisen than I recalled the origin of the word *companion*.

"Is there any bread?" I asked Mark.

Mark looked at Andrea.

"Good thing all our guests aren't this fussy. But he's right. My mistake", he said rising and heading off again to the kitchen. He returned a few seconds later, this time carrying a breadboard on which were two attractive small loaves of Greek olive bread and a pitcher of dark olive oil.

We ate in silent appreciation for several minutes.

"Very good, Mark", I said, wiping a piece of bread through a generous smear of olive oil on my plate. I looked at Andrea to see her reaction.

"Roughly what I've come to expect", she said, examining a piece of bread, almost disdainfully it seemed to me.

"Nothing less than excellent", she added and smiled as she ran an oily finger down Mark's cheek.

"Careful", he said, "or it will be a plate of peanut butter sandwiches."

But behind the banter it was easy to see great warmth.

We moved on to the dining table and to the main course, moussaka, a dish I hadn't had for some time. It was very good, and I found myself enthusing over it. And the switch in courses was paralleled by a conversational side-step into a discussion of Greece. Although we all lacked detailed expertise on things having to do with ancient Greece, I think we were all surprised at the ease with which we fell into a discussion of dramatists and philosophers.

"I've been there just once as well", I said, after Mark and Andrea had exchanged observations on their cruise in that part of the Mediterranean. "Time to go again, I think. But I'd like to be able to spend a bohemian six weeks there, maybe on one of the islands off the Turkish coast, maybe go hunting for traces of Thales, maybe see what it was about Ephesus that made them warrant their own epistle, maybe…"

Andrea and Mark both had stopped, forks partway to their mouths.

"Where did that come from?" Mark asked.

It took a few seconds for me to realize that I was having a mental earthquake. To my horror, tears suddenly began flowing from both my eyes.

Andrea was on her feet immediately. She gave me a friend's hug and wiped my cheeks using her serviette before I could start blubbering in embarrassment.

"It's okay", she said softly, sensing correctly that the long distraction provided by events associated with the skeleton and now the abrupt appearance of sights, aromas, and tastes of Greece had brought back a flood of recollections of my Greek trip with Joyce. And it was overwhelming. A tight bundle of memories, sudden and vivid. While Andrea applied her solicitous magic, Mark had risen and now returned to the table bearing a bottle and three glasses.

"Remembering is healthy, Steve, but so is a good snort. Here", he said, handing me a very generous glass of ouzo. Andrea chinked her glass against mine and took a mouthful, inclining her head to indicate I should get on with it and do the same. I did.

The strong liquor brought me back to the present with a thud. I must have been about to say something, because Andrea put a finger across my lips.

"I can't imagine what it must be like", she said softly. "No apologies. We're friends."

And then the quake ended as quickly as it had begun, and I faced two friends whose love was beyond doubt and a partly consumed, delicious helping of moussaka.

"Job's half finished", I said, digging into my meal again. "But I'm going to want seconds." I managed a smile.

Mark refilled my wine glass.

"Good weather we've been having lately", Mark said brightly, taking a deliberately gauche conversational turn. Andrea groaned, we all chuckled, and I took another mouthful of moussaka, looked at them both, and said, "Thanks."

"How's the new project going?" Mark asked Andrea. She sighed but then moved into a long discussion of an interesting task, a difficult client, and some innovative ideas that she was itching to put into play. I thought of my own work and, in one way, envied Andrea and her constantly changing problem sets.

I must have been lost in thought for a second, because I found Andrea looking at me expectantly and realized I had just missed a Mark and Andrea exchange.

"Sorry", I said. "Must have hit a bump in the road. Was there a question?"

"Not really", Andrea said. "Mark and I were talking earlier about the identity of the skeleton at John's place."

"Oh! Yes! Well, we don't know who it was, and that's brought us pretty much to a dead end."

Andrea finished a mouthful of moussaka, set down her fork, took a sip of wine, then focussed on me.

"But there are these two odd sets of events. Finding the skeleton and discovering the peculiar disappearance of Charles Ballantyre."

"Yes", I said. "But they seem to be just coincidental, nothing more."

"Well, is there no chance that the skeleton belonged to Charles?"

"No", I said, shaking my head in certainty. "The DNA rules that out."

Andrea just looked at me, then at Mark.

"Do you agree?" she asked Mark.

Mark just nodded.

"But suppose that those are Charles's bones."

"Well, but they aren't", I said.

"No. I understand what you're saying, but if you postulated that it was Charles who had been buried there, what would that mean?"

Mark and I just cast each other looks of dumb incomprehension. Mark got there first. His face brightened.

"Ah, I see", he said. "Well, it would mean that Charles was a black sheep, not really a scion of the Ballantyres. Interesting, but it doesn't move us any further along. The Ballantyres will just claim that the postulate is wrong, that the skeleton belonged to an unknown, as had been suspected all along."

"Except", I said, tapping the table. "Did you have anything specific in mind when you suggested that postulate, Andrea?"

"No. Just that there are these two events that might have occurred about the same time, so connecting them is at least a possibility."

"Except what?" Mark asked me, suddenly very focussed.

"You remember the comment I found in the Milliken diary? About people being surprised when they learned about Charles Ballantyre's birth?"

"Yes. I remember."

"Old Lorne Ballantyre was the head of the dynasty then, and he was fiercely puritanical. What if an out of wedlock pregnancy had surfaced in the Ballantyre home then? What would old Lorne have done?"

"Okay. I see where you're going. But it wouldn't have been Lorne's wife who gave birth would it? Lorne? A cuckold?"

"No. I'm not saying anything specific. If Lorne's wife somehow became pregnant by somebody other than Lorne, he would have just covered it all up, claimed the infant as his own, and that would be the end of it. Well", I said after a short pause, "that would have been the end of it publicly."

"So, what?"

"Well", I began, "let's just say that some woman in the Ballantyre household had an illegitimate child. I don't know who was living there at the time apart from Lorne and his wife and several children. But there would have been servants."

"Okay. One of the servants gets herself in the family way."

"Yes", I agreed. "Let's suppose. But then how would old Lorne react?"

"Don't know. Fire her? Ah, no. Maybe not. Then the word would be out that the Ballantyre home is really something of a leaping house."

"Leaping house?" Andrea said looking puzzled. "What… Oh!" she added, her expression displaying the recognition that the tone of the conversation had lurched downwards. "Forgot to account for the male brain."

Mark cast me a twisted smile.

"Definitely not!" I said. "I think Lorne would do everything possible to keep up appearances."

"Ah! So Charles might have had his origins under stairs."

"Could be", I said. "That was a good call, Andrea."

Andrea had resumed eating, looked up and mumbled, "I'm not so sure now."

"So now we have a hypothesis to test", Mark said, thinking out loud. "Too bad we don't have any way to test it", he continued, shifting his attention to me.

"What am I doing?" I said with emphasis. "Please pardon me. I'm being a very ungracious guest. Let's get back to this lovely meal. And I'm sorry, Andrea."

"It's at least half my fault", she said, her smile returning. "I started this."

The evening recovered quickly and soldiered on happily until almost midnight. On my way home, strolling through a warm night, two thoughts filled my head.

The recollection of my Greek trip with Joyce had come upon me in a suddenness and power that was unexpected. It had left me bewildered and my sense was that the lasting impression of it that remained with me wasn't going to fade any time soon.

Then there was the intriguing possibility we had explored briefly concerning the skeleton. Our discussion of it still exercised my mind, even though it pointed to no way forward.

These two things battled somewhat uncomfortably for my attention all the way home.

24

Implications

My watch told me it was 2:20 a.m. I had that same odd feeling I remembered from a few occasions in my childhood, when I wasn't really sure where I was, or even just who I was, and that wherever I was, it wasn't the right place.

What day is it? The unspoken question rose into consciousness from somewhere. The answer, *Thursday*, came to me from an equally obscure source. *You're not awake yet*, an internal voice said, hinting at the need for some patience.

How did I get to Thursday?

I switched on the light. It must have been the anchoring familiarity of bedspread, night table, bookcase, closet, and curtained window that yanked me back from a flight in Neverland and scrolled before my mind's eye a summary of the past few days.

Returning awareness brought with it a rapidly increasing feeling of urgency.

I was aware that I had to do something. What?

Thumbing through the routines of my life brought the recollection that work had been almost completely mechanical the past few days. There was nothing other than ordinary tasks facing me at work.

Joyce?

Of course, I could recall her face easily, and the dull pain of her absence never really left me. I remembered the emotional surge at dinner the previous evening, but that was now just an image, yesterday's lump in the throat.

What was so urgent? And why did something cause me to awaken so suddenly in the middle of the night?

Climbing out of bed, I went to the kitchen, poured myself a glass of juice, then walked to the den and sat in front of my computer. There was a moment of vague but significant expectation, what one might feel when looking at the sky, convinced that Betelgeuse was going to blow any second. Then, as though responding to a metaphorical tap above the ear, an image sharp and clear crystallized from my supersaturated thoughts.

Last night was the preparation. Now the seed crystal had been dropped. Thoughts now tumbled into consciousness one after the other.

Assume that the skeleton belonged to Charles. Okay. Done.

Write in big red letters that we knew for certain that Charles had not been born a Ballantyre. Yes. A tick mark there as well.

Work out everything that needed to be in place for that skeleton assumption to be correct. Lorne Ballantyre and his wife were not Charles's parents. All right. Follows inevitably.

Check the contradictions and loose jigsaw pieces lying around, and see what makes sense in the light of that assumption. Getting onto fresh turf now. Work needed here.

And think about where I might look for evidence to support the assumption.

Bingo! This item provided an almost clear path forward!

So now I had to get this down on paper, seek out the exactitude of precise wording.

Within twenty-five minutes, my deductions, ideas, points to pursue, and possible links to other information had filled four pages of notepaper. All but one of my bullet points documented the musings and postulates we had rolled out orally the previous evening, and in some cases clarified or extended them. But I was baffled that our discussions hadn't also unveiled the one last point: make a guess at exactly where Charles had come from.

I checked my watch: two fifty-five.

My impulse was to dive right in and start beavering. But then I would be a basket case the rest of the day at work. Better to tackle the matter in the afternoon, once I was home from the office. Besides, I had met the first action criterion for dealing with brilliant nocturnal insights: write them down in enough detail that the thread can be picked up later. At all costs, avoid that next morning letdown, the realization that the flash of genius was either trivial, ridiculous, just stupidly wrong, or, worst of all, now irretrievably forgotten.

I expected to toss and turn once I was back in bed, but I slipped back easily into the pool of sleep, and the rest of the night winked past.

At five forty-five, instead of heading straight to the shower, I went to my desk and scanned the notes I had made a few hours earlier. The hastily erected nocturnal framework of my intellectual lean-to didn't collapse under clear-eyed scrutiny in the merciless light of morning. There wasn't that sound reminiscent of a dozen kookaburras laughing their heads off.

Buoyed up by a feeling that progress had been made, I rushed through the shower and shave routine, skipped breakfast, and headed to the office. Early to arrive, early to leave, and the sooner to return to the mists swirling around Charles Ballantyre. It seemed to me that the day couldn't pass quickly enough.

But then shortly after five o'clock, I was back at home, sitting at my desk, consuming a takeout meal of pad Thai and elbowing my way back into the thin assortment of relevant fragments from the nineteenth century.

I decided to construct a large table as a first step in trying to find the right pieces and then to put them together. In no time, I was up to my elbows in paper. My notes from the Stanley family diaries and from multiple searches through old newspaper files and through

Sarah Milliken's decades of jottings all had to be reviewed again. By ten o'clock that evening, I had populated much of my table. Several insights now shone from it.

First, Charles was bright and decisive, had good business acumen, and seemed to have outshone easily his nominal uncles Graham and Arnold. That is probably what accounted for the fact that he was tipped to be head of the family businesses. Old Lorne might have had smouldering resentment at having to take Charles in as family. Everything about Lorne on the record made it clear that the value he placed on probity, both real and apparent, was high. And Lorne himself was a businessman of unyielding ambition. It was easy to see that Charles might impress him as the best choice for moving the family businesses forward.

Second, although Milliken's notes made it clear that the lower orders in all those communities where Ballantyre businesses operated were outside that family's social circle, there was a continuing flow of business contacts to Pine Lodge. Notable individuals in lake shipping, in the railway industry, and from some rival timber families were seen to come and go regularly. Elected officials, one or two high flyers from the press, and a handful of prosperous local merchants were among the favoured. The names of two clergymen were mentioned. And over a quite long period, it appeared that Malcolm Smithers was an occasional visitor.

Third, despite the efforts Lorne undoubtedly made to prevent it, rumours of family discord leaked out at frequent intervals. A broad streak of congenital bloody-mindedness probably had something to do with that. The inevitable clashes of strong wills over the best ways to direct the family businesses and handle the family fortunes no doubt played a part. But the eruption, on three occasions over a period of about three years, of disputes that seemed to be of a more personal nature, could not be suppressed. In her diary, Milliken noted one of these, linked to a nasty dispute between Charles and other members of the Ballantyre family who thought they should have taken priority over Charles to head the business.

I sat back to think.

It seemed evident to me that Charles's status as a non-Ballantyre would have been perfectly clear to his siblings. It was also hard to avoid the suspicion that this would have caused some bitterness, especially, as likely was the case, if Lorne came down hard on any break in family solidarity. When I looked at it from Charles's point of view, there seemed little doubt that he would have been on his own most of the time, constantly beset by sibling sniping, his main support being Lorne and that support always contingent on making the best business decisions.

My reverie was interrupted by the telephone. Call display told me it was Willis.

"Hello, Dr. Willis."

"Mr. Boscombe. I'm sorry to disturb you this late. I intended to call earlier, but … well, things have been busy."

"Not at all. No need to apologize."

There was a short delay here and a sound of papers rustling at Willis's end.

"I wanted to bring you up to date on some findings, Mr. Boscombe, but it must be in complete confidence I'm afraid."

"Yes. Of course", I said.

"I have completed the autopsy on Ted Ballantyre. The cause of death was indeed heart failure, probably induced by an injection of potassium chloride. But I'm not able to state definitively that that was the cause."

I wasn't really sure where this was going, but I did need to provide some response.

"Have you concluded that it was suicide?" I asked.

Here there was a long pause.

"Whenever you have the time, Mr. Boscombe, I would like to talk about this in person."

Okay, I thought. I could see the delicacy of Willis's position. But I had the feeling that something more than just professional caution was involved here.

"Do you have time tomorrow?" I asked.

"Yes. I can make time up to about two o'clock. After that, my schedule is packed."

"I can meet you at the hospital at ten o'clock tomorrow morning."

"May I suggest", Willis said, "that we meet at the bar of the Bayshore Country Club. I'll send you a link by email giving details."

"Fine. Mark Whelan might attend as well, unless you would prefer not."

"No, that's okay", Willis said. "Until ten o'clock tomorrow then."

This is interesting! I thought, after we had finished the call. And then I phoned Mark immediately.

"Are you going?" Mark asked, after I had related my conversation with Willis.

"Yes. Something's up. I'm sure of it. Will you come along?"

"I want to", Mark said. "I need to make some schedule adjustments. I'll email you to confirm within the hour."

"Okay. Willis is sending me details on where he wants to meet. I'll pass them on to you."

I was going to end the call, but then Mark continued. "Did you get any hint on what Willis wants to talk about?"

"It has something to do with what he will be giving as the cause of Ted's death. I'm fairly sure of that."

"Surely he doesn't think we can help?"

"No. It won't be that. I couldn't read it any better than that over the phone."

"Okay", Mark said, his voice expressing interest and intrigue. "I guess we'll find out."

I thanked him and Andrea again for the previous evening, then went back to my newly constructed information table. There was a lot of detail, and I began going through it item by item.

You need to step back a bit, Boscombe, try to see the big picture. My internal voice was clear and definite. And a bit surprising. But it sounded worth a try.

For twenty minutes, I tried to integrate sections of the table into larger blocks, searching for internal patterns, broader linkages that I might have missed. Nothing was coming to me and I was about to give up when I felt a sort of twinge, a distant chord. It was like seeing a vague shape through fog.

Try again. Move through the table the same way, just once more.
And then…

I could hardly believe that I had missed it. It wasn't a fact. It was a possibility. And then another possibility collided with me, one having greater momentum.

I spent the next ninety minutes searching. The possibility became firmer, and my searching became more focussed, more urgent.

Willis's message arrived providing details for the Bayshore Country Club. I passed it on to Mark immediately. Mark's email turned up about twenty minutes later saying he would be there and suggesting we meet fifteen minutes or so before the time agreed with Willis.

After a further twenty minutes of searching and checking, I sat back, a smile on my face. There would be more checks needed to confirm what it looked like I had found. And I had to remind myself that I hadn't proved anything. But I did now have the means to throw another postulate into the ring, one that might just provide the key to the whole puzzle.

25

More Details

Just before turning in for the night, I sent off an email to my boss, saying that I was taking another day of vacation the next day, Friday. By the time I was in bed and had switched off the bedside light, it was after twelve thirty.

By six thirty, I was up and dressed, had printed the table that was the result of the previous evening's labour, had packed that and the notes that had accumulated over the past few days into a leather documents case, and was cooking myself an egg, bacon, and toast breakfast. As I ate, I texted Mark and plugged in my iPad to top up its charge.

I surprised myself by thinking only about how much I was enjoying breakfast.

The trip to Cobourg was spent almost entirely in anticipating what I would hear, interspersed by bursts of recollection on the previous evening's digging. The signs flagging the arrival of the Cobourg exits reminded me to check on Willis's directions to the country club. It wasn't hard to find, and when I arrived at the car park in front of the club, I wasn't surprised to see that it wasn't a flashy whiz-bang sort of place, but a subdued, well-maintained building fronting an attractive rolling golf course. Just the sort of club I might expect Willis to join, although it would hardly surprise me if he found little time to enjoy it.

I was more than a half hour early, so I parked, had a look at the outside of the clubhouse, located the bar, then took a seat at a bench on the veranda. I saw Mark's car turn in to the drive and cruise slowly toward the car park.

"You're here early", Mark said as he approached my seat. We talked about nothing in particular for a few minutes, then at five minutes to ten, a dark Mercedes parked and Willis stepped out. He smiled briefly as he approached us, said a crisp "good morning", and invited us inside.

"You had no trouble finding the place, I presume", Willis said, once we were seated well off to one side. We both shook our heads.

"Nice club", I commented.

"Yes. Not overdone. Golfers here are decent, ordinary people. A nice place for a game. At least, it would be if I had more time."

We all shifted slightly in our seats, an indication, apparently, that the preliminaries were now over.

"I want to thank you, Dr. Willis, for keeping me informed on this case. I know you don't need to." I was hoping Willis would see this gambit for the fishing trip it was meant to be. He nodded.

"There are two things I wanted to relate", Willis began, jumping right in. "First, I have formally received a DNA sample from Gary Ballantyre, it's been tested, and there's now an official result showing that the skeleton is not that of a Ballantyre."

"That confirms what we three knew already", Mark said. "Has it upset any apple carts as a formal result?"

"Not that I'm aware of", Willis replied. "But I haven't been questioned at all on the result. And that did surprise me a little."

"Really? Wouldn't you expect Gary just to take it as confirmation that the skeleton belonged to a complete stranger? After all, having it declared not a Ballantyre makes it, in some way, absolutely anonymous. There can't be any speculation now that it was possibly a Ballantyre."

"That's true, Mr. Whelan. But Ted had made such dogmatic statements that it was a Ballantyre, I was expecting Gary to ask me for some details. DNA results give probabilities. Gary didn't ask me anything about that."

"In an odd way", Mark replied, "this has the potential to provide a link between what happened back then, and the situation today."

"Here, one needs to be very careful indeed", Willis said, his expression beaming out warning. "I'll make a few more comments about what I think we can say concerning the skeleton. But I want to stress that a careful separation needs to be made between present-day forensic results that refer to the past, and present-day results that refer to the present. We do need to keep these things separate." And Willis held us both in his gaze, for emphasis.

"Okay", Willis resumed. "I also want to state that I'm not expressing privately anything I haven't told already to those I report to. This business of the skeleton is a ragged case, not what it should be and far from what I like professionally. But I'll restate to you what I've made clear in my formal reporting. The skeleton is the result of a death that occurred a hundred or more years in the past. And that death, in my opinion, has to be regarded as suspicious. Those circumstances just aren't getting the attention they deserve. Today I'm passing on information to you, unofficially and probably illegally, because you seem to be the only people who have an interest in finding out what happened back then. And I do request again that you will keep this confidential."

We both nodded, but I wanted my own involvement to be clear.

"As you know", I said, "I got involved in this because I was concerned about commentary and gossip that might engulf John Stanley. As far as I'm concerned, there's still some risk of that happening, and that's the reason I haven't dropped the matter. But, there's really nothing I can contribute officially to this. I've got no standing here."

Willis was shaking his head.

"You're correct to say that you have no official standing. But from my perspective, it's important to find out how that man came to be dead.

I'm the one who speaks for the dead. But without the police behind me, there's sometimes very little I can do to discharge that duty."

This was really Willis's request for our unofficial help, but with very definite cautions. We looked at each other for a moment, and Willis seemed to be a bit more relaxed now that he had laid down some ground rules.

"I presume that the second thing relates to Ted Ballantyre's death", I said.

Willis nodded.

"I assume from our brief telephone conversation that you don't have serious doubts about a potassium chloride injection being the cause of death. Is that a fair statement?"

"Yes", Willis said. "And this moves us forward a hundred years, to today."

"Ted's death, and the death of the man whose skeleton was found, these two events will receive quite different levels of scrutiny", Mark said, then stopped, appearing to look for the right words. "But they're also so disconnected in time that it seems to me they'll be viewed officially as completely unrelated. Do you think they're unrelated, Dr. Willis?"

Willis's answer came without hesitation.

"Officially, they aren't related. And this is my position as medical examiner. I have no basis for any other position. But personally, privately, I'm not ready to rule out some possible connection. Although I doubt that I'll ever be able to prove that a connection exists. And I have neither the authority nor the resources to go digging for one."

"But perhaps we could focus on Ted's death", I said. "When it comes to deciding whether Ted's death was suicide, there seems to be a problem."

"Not really a problem", Willis replied. "But there are some inconsistencies. Ted was left-handed, so injecting himself in the left arm would not be the natural thing to do. Also, and this you really must keep under your hat, the police found no fingerprints on the syringe. Also, there was no note."

"So it could have been murder?"

Willis raised a hand in warning.

"Let's just say that what evidence exists is consistent with that. But I won't be drawing that conclusion just based on what we know. And I think nobody else should be doing so either."

There seemed to be little more to say about Ted's death. I waited a few seconds to shift mental gears.

"I'm going to ask you a somewhat speculative question, Dr. Willis. If you don't wish to answer, that's okay."

Willis nodded for me to carry on.

"Do you have any sense as to how the case of the skeleton, such as it is, will be wrapped up?"

Willis looked half exasperated and half intrigued.

"The police really don't want to invest any resources in a case that's probably more than a hundred years old. And I can understand that. But I don't like loose ends. And I don't like seeing suspicious deaths, no matter how old, remain unresolved, just left to sink into a cloud of uncertainty. There was a real person involved here. Oh, he might have been a scoundrel, even a criminal. But he might have been a perfectly decent human being."

And from the expression on Willis's face, it was clear that the situation did bother him.

"But … I suppose we'll never know", he added.

Willis was evidently a busy person, and it looked as though he had said all he wanted to say.

I looked at Mark, then began to wrap up our exchange with Willis. "Let me thank you again, Dr. Willis. If I come across anything new that might be of interest to you, I can pass it along if you wish."

"Please do", Willis said, then he rose. We shook hands, and Willis headed out to his car.

Mark and I moved outside onto the veranda and watched Willis drive off.

"Well. That was odd", I said. Mark nodded.

"There will be elements in this case we will never know about. I think that's almost certain."

"Meaning?" Mark questioned.

"Well, I wonder what Willis's real motivation might be for meeting us like this. He's breaking an important rule, it seems to me. And he didn't ask, he hasn't ever asked, why I have this continuing interest. I've told him that it's my concern for John, but, really, that's a bit thin now."

I looked off into the distance, then turned again toward Mark.

"In fact, I've asked myself that question several times lately. Not sure just why I'm doing this. Not sure about the future at all when it comes right down to it."

"Whoa!" Mark said, in some alarm. "Hang on a minute! Not sure about the future? What's that mean?"

I took my time answering.

"I didn't mean anything particular by that. I'm not going to jump in front of a train. It's just that … well … sometimes things seem very flat."

Mark's expression was still one of concern, but he waited to see if I would continue.

"I always had Joyce to inspire me. She was very good at that. And I always had her to talk to. But now… Frankly, Mark, my job is boring, and I've been thinking of a change for the past month. And these aren't just idle thoughts. Something inside is telling me it's time for a complete change."

"A complete change", Mark repeated. "What does that mean?"

"I wish I knew", I said and shook my head. "This is getting us nowhere. Do you have the whole day available?"

"Yes."

"All right then", I said decisively. "I think I've made some real headway on this skeleton stuff. I want to explain it to you. And there are some follow-up searches I want to do. Do you mind going to the public library? A couple of hours should be enough."

"Let's go!"

Like many of the libraries in medium-sized regional centres, the public library at Cobourg is an oasis. We found a spot to sit, out of the way of traffic, and I unfolded for Mark what I had found over the previous two evenings and what I thought we could use.

It took me forty-five minutes to relate everything I wanted to. Mark listened without commenting, shaking his head from time to time in disbelief, and I could see from his expression that he was having trouble swallowing a fair bit of what I said. When I finished, having made the whole thing as concise as I could, Mark just sat there looking at me.

"So", he said finally, "you're postulating that Charles was the illegitimate son of Mary Somerville, who was the Ballantyre family's domestic servant. But the only real support you have for this is the fact that Mary Somerville remained in the Ballantyre household until she died, something that was not common, and that you've found a legal name change document from 1875 that shows a Charles Ballantyre becoming Christian Somerville. And you suspect that Malcolm Smithers had a dalliance with Mary Somerville that resulted in Charles, but that's just an assumption. I agree with you that Smithers's death by drowning was odd and that the police report on his death looks like a whitewash. There are a lot of assumptions here, Steve, and there seems to be no obvious way to confirm them."

As Mark spoke, my sinking feeling grew, and I really did begin to wonder whether I had talked myself into something that was completely nonsensical. At least I had the good fortune to fly it past Mark before running a risk of making a public fool of myself.

I was about to tell Mark that he was right, and it was all a ludicrous mistake.

"But ... you know..." Mark began, rubbing his chin in speculation, "there does seem to be a rather suspicious line of coincidences running through all this. It's true that it was unusual for a domestic servant to be kept on long after she would normally have been able to earn her keep, and very unusual for a servant to be kept on in an employer's residence until she died."

Mark was working his way through things, so I said nothing and just waited.

"Ballantyre wasn't a common name. Isn't a common name. The name change documents were filed in Toronto. Correct?"

"Yes."

"And were they filed by Charles himself?"

I smiled. "You don't miss a lot, do you? No. They were filed by a lawyer, Ernest Castlefield, and that's probably because Charles was still out of the country in 1875."

Mark nodded. "Did you find any other Charles Ballantyres in Toronto in 1875?"

"No", I said. "Not in Toronto, and not anywhere else in Ontario."

"And you did find any relatives to Malcolm Smithers?"

"Yes. A brother. Eric Smithers. He was much younger than Malcolm and lived until 1925."

"And you say that Eric had a son, Tennyson, who Eric fathered when he was almost seventy. My God, Steve! This is wild stuff!"

I just nodded acknowledgment but wanted to see us pick our way through to the end of this improbable mess, even if that meant we would end up leaving Cobourg library, driving back to Toronto, closing the book on the whole thing, and calling it a day.

"Everything I've said is either verifiable fact or stated clearly as assumption", I ploughed on doggedly. "So I'm going to finish this odd tale. Tennyson Smithers died in 1978, but his son, Michael, is retired and lives in Toronto. I've done some serious digging for this. I might be able to find more with a lot more effort. But there are too many dots still not connected. I can't avoid the feeling that something important is missing. But I can't see what that might be, no matter how I look at this. There seem to be too many unknowns. And, quite frankly, Mark, I'm becoming discouraged."

I had been doodling with a pencil on the notepad I had shoved into my documents case. I dropped the pencil in some finality, and at that point I was ready to give up. Mark was right. It really was wild stuff. I had most likely wasted my time and not used enough common sense.

I looked up at Mark. He was regarding me closely, and there was a strange speculative glint in his eye, as though he had found a different path to follow, and that perhaps he didn't think that I had wasted my time.

"We can't prove anything with what you have here. I guess you know that."

I just waited for him either to continue, or to say, "Okay. Let's head home."

"But I'm thinking now that perhaps we don't need to prove anything. Maybe we just need to make a provocative suggestion and see what happens."

"You've lost me", I said.

"Remember what Andrea said the other night, that there's nothing to stop someone assuming that the skeleton was that of Charles Ballantyre?"

"Yes. And?"

"Suppose that that really is the case. Suppose it's Charles's skeleton. And suppose that there's a metaphorical skeleton in the Ballantyre family closet, a family secret, that they really did know who had been buried there, but it's something that's now long since repressed. Just suppose."

"Well, okay. But I don't see how…"

"If our skeleton is that of Charles Ballantyre, and the rest of your theory is correct, then Michael Smithers's DNA would show a family connection."

"Yes. But I'm not sure… How could we convince Michael Smithers to—"

"Remember. Don't approach this with the intention of trying to prove something. Suppose the story got out that we had found something leading us to suspect that the skeleton had been Charles's and that we had a credible way to test that."

"That certainly would have the potential to cause a stir. But surely that would be little more than an embarrassment to the Ballantyres. This was all more than a hundred years ago. It has no relevance today.

Even if you acknowledge that there's no statute of limitations on murder, it's still just a historical footnote."

"All true. But I'm thinking that it would be unnerving for the Ballantyres. And you said earlier that there must be something else involved here that we need to uncover if we're going to explain some of the recent happenings. Whatever such a something might be, it seems that it has to involve Charles Ballantyre. Let's say that there really is such a something. And let's say that at least one of today's Ballantyres knows what that something is. Suppose Gary and the other present-day Ballantyres begin to suspect, to fear, that we've turned up something important."

I sat back and looked into space as a new kaleidoscope image clunked into place in my mind.

26

The Plan

We sat in the Cobourg library for another hour, refining Mark's outline suggestion based on what I had researched.

We had to try to shake something loose. But it would be a bit like cutting a diamond. We had to strike at just the right place, in just the right way. We couldn't risk overdoing it and spooking them. But the message had to be strong enough to make them swallow hard.

We started off by writing down some questions as a guide.

What exactly will we say?

How will we say it?

Who will we direct it to?

What specific inference do we want them to draw?

How will we try to make sure that they'll be constrained to draw only the inference we want them to draw?

What problems do we need to guard against?

What could be possible responses by our target?

In the case of each of those responses, what would we do next?

Is there any advice we should take before we start?

We had listed all these questions and refined their wording. We kept going through them — four times, five times, six times — until we stopped coming up with any new questions. At that point, we began putting together what I referred to as a script, a sort of storyboard, a set of steps.

It wasn't easy. And the thing that made it not easy was still, always, the fact that we were trying to catch a glimpse of the *something else* we had been talking about. We couldn't see how to account for what might be behind the rather dramatic events that were unfolding in the present. There had to be *something* driving things. Whatever that *something* was, it must be linked in some way to the skeleton and to events back then, more than a century ago, that resulted in someone becoming a skeleton and in having that skeleton placed where it had been found.

We walked around these questions for quite a while, thought about possible replies to what we would launch finally, probably into cyberspace somehow. Then we took a stab at a first draft.

Too weak.

Second draft.

Ambiguous.

More drafts. But I had the feeling that we were homing in on a target.

We came down to rewriting sentences. Then we were working on candidates for individual words. We were finding fewer problems, fewer sources of potential for things to go wrong in our wording.

We walked through the main items again.

The discovery of the skeleton had given rise to a set of events and influences. Who the skeleton belonged to and why it was where it was could be matters of Ballantyre family lore. We hoped that was the case, and we hoped that there was enough distrust in the family that suspicion would attach to all such elements of lore.

***

We went through our storyboard again and again, looking back at our list of questions and then looking at the text of our draft message after each of these walk-throughs.

"Could this all go out of control?" I asked.

Mark shrugged. "I suppose it's conceivable. But the only aspect of that I think we need to worry about is whether something could come back on us."

"It seems to be general knowledge now that you and I are interested in this situation."

"Yes", Mark agreed. "And we do want information to come back to us, although not with any direct vengeance. But I think that what we have now is enough to force somebody to draw the inference that we are involved somehow and that we have detailed knowledge that could be damaging to somebody, but leaving them in doubt as to just what we know and how we came to know it."

"It's a fine line", I said. "We need to raise concern but definitely not panic."

"It's a razor thin line", Mark agreed.

After a further twenty minutes of second-guessing, postulating, and working through "what ifs", I rose and stretched.

"I think we need to pack it in now. Let's head back to town, put all this aside for a day to ripen. Does Andrea like Indian food?"

"Andrea? Yes, she loves it. Why?"

"I'd like to treat you both to takeout Indian tonight."

"I don't think she has anything on", Mark said, pulling out his cellphone. "I'll send her a text."

"We could eat at my place", I said. "I feel I have debts to pay in that area."

"That's kind of you, Steve, but I'd like to suggest our place. Andrea is never home particularly early from work, and I know she looks forward just to flopping and unwinding. I'll definitely take you up on the offer for a weekend. But if Andrea says yes, let's make it our place."

I agreed, and we began collecting our things. We were just about to head out to our cars when Mark's cellphone vibrated on the table.

"Here we are", he said, smiling, and he showed me Andrea's reply. *Sounds like a Steve idea. Out of my husband's league. Yes please. Home before eight.*

After several days of strenuous work in spurts, the even harder task of puzzling over what things mean, gaining some insights, discovering large holes, then coming up with a sort of plan, and now having shelved it all for a while, I felt more relieved than I had done for some time. Our research had brought us to some initial plateau of achievement: we had lined up a number of mallards and felt we could now see a sort of path down the field toward where the net should be. (A self-criticism arose immediately about mixed metaphors giving rise to an amalgam image of ducks playing soccer.)

The drive back to Toronto was unexpectedly peaceful. Comments Mark and I had made came to mind, one after another. We had spoken of things far from Ballantyreland, had some good laughs, and told the wider world to piss off and solve its own problems. When the first signs directing me to the Don Valley Parkway glided past overhead way too early, I realized just how relaxed I had become. I was almost home. The many tasks that life shoved in one's face constantly made their existence known again, and I began ticking off in my head some domestic items I had to take care of.

There were the arrangements we had discussed for dinner at Mark and Andrea's place. Mark would consult Andrea and look after ordering the takeout. I was in charge of picking up lager and some good gewürztraminer. Then I would turn up at their condo at six thirty.

Nice to have a plan.

Ten minutes later, I let myself into my condo in time to see a dust bunny scurry under the hall table.

"Won't do you any good, you little bastard", I muttered. After a quick sweep with the vacuum, I stripped off the day's clothes, put in a laundry load, showered, shaved, and flopped into a dressing gown to dip into a bit more of the Peter Robinson compendium that had become my current refuge for relaxation. That should take me through nicely to about four o'clock, leaving about an hour and a half for a nap. All the things I had lined up mentally got done eventually, although — no big surprise! — not in the order planned. At six thirty,

I was moving at a stroll pace toward Andrea and Mark's condo, my cargo of lager and wine clinking merrily in the bag slung over my shoulder.

As always seems to happen for guests of Andrea and Mark, the evening was a leisurely flight to eleven thirty on gossamer wings. Andrea made her entrance at about seven forty-five, clearly anticipating the meal.

"I'm starved", she said as she walked into the sitting area. "Where is it?"

"Should be here in about ten minutes."

But Andrea moved on toward the rear of the condo. Less than five minutes later she was back, changed into casual slacks and a dark loose-fitting sweater. Mark offered her a seat next to him at the coffee table, where a glass of wine and a bottle of lager awaited her choice. It was the lager's turn to languish.

Andrea took a sip of the wine, and I imagined I could literally see muscles relaxing.

"This was a brilliant idea, Steve. Great way to end a work week. I don't remember when I had Indian last."

Another sip of wine.

"Good day today down east?"

I was about to answer when Mark's phone rang.

"That'll be the food", he said.

27

Plan in Action

I sat up for a while after returning home from the evening with Andrea and Mark, partly just to bask in the glow, partly to let the meal digest a bit, and partly to look ahead. Looking ahead was needed if my recent urge to set a new course was to be acted upon. The next day was less than an hour away, but it would be a Saturday, so a late night wouldn't matter particularly, and the mood set by the evening was a good backdrop for planning. At just before one o'clock, I drank a large tumbler of water, prepared for bed, and knew I'd had a good night when I opened my eyes at nine o'clock, wide awake and having no idea where the night had gone. I slid down a little further into the bed, put my arms behind my head, and just luxuriated for fifteen minutes.

Perhaps predictably, I found that patterns of thought were lining up, like airplanes on approach. The first of these, somewhat to my surprise, was a knot of reflections focussed on my work. The second, more immediate, was a sort of cloud of anticipation, the expectation of some solid progress in moving toward the end game in the skeleton business. I would wait for that one, I promised myself, but the anticipation, not really wanting to go away, strained subtly at the boundary of consciousness, like a long sea swell. The third was different. It was the need to consider a radically different next life phase.

There was no need to prompt any thoughts on my first metaphorical aircraft: the need to take a hard look at my work, my day job. This was overdue, and the basic assessment surfaced quickly enough.

My work doesn't have a high cerebral coefficient. A lot of it is mechanical, even though there are usually problem-solving elements to it. The work tends to come in fits and starts, so some days are busier than others. But it's not really possible to do extra work and get ahead of the curve. One just follows the curve through its peaks and valleys.

But like many jobs, there's always background work that can be done. That sort of work doesn't appear naturally; one has to go looking for it. And when one looks, one finds.

I don't like just coasting on slow days, so on days like that, I go looking for background work. I'm sure this is one of the reasons why my boss appreciates my contribution, and it's also why he cuts me more slack than he does many of my colleagues. It doesn't make me the most popular guy, but that doesn't bother me over much. I have the occasional drink with two of my co-workers, but neither of them is someone I could ever call a good friend. My good friends hail from outside my workplace.

Wanting to keep busy, and the preparation work I do to remain in that state, are just part of who I am. I admit, at least to myself, that keeping busy is more important now. In Joyce's absence. Having time to think and reflect at work isn't something I want, and I'm indeed able to keep busy all day because of being prepared. This means, also, that at the end of the day, I never feel that I haven't pulled my weight.

Following the superb meal at Andrea and Mark's place, Mark and I had fixed firmly on a plan of setting the skeleton stuff aside for a while. And it worked. I fell into a routine of work and home life, and matters Ballantyre were soon a fuzzy cluster drifting somewhere near the edge of the galaxy. My boss smiled at me quite a lot, asked me to take on a special project, which lasted a day and a half, and said he hoped I was relaxed after a couple of days off. I just nodded and smiled back.

The Peter Robinson compendium of Alan Banks stories I was reading is a thick one, but in the evenings, I enjoyed stepping through it slowly, savouring the scents, sights, and sounds of Eastvale, the town in Yorkshire where Robinson's protagonist, Banks, lives.

It's fiction, I said to myself, on the evening when I had settled into this routine for the fourth day running.

But it's based on fact, my self said back.

There was no clever response, because my self was right.

You know you'd like to go there sometime, my self said, prodding. *To that part of England.*

And it's true. I would like to go there, find a nice attractive place, Knaresborough, for example, spend a month or six weeks, walk, take day trips, read, spend so much time in a local pub that I couldn't be ignored. Joyce and I had wanted to do something like that, and it was still in my mind. Would it work for me without her?

This sort of thing can be successful if one approaches it in a quite pragmatic way. But the end result would be hugely disappointing if, instead of planning, one allowed oneself to drift in some unrealistically romantic space. The sepia-tinged dream. The landscape viewed through rose-coloured spectacles. The beautiful garden seen as a well-ordered self-weeding bed of self-deadheading thornless roses. The overall image being one of happy peasants singing and dancing in the sunshine. Any reality encountered based on expectations like that would deliver a hard and merciless kick in the ass.

You need a change, Boscombe. Seriously. Here we were, back at the third thought pattern.

My self was right again. Of course. And although I knew that recognition of this need for change was recurring at increasing frequency, and more insistent urgency, I kept putting off any decision to deal with it. Deal with it! Indeed! Who was I kidding? This would need to be a big change, more than just a change of job, but a change of life. And big changes are momentous, can be wrenching, are not easy to come to terms with. Deep down I knew this.

The short-term response was simple. I couldn't focus on this longer-term stuff just now. I had to finish this … this … this Ballantyre shit. I had … I had to…

But then I did something surprising. I had a long talk with myself. Agreed that something had to give. Straight up. No bullshit. There was the expected resistance. But I was encouraged. It had been a first step. Yes, of course, I was still alone on a small ship. Compass broken. Seas all around me in tumult. But still, a first step.

"Not good enough", my self muttered in resignation.

"No", I agreed. "It's not good enough."

True. And in preparation for what needed to come next, I swept the clutter from my mental desk in one long arc. Restated that the skeleton work I had embarked on needed to be done, that I had competent assistance in Mark, had to finish all that before trying to define what should happen next. Almost before I knew what was happening, I had set myself a deadline, of sorts. As soon as we had got to the bottom of this skeleton business, or perhaps got as far as we would be able to go, I promised I would take not more than a month to look at what should come next in terms of job and life.

There!

My self was not particularly impressed. Tough! As far as I was concerned, I now had a path forward and a timeline. Just thinking about it made me feel a lot better. I shifted under the bed clothes, said to myself that if you really want to finish this Ballantyre shit, then get started. Now!

I climbed resolutely from the bed, dressed, short-circuited past a shower and shave, carried toast and coffee into the den, sat down, recorded the time at nine forty, and then found that things began happening. The notes that Mark and I had produced were rough but complete. I went through the wording of the draft message again several times, made three corrections that looked right in the light of day, and read it through once more. It looked fine, so I entered it into my computer and printed it out.

Time to become equal unto the day, and a shower and shave did that. But equal unto what?

We had chosen Monday as D-Day. There was nothing more I could do in terms of the draft email message, planning what to do once there was a response (or indeed no response), so I deliberately began making a list of things to do.

Go for a long walk.

Get out my bicycle, head over to the island, and rack up thirty kilometres.

Visit the public library.

Take a book to the park, find a bench in the sun, and read.

Find a good recipe and cook something for dinner.

Okay. That one took priority, I dragged out the cookbooks and settled on the most complicated version of shepherd's pie I could find. I decided to make something for dessert at the same time. When I checked through fridge and freezer, I was delighted to find that I had almost none of the ingredients I needed.

Therefore. Next job. Shopping trip.

Five hours later, a completed shepherd's pie and a tray of biscotti had emerged steaming from the oven. They looked and smelled excellent, and I realized that I was hungry. So tonight I would be the chef at home, selfishly enjoying the results of his day's efforts.

By eight o'clock, I had eaten and washed up. That was Saturday taken care of. When I sat down to read that evening, I was surprised to find myself yawning almost immediately. I was reluctant to go to bed early, fearing that sleep wouldn't come, and I would just toss about. But more yawning convinced me that I really was tired, so I dragged myself to the bedroom, undressed, drew the curtains, pulled back the…

The room was full of light, I felt an odd buzz of excitement, and it took me a while to realize that the night had passed. It was now Sunday morning and we really were on the countdown. Barely five minutes after I had climbed from bed and dressed, Mark called. We got to the meat of the conversation quickly enough.

"Ten o'clock okay?" Mark asked.

It was, we would get together at my place, and, as planned, we would walk through everything that was to happen from now onward.

Mark sounded energized, and I realized that I was as well. I wanted to get the show on the road, move to whatever conclusion there would be.

At five to ten, I asked the concierge to send Mark up to my unit. He entered carrying several folders, and we got straight to work.

The buzz in the air had become more insistent.

Mark walked through the arrangement he had made setting up and testing the super-confidential email account he had organized, and we spent half an hour going over how it would work. I expected complexity, but apart from an involved set of access codes, it was simplicity itself.

We walked through everything that might happen over the next several days.

"Okay. Are we ready?" Mark asked.

"We're ready", I said.

"Good. It's only fair that you send out the email. So, tomorrow morning, do that when you're ready, then let me know. I have no idea how long it will take to get a reply. We'll just have to take it a step at a time."

I nodded. It felt good to be on the road.

"You've gathered up all your notes?" Mark asked. In reply I pointed toward three bulging cloth bags that sat next to the hall table.

"Anything you don't want to keep?" Mark asked.

I shook my head. I knew that if there were any such papers, we would burn them. Everything else was going into the safe in Mark's office.

"Okay. I'm off then", Mark said. He rose and collected the three cloth bags, and I accompanied him out to the elevator.

"Break a leg", he said through a broad smile as the elevator door was closing.

***

When Monday dawned, I was still energized. By agreement with my boss, I would be working from home that day. At 8 a.m. I sent an email to Mark letting him know that we were about to go live. His reply came back within five minutes.

Stay cool. Call me when the message has gone out. I'm available all day.

Okay, I thought. *Here we go.*

The addressee was the main email account for Ballantyre Industries, the current Toronto head office for all the Ballantyre companies, and the message was to the CEO, Gary Ballantyre.

There were no second thoughts, so I prepared the message for transmission, counted to ten, and then clicked the send button. The system told me that the message had been sent successfully. I went immediately to my personal email and dispatched two words to Mark.

Message sent.

Associated with the confidential email account was a separate address for receiving replies. Mark and I were the only ones who knew how to access that address. We had agreed that I would be point man on checking that account, and I would look for a reply at 4 p.m. that same day.

***

And then, I just went on with my work day. Well, went on with it with some difficulty, because I couldn't focus easily at all, even to the minimal extent required for my work. But the day limped past, somehow. Even though it had been far from a normal work day, by four o'clock it was clear that I had done more than I would accomplish at my desk during a typical day at work, so I called it quits.

It was with an odd feeling of disconnection that I went through the protocol to check for a reply.

Six minutes past four.

It surprised me when a feeling of almost crushing disappointment mixed with relief flooded through me when I realized there had been no reply.

Four twenty. Nothing

Four fifty. Still nothing.

Now all sorts of thoughts streamed through my head. Was the super-confidential system really working? Had the message actually been received? But I wasn't going to let myself become jittery like a teenager two hours before a first date.

Five thirty. Nothing. Time for a glass of wine.

Fifteen minutes later, I was becoming despondent. No reply was one of the possibilities we had looked at, and in that event, we did have a plan for what should come next. I checked once more, now half-heartedly.

As soon as I saw the name Jackman, Welcome, and Howard appear in the inbox, I gave thanks for all the planning Mark and I had done. Here was the third in our list of possible responses: a legal firm gambit. Scanning to the bottom of the short note, the name Brian Jackman indicated that it hadn't been handed off to an underling, that our first volley appeared to have struck close to a bull's eye.

Our client requests a meeting to review your proposal.

That was it.

A careful response, probably aimed at prying loose a bit more information on who and how, admitting nothing, probably also trying to find a way to neutralize any threat, evade the problem altogether, whatever the problem might turn out to be.

Nice try, Brian. You are wondering who we are, what we know, in what detail, and whether we're bluffing or actually possess something that could be stuck into your bicycle spokes.

I thought back to our outgoing email, suspecting that Jackman, Welcome, and Howard had likely made attempts to trace it back to an origin and had discovered that no such thing was possible. The wording of that outgoing email was etched indelibly in my brain:

The bones will reveal all. Offspring unveil the mystery. You cannot hide. We will know. We will not be silent. Time to open the books. Don't wait too long.

Time to call Mark. Our chat was short and ended in agreeing to meet immediately at Mark's place.

28

Move and Countermove

Printouts of the two emails, our outgoing message and their reply, were spread before us on Mark's coffee table. Mark studied them for five minutes, then he looked up.

"I researched this Jackman crowd", Mark said. "I suppose you did as well. They're a legal firm, of course, but they're also professional negotiators, mediators, arbitrators. That tells us something. Exactly what, though, we need to work out."

I nodded. "I suppose they want to find out who we are so that they can neutralize us", I mused.

Mark just looked at me. "More likely they're looking for confirmation."

"They'll just assume that we're behind all this?" I suggested. "Or, that I'm behind it?"

"No", Mark said shaking his head. "They won't assume. They'll postulate then look for anything that might confirm their postulate."

"Well, okay", I began hesitantly. "But there's only so much—"

"No, Steve!" Mark said forcefully. "These days, most people leave a wide trail in the world. We're all connected in quite a few ways, and for someone determined enough, snooping in those connections isn't that difficult."

"But then, how do we—?"

"I'm sorry to keep interrupting you, Steve, but we're not just sitting ducks here. Ease of snooping also means ease of counter-snooping, and I know some people who are pretty good at that. So, a couple of guys I know will be on the lookout, on our behalf, for snoopers. And before you ask, yes, counter-counter-snooping is possible. But in all cases, one needs to be aware that both snooping and counter-snooping leave traces, but people who are really good at this know three things: what a snooper's traces will look like, how to leave few or no traces yourself, and how to leave misleading traces."

Mark smiled at what I expected was my expression, indicating that I was way out of my depth.

"Don't worry", he said. "They will almost certainly try to listen in on our telephone conversations and peek at our email accounts. The big difference between them and us is that they're officers of the court and we're not. When they decide to snoop, they'll expect us, or at least me, to be waiting for them, so they'll have to be careful. But I'm fairly sure that my snoopers are better than theirs."

"Sounds like cat and mouse."

"That's exactly what it is", Mark said, nodding and smiling, "but the important distinction here is that we won't be doing anything to raise a doubt in their minds that they are the cat."

"When do you think they'll begin snooping?" I asked.

Mark's reply was just that little bit delayed.

"They've already started", he said, then smiled again when he saw me jump.

"Look Steve", Mark said, putting on a reassuring face. "I'm confident they won't try to break into either of our places. Too risky."

"Then why lock everything away? Why take such extreme measures?"

"Call it a safety factor", Mark began. "We can't be certain that we haven't missed something. We also can't be certain that the other side won't try something based on a horribly poor judgment. Either we or they might make some mistake, of commission or omission. If we're the ones who make the mistake, we might or might not realize it, and they might either miss it or pick up on it. If they miss it, no immediate loss for us. If we don't realize the mistake and they pick up on it, they'll have an advantage, and we won't be aware of the fact or know how big the advantage might be."

I nodded, trying to digest this information.

"When you say they won't try breaking into our places because it's too risky, what does that mean? I get the feeling you've already considered this. So why would it be risky for them?"

"It would be risky because they will suspect that there will be surveillance cameras in place."

"But…" I began.

"Yes, I know that it's a lot more awkward breaking into condo units, and I know that they won't want to be taking time looking for surveillance, then disabling it, then breaking in, then disabling any burglar alarm. Too much can go wrong. Too many chances to be spotted or recorded."

This was more detail than I had considered, and it was clear that Mark was way ahead of me in thinking through possibilities. It occurred to me that it had all been a disconnected problem, something that happened in some distant space, well away from me. But now that we were head-to-head with the real thing, I was struggling to take it in.

"Two pieces of advice, Steve. First, and without at all intending to be offensive, you aren't familiar with this sort of thing. So it seems fearful and you might try to figure out what could happen and how to guard against it. But you would be pulling things out of the air, having no information to use in judging probabilities, and likely would waste time and mental energy focussing on something of no consequence at all. So just try not to worry about anything, and don't waste effort trying to think your way through to some exit from the maze. Second, this is all a bit like a chess game. The only reality at any given time is how many pieces are on the board, what they are, where they are, and what next moves are possible."

I nodded in agreement but was still coming to terms with it all.

"Let's go back a bit", I said. "They've already started?"

Mark looked at me steadily for a moment. "I think you trust me, Steve."

I nodded vigorously and made some dramatic hand motions indicating full agreement.

"I've taken some actions here without consulting you, and I hope you're okay with that, because it's simpler and more secure that way. But if you'd rather do things differently…"

"No. Please just go ahead."

"So there's now electronic surveillance on both our places, and on John's place. There's a close watch on our email accounts. That's where they've tried to snoop."

"On both of us?"

"Yes."

"Do they know we can see them snooping?"

"No. I don't think so."

"What makes you say that?"

"Well, they tried snooping on you first. Then, about an hour later, they tried snooping on me. I think if they had detected that there was something more than just passive security involved when they tried your account, they probably wouldn't have tried me so soon after."

"Couldn't they just be testing the fences?"

"That was probably part of their objective when they tried poking in your account. They would have confirmed then that there's some protection in place."

"How would they know that?"

"Lots of questions, Steve, but I understand why. The level of protection on our accounts includes an obvious indication that the protection's there. A bit like having a sign on your house showing the name of the intruder alarm company. It will scare off the people who might be just doing a try on."

"But they won't find anything to indicate more than that?"

"No."

There were more questions I wanted to ask, but it sounded as though we were getting close to the point where Mark would say "enough".

"There's one other thing you haven't asked me that I think you should know."

I gave Mark a quizzical look.

"How I get my updates in a way that's secure."

"Okay", I said. "How?"

"When I set up this surveillance, the security company gave me a special email account. I can't send anything from it, and the only address I can reach to look at incoming material on security updates is one that connects to part of the security company's website. There's only one section of that site I can access, and that's the area where all the surveillance results for us are located. Everything there is in code. When I set up the account, I was given a sheet showing the codes for all the information they place on our section."

"So that's how we find out what's been happening without anybody else being able to see any of it."

"Yes."

"Okay. I don't need to know any more." And having said that, I felt as though I had changed gears.

I spent some time collecting my thoughts.

"Okay, Mark. From the top. Tell me what you think."

Mark looked at me intently, then nodded, and I could see that in his mind a duck line-up was underway.

"Okay", Mark began, and he noted points on his fingers. "First point. We started things off with our cryptic email. One of the possible responses we considered was that it would just be ignored. That could mean either that they were calling whatever bluff they thought we were making or that they felt we could do nothing to harm them in any substantive way."

"But they did respond", I added.

"Yes", Mark said, "meaning, second point, that this isn't something they feel they can just let pass."

"Do you think the lawyers know the backstory?"

"I think they might know quite a bit of it", Mark said, "but that doesn't really matter. Carrying on. Third point. They're not serious about a meeting. That statement is just a placeholder, a way for them to say to us 'All right, it's your move now'. So we make our next move. And that's the fourth point. We up the ante."

"So we send another message."

"Yes."

"So I guess that means we tell them what the outcome has to be."

"Close", Mark said. "We tell them what has to be a primary result."

"Yes", I said. "Of course. We tell them that the full story of the skeleton has to become public and that it's up to them to do that."

Mark smiled and nodded.

"You're getting pretty good at this. Yes, we tell them that, but we make it clear that if they don't take the story public, we will. But, of course, we have to let them reach that conclusion. There's something else important in play here. I don't know what it is, or just why it's important, but we need to try to figure that out."

"You mean they're vulnerable somewhere."

"Exactly", Mark replied. "And we know that, as a family, the Ballantyres are not vulnerable financially. Enough is known about the Ballantyre businesses to be very sure that they're not worried about money. I'm pretty sure they're not worried about family reputation either. Times have moved on, and the things that could have raised a good old-fashioned scandal are so far in the past now that nobody will care. Whatever comes to light will be just colourful history."

"So", I continued, "their vulnerability must come from some sort of criminality or, what?"

"Well, a good fallback for the 'or what' is always personal greed."

"You mean apart from the family businesses?"

"Yes. The whole history of the family, individually and collectively, past and present, seems to point to a grasping nature that won't ever be satisfied."

"But", I said, shaking my head, "greed for what? And how would that link to the skeleton? Or would it?"

"Good questions", Mark said. "I just don't know."

I took a minute to pull together the few shreds of thought that seemed relevant.

"Our reply then", I began decisively. "How about something like, 'You're wasting time. Make the full story behind the skeleton public. Or we will.'"

"Yes", Mark said. "A little blunt, but that's not a bad thing. What do you think would be their response?"

"Not sure. Probably stall for time."

"Why do you think they would do that?"

I looked at Mark, wondering where he was going with this.

"Well, there's the embarrassment factor", I suggested. "The full story likely goes back a long way into the Ballantyre family's dirty linen. Then there's the possibility that even they might not have all the details. But I'm wondering whether they might want to force our hand. Maybe they think we're bluffing. Maybe they think they could just deny anything if it's us who takes the story public. I'm not sure."

"There's another possibility", Mark said.

"Oh?"

"Yes. There might be something important that we've missed and they want to see whether we know about it."

"Something we've missed? Like what?"

"Well, you mentioned criminality. And we talked about greed. Whatever the reason is they're playing cagey, it's likely a good one."

"Hang on", I said. "Do you think there's some money involved here?"

"It wouldn't surprise me in the least."

"But, what? Where?"

"I don't know, Steve. But there must be a good reason for them to be putting so much effort into this smokescreen. It just seems to me, and it's a strong feeling, that somebody has a lot to gain by getting things right. Or to lose by getting them wrong."

I felt like I was going in circles.

"So do you agree with the reply I suggested, or something like it? Or not?"

"Oh, I agree", Mark said. "But when we threaten to make the story public, the threat needs to be credible. And by credible, I mean that it will need to scare the shit out of them."

"So, are you saying that we don't have enough juice to do that?" I asked, cursing inwardly that I was sounding defensive.

"Well, you know that we don't have the DNA proof to nail down the real identity of the skeleton. And even if we did, that's still just a long-dead scandal. But if we pull the whole Ted business into it, well, then…"

"Ted? But we have no evidence about what happened to Ted. There's a bit of support for an interesting speculation. But even if the speculation is true, the driver behind it is unknown."

"True. We know what it is that we know but we can't be sure about what we don't know. And it's a leap on our part to drag Ted into whatever else might be their big headache today. I just have this very strong gut sense that there's some firm and maybe even direct connection between what happened to Ted and the skeleton."

"Really? But those things are a hundred and fifty years apart!"

"Yes, I know", Mark said. "But sometimes you just need to go with your gut."

"And if they do a double bluff, just brush the whole thing off?"

"Yes. An entirely plausible outcome. Although don't forget that Willis has some doubts about Ted's death being suicide. But we can go with your line. That lets them just shrug it all off. Then we deliver a story in instalments. There's always appetite for a juicy story that turns up a chapter at a time. And this one is a nice mixture of yesterday's scandal that sticks to a prominent family, an old body newly discovered, and a death today as yet unexplained. The other side knows all this. What we need to do is leave them in no doubt that we're serious."

"Okay. Let's get on with it then", I said. "Serious people act promptly. So we need to send back a message today."

"Yes", Mark said, reaching for a pad and pen. "It's six thirty now. Let's get something back to them before seven thirty."

We set to work. Five minutes later, we had a revised message.

You're wasting time. Make the full story behind the skeleton public. Explain what happened to Ted as well. Or we will.

We examined it from all angles, tried some alternative wording, looked at it from what we thought might be the other side's point of view. In the end, having roamed widely, we stuck with the initial wording. At five minutes past seven, the message was sent.

"Good!" Mark said, smiling. "I'm starving. How about a nice takeout Thai meal."

"What about Andrea?"

"No", Mark said, shaking his head. "She won't be home until after nine thirty tonight."

At eight fifteen, our Thai orders arrived, we opened a bottle of gewürztraminer, and we threw all things Ballantyre over the side for the duration.

29

Attack

The Thai food was excellent, and there was more than enough for two, so we closed the food containers and placed them in the oven to keep warm in case Andrea wanted a late snack. Our dinner was one of almost prone decadence as we flopped out in front of the television and laughed our way through a DVD episode of *Republic of Doyle*. Andrea arrived home at nine forty, running on empty, and Mark met her as she was dropping what seemed her usual day's briefcase baggage.

"Go get changed", he said, "then come and join us. There's wine and Thai food."

"Oh! I will change", she said, "but I'm not sure I can handle Thai at this hour."

Twenty minutes later, she had eaten almost as much as each of us had done, was on her second glass of gewürztraminer, and seemed more than equal to what was left of the evening.

"Good day?" Mark asked.

"Long. Difficult. Frustrating. But, yes, it turned out to be a very good day."

She took a long slurp of wine.

"Good meeting. Well worth all the preparation. We now have another largish contract." And that apparently called for another long glug of wine.

"Another contract?" Mark said. "That's the third new contract this month. Are you going to be able to get all the work done?"

"No worries. I'll just buy a bigger bull whip."

I sat back in a green curry glow and listened as they told each other about their day. Mark's narration of our day departed, at a number of points, from what I remembered, but green curry and wine can often account for divergent recollections. It was a pleasure just to be invited into the conversational glow that reflected the nice mixture of tension and contentment that characterized the life of this pair of people.

We flopped around, talked about all and sundry for a further half hour, but then, when Andrea drained her glass, leaned back in her chair, and sighed contentedly, I noticed how pronounced were the grey crescents of exhaustion beneath her eyes.

"Okay", I said, setting down my own glass and rising. "Time for me to be off."

There were modest protests that I not rush off, but I pleaded tiredness and ongoing work load, and I soon had said my farewells and was strolling home through the night. As I walked, I had the feeling that we were wrapping up this skeleton business, and that we could soon all settle back to something more normal. The feeling was satisfying, in an odd, relieved sort of way. But then, when I thought back over just what it was we had done, I realized that many hours, much thought, and some very long days had gone into this effort. Hardly surprising that there was relief, if what had given rise to all this was about to be cleared away.

As I passed one of my local watering holes, the Jason George on Front Street, two familiar faces smiled out at me, there were waves of recognition, and I waved and smiled back.

Ten minutes later, I was approaching the north entrance to my condo building through a small but well-lit laneway beneath two large maple trees, both of which cast an enfolding shadow of welcome over the final few metres to the entrance. My key was out, a minor belch reminded me of the excellent meal we had just enjoyed, I was looking forward to a large tumbler of water and flopping for twenty minutes before climbing into bed. And just then, the power failure occurred.

There was no good reason for me to have even a modest hangover, like this one. And I was puzzled as to why my bed, normally very comfortable, was so hard and unyielding. Most of all, I was confused as to why Mark was there, patting my cheeks. Had I overslept ridiculously? And why was it so cold? And why was I still wearing my clothes?

"Steve!"

There was something wrong here.

"Steve! Can you hear me?"

I propped myself up on one elbow, and, when I looked toward the voice, was surprised to see Mark.

"What happened?" I mumbled. "Did I trip and fall?"

"Can you sit up?" Mark asked, but I was already there, and I began rising to my feet. A bright light was in my eyes.

"Ahhh!" I said. "Must have hit my head." I put a hand to the back of my head.

By now I was standing on my own.

"Look at me", Mark said, and he looked closely into my eyes. I recalled, for some reason, that Mark had had some EMS training.

I had by now gathered some ragged sense of what was going on. Something or somebody had hit me over the head. Mark's hand was gripping my upper arm, and he guided me as I walked around for thirty seconds.

"Do you have a headache?"

"No", I said, "just a sore patch on the back of my head."

The bright lights that had been blinding me were car headlights.

"Okay", Mark said, "I think you're all right. But you're coming back to my place now." We headed toward the headlights, which were on Mark's car. He had driven off the street and up onto the large, bricked space around the condo entrance, knocking over a planter in the process. The two of us managed somehow to get me into his car, and without bothering about seat belts, Mark pulled away from the entrance and back onto the street, and we headed off. I closed my eyes and willed the sore head to go away. It's not more than a five-minute drive from my place to Mark's. I recognized the streets and was beginning to feel better when Mark drove into his parking garage.

It was a short walk from the seventh-floor elevator lobby to the entrance to Andrea and Mark's condo, and Mark's firm grip on my upper arm guided me along the corridor and through the door to his unit.

"Mark? Is that you? What's happening?"

Andrea.

She appeared at the end of the hallway in a nightdress, and her mouth fell open.

"Oh my God! Steve! Mark! What the…? What happened?"

"Get a pillow", Mark ordered, closing off the immediate possibility of more questions.

I was soon sitting in a large wing chair, Andrea was holding a wet facecloth, and there was a cool pillow behind my head.

Andrea's expression had passed quickly from one of uncomprehending shock to hardened anger.

"Someone coshed him at the entrance to his condo building", Mark said. He looked at Andrea. "After Steve left to go home, and you went off to bed, I checked our lobster pots, found something interesting, and called Steve. Called him three times. He was pretty hyped when he left here, so when there was no answer at the third try, I was worried and went out to look."

"We need to call the police", Andrea said.

"In due course." Mark fussed around a bit more. Andrea raised a glass of deliciously cold water to my mouth. Several swallows had me feeling somewhat better almost immediately.

We talked a bit more, I told them what I remembered, which was very little. I hadn't seen it coming at all, had no idea or memory of who it was. The next thing I knew, I was in a strange bed and light was streaming into the room where the curtains didn't quite meet.

It was eight forty.

"Hungry?"

I looked up to see Mark standing in the doorway to their spare room, smiling.

"No. But I'm thirsty", I said.

"How's the head?"

I took stock. The back of my head was tender but no longer sore.

"Well", Mark said, "we have a house rule of no eating in bedrooms. Guests are invited to the kitchen. Next door to your right you can take a shower. Then I propose to pump you full of orange juice and coffee."

Another smile.

"Take your time, Steve."

The shower felt good, although I stopped short of washing my hair. There was no headache, no dizziness, and I was as ready as I could be to face the world again.

Andrea had gone to work at least an hour earlier, but not before giving orders to keep her updated.

Having borrowed Mark's deodorant and climbed back into my clothes, I appeared in their kitchen, where there was toast, an omelette mixture ready to be cooked, orange juice, and coffee. Mark waved at the omelette mixture, I said yes because the aromas of toast and coffee made me realize that I actually was hungry, and within a few minutes, we were working our way through omelette on toast. The missing details from the previous evening were filled in quickly.

"I don't remember anything about being struck", I said.

"Do you remember me driving you here to our place?"

"Yes."

"And do you remember me and Andrea putting you to bed?"

"No. Nothing until I woke up this morning."

Over breakfast Mark filled in a few more details. I learned, not to my surprise, that Andrea and Mark sat up discussing what had happened. Andrea was not pleased at all.

Mark had filled in the situation for her.

She still wasn't happy and reminded Mark about his promise to avoid physical nastiness in his work.

There was apparently an uneasy truce, and they left it at that.

After my third glass of orange juice and second cup of coffee, I was feeling a lot better. I used Mark's computer to send an email to my boss saying that I had had a minor accident and was taking the day off.

I fixed a long look on Mark. He had found me on the ground outside my condo building. Which meant that he must have arrived there fairly soon after whatever had happened. Otherwise, another resident would have found me. I was quite sure that Mark knew more than he had said. But once again, Mark got there before I did.

"I'll try to explain what I know and how I know it."

I nodded and gestured that he should go ahead.

"About ten minutes after you left here last night, I thought I would check the secure incoming email address once more. I was a bit surprised to find something in it. I wanted to discuss it with you, so I tried phoning. You would have made it home by then, and I figured you would likely sit up thinking over some of the things we had talked about. When there was no answer to my third call to you, I decided something was wrong. So, I drove to your place. I looked down the lane toward the entrance to your building and saw someone lying on the ground. You know the rest."

"What's going on, Mark? What did the message say?"

"It was odd", Mark said. "The message was short. It said, 'Going ahead. We'll be in touch.' Here", Mark added, turning his laptop screen toward me. "Take a look."

"What does that mean?" I demanded.

"It might not mean anything in particular."

We looked at each other.

"I know who struck you outside your building."

"Oh? And how do you know that?" I didn't care for where this might be going.

"Here's where things become sticky. My information doesn't come legally. I installed a miniature device up on the wall by the door to your building. I've removed it now. But it did record you arriving at the door to your building, your key in your hand, and there's a clear set of images of somebody coming out of the shadow behind you and striking you."

I was shocked and I could feel anger growing.

"Christ Almighty, Mark! This could get us both into some really serious shit!"

Mark gave me a hard neutral stare.

"Do you have any idea, Steve, how many cases the police and public prosecutors just have to let go because they don't have the evidence to move forward in a case where they're convinced they know who committed some serious crime and why? Don't bother trying to answer. It's a rhetorical question. But a good answer would be 'a lot'. I'm almost convinced that Ted Ballantyre's death was a murder. There's somebody out there who wants things to go a certain way for certain reasons, and it seems clear that he or she will do anything to try to guarantee that outcome. You're in all this up to your neck, whether you want to admit it or not. And you're in it partly by chance but mainly because you want to help John Stanley. It would be really easy for me to say 'You don't want me to try to unravel this for you? Fine! I'm out and you're on your own.' But I'm not made like that, and I'm your friend. So I'm going to do everything I can to get you clear of this crap."

We just sat there looking at each other for a minute.

"Do you have any brandy?" I asked finally, and I couldn't help breaking into a smile. Within fifteen seconds, we were both laughing uncontrollably. Mark found a bottle of Hennessey, said that it was happy hour someplace, and we shared a drink. It wasn't yet ten o'clock in the morning.

I waved at the table, where there should have been some printed images.

"And I assume that you've downloaded things from that snooper camera?"

"Yes. And I've gone a bit further than that. The man who struck you is called Harold Gray."

"Harold Gray? I don't know any Harold Gray. Who's Harold Gray?"

"He's a minor hood for hire as muscle. But the important thing is that he lives in Cobourg and operates in the area between Bowmanville and Kingston."

My earlier anger had faded, but having my assailant identified soon caused that anger to be replaced by determination. But before I could ask another question, Mark continued.

"You might know that I do work for clients across quite a large part of Ontario. You won't know that I have many professional connections and that I've come across quite a selection of unsavoury characters in the course of more than ten years. I try to keep that network well oiled. Never know when you might need to use it. Well, that regular oiling paid off this time."

Mark closed his laptop, I think to focus exclusively on what he was saying, and he seemed to be choosing his words carefully.

"I want us to focus on just a few specific items, Steve, so I'm going to ask that you forget all about surveillance devices for the moment. We can talk about the whats, hows, and whys later. Right now we need to think very clearly about what we do next, so I'll explain just enough to allow us both to focus on that. Okay?"

Wanting to get on and do something, but having no real idea what that should be, I had no option but to agree.

"It took only a few minutes to produce a good, fairly clear image of your attacker, and I consulted four sources to try to identify who it was. One of them came up with the name Harold Gray. Once I had a name, I could dig further. Mr. Gray is evidently a slippery fish, but the bush telegraph has linked him to many jobs, although nobody's ever been able to pin anything on him and make it stick."

"So, are we any further ahead? Do we get somebody to find Harold Gray and beat out of him what he's up to?" My confidence of just a few hours earlier, that we were coming to the end of the mess we had found ourselves in, now seemed as distant as Saturn.

"No", Mark said, shaking his head decisively. "That wouldn't work."

"So then … what?" My tone was accusatory, but I didn't care.

"The piece of information that really caught my eye, and there's no way I should have it, is that Harold Gray is a confidential informer to the OPP."

"But how does that help us?"

"Well, directly, and on its own, it doesn't. But I can dig into the social septic tank where Gray and his like frolic. I'm pretty sure someone there who doesn't like him will have information we can use. But it could get messy. Before I do anything like that, I need to know if you're in."

"A hundred and sixty-one percent", I said, without hesitation.

Mark nodded.

"Okay. I'll get to work."

"How long will this take?"

"There are certain protocols to follow, even in the social septic tank. But I think I should have something this afternoon."

"Good", I said. "What can I do?"

A smile tugged at the corners of Mark's mouth.

"Go to work. Or better yet, go home. Flop on a couch. Read a book."

30

Meeting Hal

And so, resolving to do both, I did go home, got changed, and turned up at work just before noon. I went straight to my boss's office, apologized for appearing so late in the day, said that I had been mugged the previous evening, but that I was fine and ready to roll up my sleeves.

"Mugged? Good God, Steven! Where? Why? But then… No. You need to go home. Take the day. Better yet, take two days."

"No. Really", I began. "I'm perfectly capable—"

"No Steven. I won't hear of it. Off you go. Let me know tomorrow how you feel, then we'll decide."

And he made some energetic shooing motions with his hands, already beginning to turn his attention back to what lay on his desk. I thanked him and left.

It was a pleasant day, and where I worked was only about a twenty-minute brisk walk from where I live, so I went home on foot. As I walked, I called Mark and explained the situation.

"Good", he said. "The rest will likely do you good." We talked briefly.

"I'm just about to dive into the septic tank. I'll call you when I have something. Probably late this afternoon."

And we left it at that.

I arrived home at about quarter to one, gave the condo a thorough cleaning, then settled down to some reading. It was luxurious, but I still felt a bit ruffled. When my cellphone rang, I looked at my watch and didn't understand where two and half hours had gone. After all, I was still only on page nine of my book.

"Steve. Can I come over?" It was Mark.

Of course he could, since there was a chance he would admire the results of my vacuuming skills. He arrived after a time lapse that seemed far too short, and then he jumped right in.

"Are you free for the rest of the afternoon?"

"Well ... yes... But, why?"

"We should go to Cobourg."

"What, now?"

"No", Mark said impatiently. "Not now. Right now!"

Evidently there was something important to be dealt with, and soon we were once again in Mark's car and flying toward Cobourg. On the way, Mark filled me in.

"The world I often need to move in has its own communications network. I'm tuned into most things at a big picture level, but there's a local guy at Cobourg I rely on quite frequently. Hal Bennet. Good man. Keeps his ear to the ground. Not too surprisingly, he knows about the skeleton. I called him, and even before I could outline the full story for him, he said that something big was going down. The telegraph lines were singing like he'd hardly seen before. 'Better get down here.' Those were his words."

"What else did he say?"

"Very little. Didn't need to. He's normally a placid guy. Doesn't say much and says it carefully, but every word counts. This was the first time I've heard him speaking quickly. It was pretty much the equivalent of anyone else in full panic."

"What did you ask him to do?"

"You mean originally? Just wanted him to tune into the local chatter about Ted Ballantyre. He got back to me less than an hour later. That's as good as instant turnaround."

"What did he say about Ted?"

"It wasn't the direct news about Ted. It's the connections that have started jangling. He said that Harold Gray is dead. Said that nobody could get hold of the local police chief."

"What? Dead? How…?"

"Never mind that now, Steve. I realize it's shocking. But alive or dead, Harold Gray is a minor item in the overall picture. So try not to think about him just now."

I shook my head.

"Okay. All right. I'll try. But what are we going to do?"

"Well, I want to get some first-hand information. Hal didn't want to say too much on the phone, so we'll see him first. But I have to say that if what my gut is telling me is anywhere near correct, then things have really heated up. Hal said he'd get in touch with me again."

We rode in silence for a minute.

"What do you think is happening?" I asked.

"Well", Mark began, "I doubt that it's quite the end of the world, but it's a much stronger reaction than I expected to our email prods, if that's what's behind all this. And it might well be something else. We need to see."

"And if it was all triggered by our emails?"

"Then the something big we've been speculating about really is big."

I began wondering seriously now. In trying to fix a minor drip leak, had we ruptured a water main? Mark must have read my thoughts.

"Don't go too quiet on me, Steve. We've committed no crimes. If there's been some kind of eruption, it was ripe to happen sooner or later. If anything has set this off, it's that skeleton. I don't expect—"

Mark broke off to answer his cellphone, which was in its hands-free slot on the dashboard.

"Whelan."

"Where are you?"

I had to assume it was Hal Bennet on the other end.

"Just coming up to Port Hope. We'll be in Cobourg in less than ten minutes."

"Okay. Meet me in the car park of the Comfort Inn. You know where that is?"

"Off Division Street?"

"That's it. Blue Audi."

The connection was broken. The entire exchange had required less than twenty seconds.

Mark looked at me.

"Yes. Man of few words. But that was clipped even for him. Whatever it is, it must be juicy."

We drove on.

"Can you call Willis?" Mark said to me. "Use my phone. His number's stored."

Willis answered before the second ring.

"Willis."

"Dr. Willis. This is Steven Boscombe. Mark Whelan and I will be in Cobourg in about ten minutes."

"Good. Something's happening. I don't know what. Come and see me please. As soon as you arrive."

I looked across to see Mark's nod.

"Okay. We will. We'll call first. At the hospital?"

"Yes. I'll wait for you at the main entrance."

That connection was broken as well. It was becoming a day of staccato exchanges.

Hal Bennet had found an isolated section of car park at the hotel, so his blue Audi was entirely conspicuous. We pulled up beside his car. He was at the driver side window before Mark came to a stop. Even though he was seated, it was clear that he was wiry and strong, had steel-grey hair, and appeared to be in his mid-fifties. He needed no prompt to start talking.

"Gray was shot. Execution. Found at the entrance to Union Cemetery. Nobody can get hold of the police chief. All seems to be related to Ted Ballantyre's death. There's been a tip-off. Something about a photo."

"Photo? Where?"

"Chasing it."

"Others?"

"Yeah. Two that I know of."

"Who has the inside track?"

"Me."

"Can you get it?"

"Trying hard. It'll cost."

"Doesn't matter. Pay. We have to go and see Willis now. Stay in touch."

And then Bennet was back in his car, and we sped out of the hotel car park.

"What's the photo?" I asked, feeling completely at sea. "Something to do with the execution?"

"No. You'd never get a photo of an execution. No point. I think it has to do with Ted's death."

"What though?"

"I'm hoping it's an identity."

Mark was concentrating on his driving, so I just swallowed my dumbfoundedness and let him drive without distractions. Willis was recognizable immediately as we entered the hospital car park. We skidded noisily to a stop not far from him, and he was in the back seat almost immediately.

"What do you know?" Willis asked bluntly.

"Steve here was attacked last night outside his condo building. We know who did it. He was found this morning, executed, and the usual contacts here seem to have gone quiet. Anything new from your side?"

"Only something ridiculous. I've been instructed to speak to nobody about anything." Willis's lip curled. "Nobody gives me blanket instructions like that!"

"Who was it?"

"Said he was an assistant to the police chief. Don't know his name. And on the telephone, for God's sake!"

"What do you think is happening, Dr. Willis?"

"Call me Frank. I think we're getting our first peek into some dark Ballantyre corners."

We waited for more, but Willis just sat behind us, fuming.

"What are you here for?" he asked after a pause.

"I have some contacts to speak to", Mark said.

"Well, keep me up to date", Willis commanded. "I have some very old bones and two recent cadavers in my morgue, and I'm damn well going to find out what their stories are. You have my cellphone number."

And without waiting for a reply, he opened the rear car door, rose forcefully from the seat, and strode toward the hospital entrance.

"Well", I said, "I guess he's made his—"

Mark's raised right hand as he reached for his cellphone and told me to hang on.

"Whelan."

Short rapid-fire sentence from the other party.

"Where?"

More rapid fire.

"Have you got something?"

The reply was a few barks, although I couldn't make out any words.

"Is it the real thing?"

Another bark that could have been only "yes".

"Be there in five."

Mark's car roared to life, there was a screech as we lurched backward out of the parking spot, then we squealed our way toward the exit from the hospital car park and announced our departure through a long shriek of rubber.

"Where are we going?" I asked.

"A grubby little restaurant called Stumpie's, and no, you wouldn't go there because of the name, but yes, the food is fantastic."

I assumed we weren't going there to eat.

We weren't.

31

Stumpie's

Stumpie's is down a back street not far from the port, close to the lake but just beyond the eastern limit of Cobourg. The entire street looked like a candidate for being condemned. Many buildings were boarded shut, a few staring windows had met the fate that such areas attract, but the knot of cars and pickups near the end of the street indicated one spot that retained a strong pulse of economic life.

The restaurant itself was small but packed. And the clientele included far more than just coffee addicts. The windows seemed to be mostly a space for signs and notices of all sorts, and a preferred surface for condensation, but through the few clear spots one could see tables laden with plates and crowded by diners.

We entered and were struck immediately by a front of warm, damp air, an aroma of meatloaf and gravy that managed to be at once overwhelming and inviting, and a wall of sound. Almost all the diners were men, but about ten women added their soprano lilt to the acoustic roller coaster, and the discussions were punctuated by fingers, hands, and cutlery swooping through the air.

Through the kitchen hatch, a large florid-faced man broke off scowling at underlings to glance occasionally over his band of customers. He spotted Mark immediately, and his face erupted in a smile.

"Ah, Mark!" he boomed. "Welcome! Good to see you! Even though this can only mean there's evil afoot!"

Mark smiled and waved back, evidently deciding that any response attempting to override the background roar would be a non-starter. It took him no time to find Hal, sharing a table with two others in the far corner. He rose from his chair as we approached, and they greeted each other simultaneously.

"Hal."

"Mark."

They shook hands. Hal inclined his head to what looked like the door to the toilet, and the two of them moved off. I hesitated. Mark turned to me, and the slight jerk of his head indicated that I should come along and be quick about it. A threesome in what would almost certainly be a small and odorous loo was not appealing. But it turned out not to be a loo. The door opened to a narrow corridor, leading to a right L-bend, and another door gave onto the rear ground space of the restaurant. But it wasn't the depressing scene I expected, one of waste bins overflowing week-old swill, bits of broken and rusty machinery, and a tumble-down wooden fence which would have recoiled in fear of the unknown at the sight of a paintbrush.

Instead, there was a covered area sheltering clean and almost odourless waste bins, a nicely gravelled and weedless parking spot, and shiny metal fencing in matte robin's-egg blue that enclosed what looked like a quarter acre of land. A gravel road ran along behind the metal fence, and there was a clear view down it both ways for at least two hundred metres.

Mark and Hal appeared to pay no attention to all this. They began a rapid-fire exchange and the effort to focus on it blanked out all my other sensory input.

"Okay. Where are we?" Mark asked Hal.

"We have the picture", Hal said. "Cost seven big ones. But there's now a face. Made some prints." He handed Mark an envelope. "I expect to know the face's owner within the hour."

"Who took the photo?"

"Muckraker. Skilled. Informed."

"He must like risk."

Hal just snorted. "He's doomed."

"Competition?" Mark asked.

Hal nodded.

"Two of them. A third dropped out. They know we have it. Know that copies will be around. Too late to suppress things."

"But they could try for delays."

Hal nodded again. "That's where we need to be careful", he said.

Only at that stage did Hal glance my way and incline his head.

"Friend", Mark said, and that seemed to suffice.

Hal turned back to Mark.

"So", he said, his hand gestures signalling the question "What next?"

Mark nodded.

There was what seemed like an immense delay here, although it couldn't have been more than about five seconds. But for me it broke the spell, so to speak. A second glance at our surroundings showed me that the fence enclosed more than just land. It was a well-maintained vegetable and herb garden the sight of which probably made everyone who saw it smile. Here was one indication why the food served within was good.

"Good work", Mark said to Hal, resuming their exchange. "Find a name for the face. Locate him if you can. Do you think he might be a big fish?"

"Probably not", Hal replied. "Likely a pro for hire."

"Has he disappeared now?"

"Probably", Hal added, "except for…"

"Muckraker?"

Hal nodded.

"Have you done anything?" Mark asked.

Hal nodded. "Yes. The word's out."

"There's cash in the account", Mark said. "Take what you need. Usual process for receipts."

Hal nodded, gave a wan smile of thanks.

Mark widened his regard to take in both of us.

"I'll be back in a minute", he said, then turned and walked through the open gate to the parking spot and disappeared to the left around the corner of the building.

Hal looked at me and smiled neutrally. I was very much aware of how scary he would be as an enemy.

A minute later, Mark's car appeared on the gravel road. Hal had begun walking toward the gate and parking area, obviously headed for Mark's car. I followed. We climbed into the car, Hal indicating the front passenger seat for me, and we drove off.

There was no conversation. We drove around on country roads for about ten minutes, Hal indicating where to turn at various intersections but saying nothing except "here left" or "here right". Within a minute, I was fully disoriented and didn't realize until we began coming to a stop that we were once again on the gravel road behind Stumpie's but approaching from the opposite direction.

"Stay in touch", Mark said as Hal began opening his door.

"As soon as I have anything", Hal said, waving his cellphone. He closed the door, then strode through Stumpie's parking area toward the front of the restaurant. Mark waited until the blue Audi flashed past the narrow drive next to the restaurant. Then he pulled away.

I didn't know what to say, so I just croaked hoarsely, "What next?" I wasn't at all sure whether I meant "Where to now?" or "What new grim situation awaits us?" Mark seemed to assume the former.

"We're going to talk to Willis again. But first I need to check something." There was no clarification on just what was to be checked, but I was happy to wait for it. I knew I was not only out of my depth but also in some sea of confusion, far from the sight of land, too deep to be able to see the surface, and in a place where no glimmer of understanding was reaching me.

We carried on along the gravel road, turned left at the next intersection, and headed north. We were still on the edge of Cobourg, but after a few more turns we were moving back into the city and eventually into the older, original part. There were two stops for lights. I didn't recognize where we were but felt that we were nowhere near the hospital. We made another left turn into an area of old warehouses and factories, many of them in the initial stages of renovation. A right turn led us into a narrower lane passing between two large old warehouses, abandoned but still in reasonable condition. An unexpected left turn took us into another narrow lane that led toward a street that had occasional traffic, about a hundred metres ahead of us.

Mark stopped suddenly and turned off the engine.

"Stay here", he ordered, then opened the door and climbed out quickly. A fan further down the alleyway was venting air noisily from one of the buildings.

I looked around to try to see where we were and what was happening.

There was a car stopped behind us, not ten metres away.

A burly man was climbing out of the driver's seat, and as he did so, he was reaching inside his brown leather jacket. Mark was walking quickly toward him.

But the scene rapidly transformed into a nightmare. Burly Brown's hand emerged from the jacket. In it was a long, dull revolver, and it rose to point at Mark.

32

Unwinding

It has happened to me very few times, but it happened then.

Events around me appeared to slow to a crawl, but my thinking went into warp drive. Past situations that posed serious threats have elicited different responses from me. The most common, and the one I am most eager to forget totally, is that of the gibbering idiot, where panic results in either complete seizure of all mental processes or a wild synaptic storm that just as effectively robs one of any ability for useful response.

On one memorable occasion, during my only serious single vehicle accident, I experienced that sense of control and serenity in the midst of what threatened to be final moments. I had been travelling at a sedate fifty kilometres, or so, an hour. The road was snow-covered, but traction seemed good. At least until I felt an unaccustomed back-end sway. At some point, the underlay to the snow had abruptly stopped being asphalt and became smooth ice. In less than four seconds, the car was turning circles in the road while still plunging forward at a frightening speed. But in the world around me, I suddenly realized that everything was advancing at a slow crawl. Although my car was in a frantic spinning skid, I saw it as a very slow-motion ballet, where I understood every move and knew exactly what to do. And my mind, although racing, was clear and deliberate. I did everything right, as it turned out, scraped one side of the car lightly, but soon had it stopped and facing in the right direction. My hands shook the rest of the way home.

Now, I turned in Mark's car to look backward. My thoughts all seemed to be falling into a mental sack marked "To Be Examined Later". There was no panic. The driver's door on the car behind us opened slowly and Burly Brown, the driver, began to rise from his seat. Without apparent effort, I took in all aspects of what was behind us, the car, the man, his clothes. All particulars of his brown leather jacket — the stitching, the texture, the shape of the collar, the slant on the pocket zippers — were crystal clear. The image of the man himself was being recorded in full detail. I could see the small scar on the right side of his chin. His thin and almost absent black eyebrows, the steel-grey eyes, the pinstripe orange and blue lines on his shirt, these were all sharp and clear, and I seemed to have almost unlimited time to take them in. I opened the door and stepped from Mark's car. I don't remember even a hint of fear. Burly Brown turned his head slightly to look at me, and the angle of his revolver barrel swung marginally away from Mark.

And then there was the hand. It was large and it seemed to come out of nowhere, and it dropped with force onto Burly Brown's right shoulder, near his neck. I saw his eyes close, his face twist in anger or pain, or both, but he had no more time to react than that. He was spun through ninety degrees and his head cracked down hard against the windshield of his own car.

There was blood. Then Mark and Hal were all over him. He was slammed against the brick wall next to his car, and he doubled over as Hal caught him in the midsection with what looked like a powerful blow. I looked further along the alley and saw Hal's blue Audi parked across the entrance, blocking any escape for Burly Brown's car.

Mark turned to me.

"Get in the car! Drive! Wait at the other end of the alley! Then follow us!"

When a second went past and I hadn't begun to make my move, Mark gave an imperious hand signal that clearly meant "Now! Or else!"

So, of course, I did. At the end of the alley, I waited barely two minutes. Hal's blue Audi swung around the corner to my right, Mark driving. He drove across in front of me, motioned me to follow, and within five minutes we were leaving Cobourg behind. We drove for about fifteen minutes, fast enough that I had to work to keep up, and we made quite a few turns. The last turn was onto a road labelled Concession 7, but I couldn't see the name of the municipality or township. And then Mark turned left off the concession road. We passed along a lane between two lines of mature trees and stopped beside a small church about fifty metres away from the road. We were on the north side of the church, screened from the view of anyone on the road, and before us lush farmland undulated away toward the moraine, a dark ridge quite a few kilometres to the north.

Burly Brown was hauled from the car and dragged to the church where he was dropped next to the wall. His hands had been bound behind him. There was blood caked around one side of his nose.

It was Hal who spoke first.

"Okay, Jackson. Start talking."

There was a flicker on the man's face, but apart from that he remained impassive.

"Detroit, I guess", Hal said. "Well, you certainly made a wrong turn someplace. When your boss finds out where you ended up, I'm guessing he'll be a tad pissed."

"We're not going to get anything out of him", Mark said. "Maybe we should—"

But Hal's hand went up as he looked at his cellphone. He read for a moment, then turned the phone so that Mark could read it. Mark nodded.

"Okay. Back to Cobourg. Just leave him here?"

"Yes. We'll bind his ankles as well. He won't be going anywhere."

"You have his phone?"

"Yes."

Hal turned to Jackson, bent down, bound his ankles, then rose and looked down at him.

"Information networks and cellphones with cameras, Jackson. Thanks to them, we've been able to find out who you are, who your boss is, and some of your background. And we're not going to leave you here without telling anybody. I'll send your boss a message saying where he can find you."

Another flicker, somewhat stronger, went across Jackson's face.

"Oh, don't worry though. I'm not a completely heartless bastard. I'll make sure that an anonymous tip is left with our own boys in blue. We'll see who finds you first."

Hal turned to leave.

"I'll tell you", Jackson said.

Hal stopped and turned.

"You're too late, Jackson. You see, the message I just received tells me everything I need to know. You're yesterday's news now. I do hope, you know, that our guys find you first. They'll be a lot gentler. But, given the crime wave that's swept over Cobourg, they've been busy, and, well…"

Hal shrugged, then turned and walked toward his car, ignoring the shouts of "Wait! Wait!"

At the cars, we had a short conference. Well, at least Mark and Hal did.

"We're going to see Willis now", Mark said. "I'm letting him know when we'll arrive." He typed a short text message on his cellphone.

"I need to send some messages too", Hal said, "so I'll find a quiet place to do that. There's likely to be activity this afternoon. Close contact?"

"Agreed", Mark said. Then we climbed into our vehicles and drove off.

Mark and I were quiet for a few minutes in his car.

"I'm sorry you had to see all that", Mark said eventually. "My world. It can be a really shitty place."

"It's the cost of getting to the bottom of all this", I said evenly, my tone evidently so even and worldly that Mark turned and looked at me sharply.

"It seems to me", Mark said in reply, "that all this is slime from the present day, dragged into the story because of whatever monstrosities are buried in the Ballantyre past. I'll be glad to see the whole thing aired and laundered, so we can be done with it."

"What about Jackson?" I asked. "Will the police from Cobourg pick him up?"

Mark shook his head.

"No. Most of what Hal said back there was nonsense, although it looked as though Jackson bought it. Just one policeman will go to pick up Jackson. But he's special. He's entirely focussed on results, and he hates any sort of crime syndicate. Jackson will be picked up. And he'll talk. Believe me. For this guy, he will talk."

"Do you think that all this has been unleashed by our emails?"

"I do now", Mark said. "Yes. It does seem to be bigger than we expected. I'm beginning to wonder whether it reaches into the ranks of the police. But I think this train of events started when the skeleton was uncovered. It had been buried there so long that I suspect all living memory of it just faded, and for everyone else its status also sank from ancestral lore to mists of time. But then the skeleton appeared. Something must have clicked for someone. And once they realized just what had been activated, they knew that it threatened to become the thread that unravels the carpet."

Of course, all this was only part of the story, and I was struggling with other pieces.

"The intruder at John's place? The drone? The evidence you found that someone probably had broken into John's buildings? What's all that about?"

"That's the kicker, Steve. It seems just such an overreaction. I don't know what to make of it. It seems that somebody was panicking. But at the moment I can't see why."

"And then Ted's death...?"

"Let's call it Ted's murder. Suicide doesn't seem to fit at all."

"So now, the attack on me, somebody being foolish enough to try to muzzle Willis, this Harold Gray, maybe more information on who killed Ted, and now the Jackson oaf… Where's all that coming from?"

"We'll see", Mark said, "and soon enough, I would say."

"This business of Harold Gray being a police informant. Isn't that just very odd?"

I could see Mark shaking his head. "Irregular, but not unknown. Quite often the police need to get information wherever they can."

We were now approaching the hospital, and even before we turned into the car park, we could see Willis, hands in pockets, pacing at the hospital entrance. We drew up next to him. He climbed into the back seat.

"Drive", he ordered. "To Gary Ballantyre's place. I have a message for him."

It would take only a few minutes to reach the Ballantyre residence, but Willis seemed determined to bring us entirely up to speed well before we got there.

Willis told us that it now seemed as though the local chief of police had abandoned his post. He hadn't been reachable for hours.

Willis had tried calling the chief's office to find out who gave him the message to back off, but the person who answered had no idea and seemed to be stressed well beyond his pay grade.

"What message do you want to give to Gary?" Mark asked.

"The same one I gave to the Solicitor General twenty minutes ago, that I'm paying no attention to any attempts to cause me not to meet my responsibilities."

"The Solicitor General? What did he say?"

"Don't know. Didn't speak to him directly. But I was very undiplomatic. I think the message will be passed on."

There seemed to be nothing to say to that, and we drove on, reaching the Ballantyre mansion about five minutes later. None of us knew the person who opened the door to our knock. Willis moved forward past Mark and me.

"I wish to speak to Gary Ballantyre", he pronounced.

"I'm sorry, sir. He's not here."

"Where can I find him, please?"

"I'm afraid I don't know, sir."

Willis's glare could have blistered paint easily.

"My name is Frank Willis. I'm the local medical examiner. You'll need that information when you contact Ballantyre. But right now", Willis said, turning toward Mark, "this gentleman is about to take note of your name, the date and time, your answer to my question, and the presence of witnesses."

The man swallowed hard.

"I'm sorry, sir. I just don't know."

"And your name?" Willis asked politely.

"I don't see—"

"No matter", Willis said through a cold smile. "We should be able to find out easily enough."

And with that, Willis turned and walked resolutely toward the car, leaving us little choice but to follow.

Before we reached the car, Mark pulled his cellphone from his pocket.

"Hal, talk to me."

"I'm in Albert Street, behind Cobourg city hall. Better come here."

"On our way."

"What is it?" Willis asked as we climbed back into the car.

"Don't know", Mark said. "But I can guess."

We accelerated away from the Ballantyre place, probably so that generous amounts of gravel could be thrown onto the grass.

It took less than ten minutes to reach that gorgeous structure in central Cobourg known as Victoria Hall. We turned down George Street and saw almost immediately that a section of Albert Street was closed off. The flashing lights of emergency vehicles were everywhere. We parked on George Street and saw Hal approaching us. Mark left the car to meet him. Willis and I climbed out and waited to see what was happening.

"They shot the muckraker but didn't manage to kill him. He's been taken to the hospital."

"What do you think?" Mark asked.

"Don't know. Looked bad. He might not make it."

"Shooter?"

"The police killed him." Hal pointed to a group of policemen along the street. Willis's professional interest spiked.

"My cue", he said, almost under his breath, and began walking briskly toward the knot of policemen.

"Did you see the shooter?" Mark asked.

"Yes. He's our man, the guy in the picture."

"How did the police manage to get here so quickly?"

Hal looked absently toward a group of trees to his right.

"I might have let something slip."

For some reason, we all checked our watches at the same time.

"What now?" Hal asked.

"We should find somewhere to talk. Just down here in the park would be good. We'll take my car. Where's yours?"

"In a car park up the way", Hal said. "Safe and innocent."

"Are you okay to leave?" Mark asked, indicating the scene further along Albert Street.

"Me? Yeah. I'm just a bystander. Didn't see anything."

We found a picnic table, and Hal and Mark began a walkthrough of events. It sounded like ticking off main items, then ticking off possible loose ends, aiming for a wrap-up. The bottom line seemed to be that the major players were either dead or were missing and would soon be tracked down. How and why the skeleton came to be what and where it was might never be worked out, but Charles Ballantyre seemed to be a good candidate for the person whose frame it had been. The discussion went back and forth over small details and finally ground to a halt.

"So", Mark said, after a long pause, "I guess there'll be many details we'll never sort out. But the big picture looks like a case of family jealousy, some event that resulted in Charles's violent death, some other event that ended in Ted being killed, and then a series of cover-ups, various attempts at intimidation, and then the whole thing unravelled."

Hal made some hand signals, indicating he had things to do. Mark nodded and waved him to carry on.

"Later", Hal said, then smiled at us both and walked off.

I had been listening to their summary of events, and I could also tick off things in my head. But I was distracted now and then by all the flashing lights behind us, by the day, which was sunny and warm, and by the always attractive play of light off thousands of waves out on the lake. The park was delightful, and that day it was being enjoyed by many people. There were families walking as groups, couples pushing prams, a group of skimpily clad youngsters tossing a Frisbee, quite a few elderly ladies chatting on benches, and three or four older gents, leaning on canes, out in the sunshine going for a hobble…

Hobble…

A picture came to mind.

I suddenly realized that it was a complete picture.

And then it was as though I had recognized a long-lost Rubens… I must have just stood there, looking as though I was listening to Mark when I was really off somewhere else.

"…so, I suppose we can pull the plug on this one", Mark said conclusively.

I came back to the present with a bit of a thud.

"You mean in terms of your active involvement?" I asked Mark.

"Well … yes… I mean, I don't see that there's much more I can do. There are loose ends, but I expect that's more a mop-up job, something for the police."

Things were still falling into place in my mind. I stood there, mute, and probably looking vacant.

"Do you disagree?" Mark asked, perhaps thinking I was quietly worrying some problem.

I looked directly at him for a few seconds.

"I should have seen much earlier what I've just realized. The body under the tree at John Stanley's place was that of Charles Ballantyre. I'm virtually sure of that now. It was almost certainly Gary who killed his brother Ted. There was strife between Gary and Ted, and I think I know why. I'm also now sure why Charles crossed into the US then returned a couple of years later."

33

Eggshell and Pieces

Mark looked at me uncomprehendingly.

"Okay", he said. "I'm all ears." But even as he spoke, I could see clouds of doubt closing in across his face.

"It's a theory", I began. "And it's true that it all fell together in my mind just now. So I won't be surprised if holes can be poked easily."

I stopped here to collect my thoughts and find a logical way to say what I had to say. It was reassuring to see Mark's features soften in encouragement.

"Let me start with a couple of things Willis said. One was that he thought whoever the skeleton belonged to suffered from Paget's disease. I've come across items, from Milliken's diary for instance, indicating that Charles moved with difficulty. This proves nothing, of course, since arthritis could easily raise the same comment. But I've also done some digging. Paget's disease wasn't identified as a condition until after Charles had left his position as head of the family businesses. So we can't compare a diagnosis while Charles was alive to a post-mortem judgment on the skeleton. It's one piece of evidence. Not conclusive at all on its own.

"Willis also said that the owner of the skeleton had lived with the condition that has been described in legal terms as eggshell skull. Even I noticed the hole in the skull when Willis pulled it from the earth. He said that it was most likely the cause of death. So whoever inflicted that injury might have had no intention of killing him. If that's the case, then the death would not have been an execution or a premeditated murder. It could equally have been an attempt to get the person to talk. But maybe they were a bit too rough, and it all went wrong.

"I've also done some digging on the Ballantyre businesses. It's not easy, because the disclosure requirements and accounting practices in the nineteenth century were all over the map. It was boom times for the lumber business. The Ballantyre company was doing very well. They were making a lot of money. As were all the other companies in the timber business. Almost all the squared timber from Ontario went to England or the US, and for the Ballantyres, the trade to the US was huge. They had their own company office in New York, just to handle the paperwork and banking."

I stopped for breath here and to decide how to present the other items I had.

"This doesn't really point to anything specific", Mark said, looking slightly disappointed.

"No", I replied, fixing a gaze on him. "That's because the best is still to come. I came across another company, or I guess the term 'business entity' would be better. It was in New York, as well, and was called Somerville Investments. It began operations in 1872 and was wound up in 1876. The documents describing it don't say what the company was involved in, but it was owned by one person: Charles Ballantyre."

I gave Mark a moment for that to sink in.

"I began looking for other business entities that Charles might have been involved in. Not easy. There seems to have been no standard in those days on documentation for companies, but I did come up with one. It was registered in Toronto."

"Let me guess", Mark said, the light of suspicion now glowing brightly in his eyes. "It was also Somerville Investments and was owned by Charles Ballantyre."

"Not quite", I said. "It was called White Receiving and was owned by Christian Somerville."

"Who was Christian Somerville?"

I smiled and took my time.

"I also found a legal name change. For someone to change their name then was easy enough to do. Back then, systematic searching of companies on a regular basis really wasn't done. There would have been the crude equivalent of what we'd call 'competitive intelligence' today, but likely it would have been used much less. It was easier to keep secrets back then, and harder to seek them out. But back to your question. The person who changed his name to Christian Somerville had been none other than Charles Ballantyre."

"What? Does that mean he would have been operating as two separate people at the same time?"

"Looks very much like that. I've asked around. As long as he was careful enough not to have those names cross in a single context, there should have been no problem."

Mark ran his hand through his hair and cast me a speculative look.

"Well! You crafty bastard! You've been busy! When did you unearth all this stuff?"

"Over the past two weeks."

"And you didn't tell me?"

"No. Remember. It all just came together for me a few minutes ago. Up until then, it was a bunch of apparently disconnected facts. Besides, you've been busy enough. I certainly suspected that there was something big somewhere in the background. We both did. And I must have had a sense these things were related, somehow. Otherwise, it's unlikely that I would have kept digging for so long."

"All this sounds rather elaborate. Are you sure it passes the sniff test?"

"I think it does. I've had a suspicion about Charles for some time. Living in the Ballantyre family must have been a challenge at the best of times. But if you were Charles, I think it must have been barely endurable. The other scions of the family almost certainly would have known or suspected that Charles was a cuckoo in the nest. And yet old Lorne put him in the position of power in the family when Walter died suddenly. The others were likely just entitled snot rags, with no real business skills. Charles could probably have outrun them in his sleep, from a business point of view, and Lorne almost certainly made the right business decision. And I expect that old Lorne wouldn't have hesitated to draw public and invidious comparisons between Charles and his nominal siblings. Fits the Ballantyre behaviour trademark. So I doubt that there was any love lost at all between Charles and the wastrel uncles, Graham and Arnold. Furthermore, Charles was bright enough to have guessed himself that he was an outsider. He couldn't possibly have looked forward to years or decades of a life in that sort of toxic environment. So I think that Charles probably had made his own plans not long after he had the reins of power, and more likely well before then."

Mark was shaking his head.

"You're going to make me work it out for myself, aren't you?"

"No. As I said, it's a theory. Charles decided that he was going to line his own nest good and proper. There was a river of timber money surging through the Ballantyre commercial empire. I think Charles set up his own commercial entity in New York secretly. Somerville Investments. He then siphoned off money from the main Ballantyre company in New York and diverted it into Somerville Investments. I suspect that he was capable enough to do this without anybody finding out. Old Lorne would have backed well away from day-to-day operations by then. He was astute enough to have smelled a rat, but by then he had taken himself out of the picture. The rest of the family were either too dim, too uninterested, or too busy squabbling to concern themselves with mere business. As long as there was enough money to keep them happy, they just enjoyed a life that probably was fairly debauched for the times."

I could see that Mark was concentrating.

"Do you have any proof for all this?"

"No. None at all."

"So, then…"

"Let me finish my story. There's that record of Charles crossing into New York State and then coming back a few years later. I think what he was doing then was recovering the money that had been transferred to Somerville Investments and getting it in a form that could be moved out of the US fairly easily."

"What form would that be?"

"Don't know. But to carry on, I think he did get the money out of the US, but what happened next, I can't be sure. He might have had some very bad luck. Maybe one of the Ballantyres began to suspect that Charles had pulled a fast one. They couldn't prove anything, of course, but they would have been prepared to believe the worst. So I suspect that some of the Ballantyre clan took Charles off somewhere for a chat that likely was none too quiet and none too gentle. But they went too far, got too rough, and his eggshell skull fractured. They killed him. They had to get rid of the body, so they buried it on the Stanley property, hedging their bets in case someone found it."

"I know that the eggshell skull has a prominent place in legal precedent today. What about back then?"

"I've asked around. From what I've been able to find, it doesn't go back anything like that far. But I haven't had time to consult a legal expert. Willis is obviously familiar with it."

"I'm coming to the conclusion", Mark said somewhat sardonically, "that there's not much that Willis doesn't know at least something about."

We looked at each other for a moment.

"If Charles came back to Canada, there must have been a good reason", Mark said.

"What do you mean?"

"Well, he likely had the money in a form that could have been shifted anywhere. Why not just get out? Take it all off to Europe. Disappear. Live out a long and worry-free life of luxury. If he wanted revenge on the Ballantyres, getting his hand on their money would have satisfied that."

"Well", I began, "there was his mother. I have a feeling he felt close to her and couldn't just abandon her. Maybe he was working out a scheme to have her leave the Ballantyre house without causing anybody to wonder."

Mark considered that and nodded.

"I know it sounds like a stretch", I said, "but I think it does hold together — I mean this business about Charles's mother. By then she was a fixture in the Ballantyre household. After Charles disappeared, and some time had passed, there could have been no real concern left. Old Lorne certainly wouldn't have known about Charles being murdered. The young snot rags who had done it were still living a life of ease, and they wouldn't want that apple cart to be upset. So things just drifted on. Eventually the old lady died."

"Yes", Mark said. "Yes. It does make a certain kind of sense. Is that it?"

"Well, I don't think I can go any further. But as far as I'm concerned, there's enough information available now to have serious suspicions about who the skeleton belonged to, how it got where it was, and why."

"What about Gary?" Mark asked.

"I think Gary knows about as much as we do. There's the possibility of quite a lot of money being out there someplace. The money that Charles siphoned off and might have spirited back into Canada. I think that Gary and Ted figured out the main outlines. They wanted that money. But they really had no idea where to start. All that fumbling around in the dark — the intruder at John's place, the drone, apparently hiring a professional burglar to do a break-in — they had no idea and they were just bumbling around looking for clues. But they must have had a falling out of sorts, not hard to imagine in a family as nasty and grasping as they were. Gary was the more strategic of the two. Ted must have got Gary worried that he'd do or say something stupid and give the game away for both of them, so Gary pinched off that possibility."

It was clear that Mark could see gaps in all this.

"Would Gary have done something that extreme?" he asked. "I mean, he was hardly wanting for money. Why would he risk everything just to go after a bit more loot?"

I nodded acknowledgment.

"I think it was bigger than just the money", I began. "And it all might come back to something Willis said. What if, over the years, other people had become involved? Suppose someone in the police department had been providing a service to the Ballantyres, particularly Ted, for a fee? When Ted began declaring that the skeleton had been a Ballantyre, that, I think, is when the whole mess began threatening to unravel. And once that started, it would have been difficult to stop. That's the last thing Gary would want to happen. I think he had every incentive to jam the lid on it."

Mark was nodding at this.

"Yes. That much certainly does fit."

"What I'm not sure of", I said, "is how the attack on me fits into all this."

"Well, we're speculating about a fairly large theoretical superstructure here, but if there's truth to it, I suspect that that attack came from another quarter."

"Oh?"

"Yes", Mark said. "The Ballantyres appeared to get into a lot of scrapes and tight spots locally. They would have needed a backstop, a protector, someone who could make a lot of it just go away."

"Ah, yes!" I said, as the full significance of my own suspicion dawned on me. "Someone in the police would have their own ass to protect."

"Yes. And then there was you", Mark said, smiling at me rather conspiratorially. "John was happy just to let the whole thing ride, let all the skeleton gossip just burn itself out. Wait for it all to go away on its own. And it might have done. But you started digging, and it looked like you weren't going to stop. You brought me in, and I'm vain enough to suspect that they weren't going to take the risk of trying to intimidate me, possibly have me unmask somebody or something important."

"So that was just trying to scare me off?"

"That's what I suspect", Mark said.

"Doesn't sound like it was well thought out."

"None of this seems to have been well thought out. It seems to have been a series of stop-gap measures trying to keep things under control, and when each measure failed the next one had to be more extreme."

And that seemed to be something of a conclusion.

"What will happen now?" I asked.

"Well, I think we can just walk away from it, apart from one small puzzle that you and I need to discuss. The police have a lot to do to work out who was working for who, who killed who and why. And Willis, I'm sure, is going to be turning over every stone and pinning up every creepy-crawly he spots. Not a man to cross, I would say. But apart from that, it's all a bit like a Puccini opera. The main characters are all dead, there's basically nothing left for honest folk like us to do but go off somewhere and have a drink."

"Okay", I said, rising decisively. "I guess that's what should happen next."

34

Restart

It was a warm day, not hot. The sky was a playground for fat, cherubic cumulus clouds, the signature of fair weather. Out in the open, it was pleasantly gusty, but here in the forest, the wind could be seen rather than felt, and air moved past us in gentle zephyrs, only as allowed at the pleasure of the giant pines.

John and I had taken another long walk through the forest, and now we were once again next to Big White, sitting on the old log, which was our habitual spot here, to rest and keep the trees company.

As the breeze moved through its branches high above, Big White sighed, its ancient voice of enduring youth welcoming our visit, transient creatures it would outlast by multiples of our lifespan. I had things to say to John, but for the moment I was happy just to sit, ponder, and be bathed in the forest's terpenic scent. The forest was the same as I remembered it, although, being a dynamic thing, a forest is never constant, it is always changing. But I looked beyond all that to query my feeling that something was different. Was there some recognition that our resolution of the story behind the skeleton had brought about some settling of arboreal accounts?

"I love these old trees", I muttered, not quite to myself.

"Not going anthropomorphic on me again, are you?"

John and I had this gentle disagreement, as insistent and as unlikely as would be a shared war wound.

"Now John. Just because you don't really buy into the fact that these old trees are living beings—"

"You know that's not true—"

"That the dividing line between sentience and dead matter isn't really a line, it's more probably a grey area—"

"And as a forester, how could I possibly not believe that these trees are—"

"And that you're more like a disengaged physician, patients being just cases, trees being just—"

We looked at each other, then broke into laughter. I knew that we both loved this forest passionately, out of long and close familiarity, and it was just that we had different ways of expressing it.

"I'm thinking", John began, looking at me closely as he spoke, "that you would love to project a sense of something close to the sacred over these trees."

"Well, actually, I think they're projecting it to me."

As if on a cue, we looked up and around.

"How do you think your ancestors viewed these trees? A lot of the trees we're looking at now were trees they saw as well. I wondered about that as I was going through your family diaries."

"That's a question I can't answer. I'd love to know. But I suspect it might be impossible to know the mental state of someone who lived two hundred years ago. There have been so many changes."

"But they did defend these trees. They must have been concerned for them, had some feeling for them, in some sense."

"No doubt", John said, still looking at me levelly, "but I can't get into their minds."

"And what about the loggers, the guys your ancestors drove off, the guys who wanted to cut all this down?"

John smiled.

"We've been through this before. I guess you really don't believe that a defence for what happened back then can be sustained."

"I remember all your arguments", I said. "It just seems to have been such a frenzy. Even the foresters in the early decades of the twentieth century considered that clear-cutting a rape. Although they didn't use that word, of course."

"Yes", John began. "They saw the impacts of the combined clear-cutting and attempts to farm land that really wasn't arable. They saw the drifts of blow sand and the erosion. It must have been heartbreaking. I think there had already been something of a paradigm shift though, even by then."

"But it was too late", I said, almost as a bark. "The trees were all gone by then."

"Steady on", John warned. "You having an infarct won't help anything."

The trees sighed again, but I didn't know which of us they were agreeing with.

"I guess you put the Ballantyres in the same boat with all the other lumber barons."

"Well", I said, sounding defensive even to myself. "That's what they were."

"But we have the additional reminder of our skeleton. Does that make them even worse scoundrels?"

I thought about it for a minute, wanting to get my ideas straight.

"Probably", I said in the end.

John raised an eyebrow.

So then I launched into my indictment. The skeleton made it all real, immediate. Somehow the mood of the times back then, whatever it might have been, had burst through to the present. A link to today from back then made it more than just faded photographs and a disembodied historical account. The huge trees, here today because of the actions of a handful of Stanleys back then, provided a living link to those vast forests of white pine that were at the centre of all the action a century and a half ago. It took a particular set of events for that body to be buried in what became John's property. There was an entirely unremarkable indiscretion involving a domestic servant, followed by what must have been a volcanic reaction of the puritanical head of the Ballantyre family. The emergence of a very capable man of business. Then the envy and jealousy of the duller knives in the family drawer. And, finally, a series of events we can only guess at, and a jealousy and rivalry that went too far. No matter how one spins it, it would end up being a murder. And then there would have been the hope, and the expectation, on the part of the perpetrators, that the whole thing would just fade from memory and become something that never was. But as a sort of insurance, the body was disposed of such that if it had been discovered, the blame could have been directed elsewhere, away from the perpetrators.

And then there was the mood of the times, the rampant capitalism, the domineering and argumentative family itself, and the whole slash and burn mentality of the logging industry back then. The body was the powder keg to which all that had led. Now, more than a hundred years later, the keg had exploded.

I must have ranted on at length. But John replied in his usual measured way. His words were mild, but his rebuke was telling.

"We can't walk in their shoes. If we could, I'm sure it would be a searing experience. Life was hard. Back then, any kind of social safety net was many decades into the future. They all had to live in whatever way they could. I expect a lot of them failed in that. There was a continuing threat from the United States. The demand in Britain for timber was colossal. The resource here seemed limitless. It all led to a situation that made the clear-cutting of the white pine pretty much inevitable."

John paused here.

"Besides", he said looking at me squarely, "consider our present-day frenzy of fossil fuel burning and our cavalier disregard for the fate of our billions of tonnes of plastics. Have we really learned all that much? Have we earned any right to criticize?"

I was in a corner, and there was wet paint a metre deep all around me.

John then launched into a discussion about foresters, and although it sounded restrained, I soon realized that it was deeply passionate.

"Foresters know a lot about trees. They know more today than they did fifty years ago. But foresters are just people, and, like any group of people, they're all over the map. Even today, many of them work for organizations that have an interest in harvesting wood, and the interest is, always has been, for more harvesting and not less. And I remind you of what a forest is and the many things that affect its status and its ongoing stability, the state of its equilibrium. We've talked about this often."

I nodded, feeling somewhat humbled. But when John continued, I knew that he had sensed my mood, embarking on a theme he didn't express often.

"I know I'm different from most foresters", he said. "For me, the forest here is part of my life, something I have a duty toward, something almost mystical. But then, unlike many, I see magic all around me. That's certainly true of this forest here, my forest. It's magic. And it speaks to me."

For a few moments, John just looked into some far distance. But then, as if coming out of a trance, he looked around, wondering how he had managed to sleepwalk here.

"Shall we go back?"

Dougie, who had been sitting quietly at our feet, knew what that meant, and he rose abruptly and began trotting off homeward.

"I thought we might have toasted cheese sandwiches for lunch", John said.

"I didn't, I didn't mean to rant back there. Sorry."

John laughed.

"Of course you did. These things matter to you. If you hadn't said something like that, I would have been sure you weren't well."

We walked on.

"The sandwiches?" John prompted.

"What?"

He laughed, a huge guffaw.

So we talked about toasted cheese sandwiches, I agreed entirely, quickened my pace when a good dark ale was mentioned, but at the same time I resolved to get a better handle on what had happened during the last half of the nineteenth century.

Back at John's place, Dougie lapped flamboyantly at his water bowl, throwing water everywhere, and ended in a flourish that looked almost like a bow to his audience. John and I collaborated on the cheese sandwiches, and we were soon seated at the picnic table, complete with our Greek chorus of sparrows. Then we glided down the long dark ale exit ramp from our meal.

I took a sip of my ale, set the glass down on the table, and looked across at John.

"I've put my condo up for sale", I announced, without any preamble.

John didn't respond for a second.

"I didn't realize you were thinking of moving. I suppose you've found a better place? More suited to one person?"

We continued looking at one another. I didn't respond immediately.

"I've also quit my job."

John blinked once, about the closest he would come to a double take.

"You've quit?"

"Yes", I said, smiling as I anticipated the changes I was setting in motion. "I'm moving to Cobourg."

An expression of disbelief formed on John's face. But he continued looking at me, waiting for some explanation.

"Well, not exactly Cobourg. I'm looking for a place somewhere close by, near the forest."

"Is this something you've been thinking about for some time? Or is it recent? And what triggered all this, if I might ask?" John continued regarding me, but his expression was becoming speculative.

"And what will you do?" he asked. "Surely you're too young to retire."

I shook my head.

"No, it's not a retirement move. I've been asking around at small companies in Cobourg. I think it looks pretty promising."

John shook his head.

"This is quite a surprise", he said at length. "I didn't expect anything like—" but then he stopped and looked directly at me.

"No, Steven. I don't believe this. There must be something more to it. Has it got to do with Joyce? And when you say, 'near the forest', what do you mean by that? How near?"

"No. It has nothing to do with Joyce. I'm not running away, if that's what you might be getting at. I've come to terms with losing Joyce, although … it's still… No. Joyce will always be near me."

Even as I said this, out loud for the first time, the truth of the statement was evident to me.

"And, near the forest means as near as possible."

John drained the last of his ale, then set the empty glass down in front of him. He gave me a focussed look.

"Well shit, Steven! Then come and live here! There's more than enough room—"

"No, John. I'm not looking for a free ride. I'll make my own way."

"Free ride my ass! Look! I'm an old man! My dream is to be carried out of here feet first. Although, not for quite a while yet!" he said, smirking. "But my great worry is not being able to look after this place anymore. This could be the perfect answer for both of us! We need to talk about—" But then John stopped abruptly once more. It was clear that a large doubt had risen in his mind.

"No. This can't be right. There's something more. I'm sure of it. What's going on, Steven?"

I looked at the man who had been guide, then father figure, then teacher, then mentor, always companion, always friend, now almost equal. Someone I had loved in different ways through all that time, but it wasn't that simple. Odd that we have only one word for the concept of love. Ancient Greek had three. But ancient Persian had eighty.

"You're right", I said, "at least in part. Joyce spoke to me just a few weeks ago. The message was that it's time for me to move on." I stopped and took a grip before continuing.

"And it is time." Although John was my immediate audience, I felt that I was speaking to some distant place, from some other distant place.

"Joyce was such an extraordinary person. I miss her so much. Guess I always will. But it really is time for me to move on. My job was okay, but only just okay. I have friends. I think I'm on an even keel. But a big piece of magic is gone from my life. And I have this fear that I won't be able to avoid falling into the most desperate rut."

I stopped and spent a long moment looking around.

"This forest here was such a brilliant beacon for me for so many years. It can be again. I know this is the right thing to do."

John sat looking at me, waiting.

"Well then, Steven, we have a great deal to discuss."

Another long pause. And then John spoke again.

"But I still think that's not all. There's something else, isn't there?"

I had to smile. And I couldn't help thinking, *What a man to have on my side!*

"Yes. There is something else. It's complicated. And it was all started by that skeleton. There's little doubt now that it was Charles Ballantyre who was buried over there more than a century ago. And somehow it seems to involve me. All the years I spent here with you in the forest. Getting to know about trees and, in fact, feeling that I knew the trees themselves. Then the wild ride touched off by that skeleton being unearthed, learning about how these pines are here because of several generations of Stanleys, the nineteenth-century logging fever, the whole mad Ballantyre clan. And then the feeling that the camouflage was being torn away, the secrets were being revealed. If I had seen it as an outsider, I probably would have dismissed it all as an elaborate soap opera. But I saw the skeleton, I saw the Stanley family journals, I saw personally how awkward and entitled the Ballantyres could be, even today, and now we have several dozen pieces of the puzzle laid out. We can make out a picture. But there are pieces missing."

I stopped to take a breather having talked myself into something of a mild frenzy.

"I can't stop now, John. This puzzle… I can't let go of it. I'm going to see it through as far as I can take it."

John was now looking somewhat less sceptical.

"How?" he asked.

"Mark Whelan is with me on this."

"You mean he's going to keep on investigating?"

I shook my head.

"No. We won't be doing any field work. It's all too high profile now. The formal inquiry has risen well above the level of corrupt local police, the practices of catering to Ballantyre influence and privilege and keeping things under wraps locally, and all the instances of ham-fisted, half-assed investigation that stretch back God knows how many years. Mark and I can't be seen to be anywhere near all that."

"Then what?"

"Well, we'll be going over everything again. Now that we have some hard information on who did what, when, and why, I think we'll be in a better position to find homes for some of the items that seemed to sit out on their own."

I drained the last of my ale.

"And we're going to write a book", I said, with some finality.

"No! Er, I mean, why?"

"There's so much history involved here. I'm not going to let it all just sink back into the mud."

I looked at John for a moment.

"Like another ale?" I asked as a suggestion.

"Yes", he said, and I waved him back to his seat, heading off myself to get us a couple more. I returned, our glasses were soon refilled, and then it felt absurdly almost like a "where were we" moment.

We clinked glasses and sipped in silence for almost a minute.

A slow smile formed on John's lips.

"I know that look", he said. "Come on. Out with it."

I couldn't help it. I had to smile as well.

"There is something else we want to focus on", I began. I took another long drink of ale.

"And is it so secret that you need to wait until after dark to tell me?"

"It's Charles Ballantyre's nest egg."

John laughed and shook his head.

"Well, I'd say that either you've had too much ale, or not enough. Charles Ballantyre's nest egg? Surely that's just a story. A pipe dream."

"No", I replied, looking at my lifelong friend and the forest that had been my home, my once and future home.

"We have a lead. We think we'll be able to find it."

www.ingramcontent.com/pod-product-compliance
Lightning Source LLC
Chambersburg PA
CBHW031941010726
47493CB00007B/2020

*9 7 8 1 7 7 1 8 0 6 6 9 5 *